NEXT

by Matthew Davis

A light sea breeze pleasantly caressed Laurus's tanned face. He stood bare-footed on the hot sand of the sun, his legs spread wide and fixed his tenacious, penetrating gaze somewhere beyond the horizon. At that moment, he probably imagined himself to be such a Sinbad the Sailor, to whom any element was subject. External resemblance to the legendary fairy-tale hero, in fairness it should be noted, after all it was. Dark, short-cropped hair, slightly slanting eyes, a distinctly contoured profile. In addition, Fedor was perfectly physically fit, and the bronze tan only emphasized the natural to become.

Warm gentle hands lay Laurel on his shoulders, and the man shuddered in surprise.

- Dreaming about long journeys? - the lovely female voice cooed in the very ear, and then sharp little teeth bit into the lobe.

Laurel turned with a smile. Katya has already managed to change clothes and is now appearing before her gentleman in all her glory. Inexpensive, modest, even by Soviet standards, swimsuit tightly wrapped around her miniature chiseled figure. Fedor unwittingly admired the appetizing elastic hips and defiantly sticking out bust, although he saw all this not for the first time. The girl felt that she was mentally admired, and took an even more graceful pose, as if imitating the girls from the magazine photos.

- Looks awesome! - sincerely told Laurus.

- Thanks for the compliment. - Katya playfully squinted. - So you go swimming?

Without waiting for the answer of her bewildered cavalier, she quickly ran away and, raising behind her the small fountains of spray, rushed into the water with a shriek. Her head disappeared under the crystal clear surface of the Black Sea. After a couple of seconds, Katya emerged, shook her hair, defiantly laughed, and waved Lavra with her hand. Yesterday, the zack with a smile continued to watch her, standing on the shore.

More than a week has passed since he met this charming girl here in Sochi. And about two months, as a twenty-seven-year-old prisoner left the confines of a strict regime colony. Alas, this was the case. Laurel, a very young man, had already managed to spend a considerable part of his life in places not so remote. The previous move was in his account for the second. The first time Fyodor pleased the court by a youngster. But the question was different. Will this raid be his last? Most likely no. Before Laurel clearly loomed the prospect of taking in the criminal world is not the last place. Who knows how high it will be possible to climb, but it was worth the test. Perhaps in the future, and the crown will receive. Why? You never know?

But Katya ... Fedor's thoughts returned to reality. This playful and, beyond any doubt, beautiful girl he liked more and more. He felt that he was becoming attached to her. But if the thieves' crown is considered the goal of all life, then Laurer had no right to allow such weakness in relation to the fair sex. Hard traditions do not approve of a serious amorous relationship, and even more so there can be no question of marriage. A thief must be a free man.

- Dive! Katya shouted to him, and the wind carried these words to Lavrikov.

He did not begging himself anymore. Pulling up the trunks, Fedor ran away and went into the water with a fish. Katya lost sight of him and screamed in fright only when Laurus quickly grasped her leg and then emerged from the water just before the girl's face.

- Crazy! - Kate slapped his palm on the muscular back. - I could have a heart failure.

"No," Lavr disagreed with her and gently pulled both hands around her slim girl's waist. - I'll have a heart break soon. From love to you.

- You're lying all. - She tried jokingly to escape from his tenacious embrace, but Fedor squeezed her tighter.

- Want evidence of my sincerity?

- Want.

It was an outright challenge. And every challenge Laurel always took. Whoever it comes from. Tight men's lips easily found her tender and supple mouth. Katya threw back her head. Before my eyes, everything spun in a rapid waltz, and she lowered her eyelashes. Did the girl love this rude man of nature whom she knew for only eight days? Oh yeah! "Does he love me?" A desperate question flashed in his head, but the next moment Katya had neither the strength nor the desire to reflect on the possible answers. And do not care about the fact that they were on the Sochi beach is not alone. And the fact that from the shore they are, of course, observed by several overly curious pairs of eyes does not mean anything. But neither Laurus, nor his beloved could not stop such a trifle. Even the likelihood that they would have to spend the night in the local "monkey" for their immoral behavior in public places, now simply did not exist. Nature has once again taken its toll.

- Look! - Kate waved her hand.
- What is it? - Laurel squinted and raised his hand to his forehead, trying to understand what Katya meant. Interfered with the sun.
- Not what, but who. A photographer, she answered. - Maybe click on the memory?
- I have nothing against it.
- Who knows? - In her voice appeared sad intonation. - Suddenly, we will never meet again. Then I will have at least your photo.
- Stop doing that. - Laurel pulled out of the breast pocket of his shirt, thrown directly on the wet body, a pack of unchanged "Belomor", crumpled the sleeve of one of the cigarettes. He struck a match and lit it. "I won't leave you now."
Fedor was really thinking about it. God bless her, with a criminal career. It is not known yet how it will be formed, whether it will be possible, but here the happiness is quite real, tangible. Hold out your hand and touch it. He did just that, pinching Katya slightly below the waist. She only laughed back.

So they took pictures. Happy, smiling, belonging only to each other. Katya seemed to glow from the inside. She had never felt so cheerful, filled with energy. Straight from the beach, a young thief took his lady's heart to a restaurant. Along the way, they, however, had to jump into the hotel, to their rooms, and Laurus thanked God that he had not found his accomplice and faithful friend Alexander Moshkin, nicknamed Sancho, with whom they had been drawing together in prison for juveniles. Two months ago, Moshkin met Lavrikov in Moscow, and it was he who initiated this trip to the south, motivating it with the fact that the Lavra should have been unraveled. But the relationship with a friend Katya Sancho did not approve, looked at them more than sullenly and unkindly.

That evening Fedor organized a candlelit dinner in a private booth. In the light of Katina's mischievous dancing flame, her eyes fascinated, beckoned Laurus.

"Why are you looking at me so strangely?" - The girl was even embarrassed.

"I just admire you," Fedor replied, glittering with his teeth. "And then ... I thought about something else ..."

- About what?

- What would you say, Katya, if I offered you to marry me? .. - Laurus looked down. - No, I understand, of course, that not enough time has passed since our acquaintance ... but ...

- I love you. - Instead of any answer, the girl just bent over the table, almost knocking over a glass of champagne on a calico dress, and kissed Fedor on the lips.

Laurel felt arousal.

"Close the door, Katya," he said shortly.

- Where the hell have you been, Laurus? - attacked Fedor Sancho, as soon as he crossed the threshold of their common hotel room at half past one in the morning.

"I was on a date," he answered simply, sitting down on the armchair and methodically undoing the buttons on his shirt. - Something happened? Fire? Flood?

- Not.

- Then why such a panic?

- In the lives of our people with you profession, Laurus, sometimes things happen more serious floods. - Moshkin came close and hung over the sitting Laurel, like a rock above the raging expanses of the ocean.

Fedor looked at him. From the expression of the comrade's face, from his tense, athletic-folded figure and, most importantly, from the intonation with which the last words were spoken, Lavrikov guessed that this was really something very serious.

- What is the matter, Sancho? - The hand automatically reached for a cigarette.

"Chernets called," Moshkin informed Lavra. - They want to see you at the gathering. Tomorrow. We must urgently return to the capital. I already took the plane tickets for five in the morning. Hurry up, Laurel. Such a chance is given to a person only once in a lifetime.

Fedor himself understood it. Chernets simply would not call him to the gathering. It was this titled thief in law, with whom Lavr happened to cross the zone, and hinted in his time to the young boy about the possible take-off of his career, about the prospects before him, Fyodor Lavrikov. And now, it seems, the day "X" has come. But Katya ... Laurus instantly grew gloomy. Insightful Sancho caught this change and easily predicted the train of thought of his friend.

"Forget the girl, Laurus," he said intelligibly. - Such as she, you still will have a dime a dozen. And here ... Dream, Laurel ... Authority, position. Are you going to give up all this?

- A black "Seagull"? - Fedor slyly squinted and released smoke through his nostrils.

- What is a black "Seagull"? - Sancho didn't get it.

- I will have it too?

"There will be, Laurus, everything will be," Moshkin hastily assured him. - So are you flying or not?

Lavrikov threw a cigarette in an ashtray, without even bothering to repay it, springily rose to his feet and swayed slightly on his toes. Katya or the crown. The choice was his. Today or never. Sancho awaited the decision with trepidation.

- Klavochka. - Catherine's voice in the handset was very sad. Noticing this fact was not at all difficult. - I'll fly out tomorrow. Twelve o'clock flight. Will you meet

"Of course, an appointment," her sister answered brightly. - Why are you so upset, Katya? What happened?

Instead of answering, the girl completely unexpectedly for the interlocutor loudly burst into tears. Klava's heart sank painfully. The fate of her sister was never indifferent to her, and even when Katya was so far away from her native penates, the anxiety for her fate doubled. And suddenly these strange, but so sincere sobs. Lord, what happened to her there? Last time, when Katya called from Sochi, she, on the contrary, was very happy. Chirping, like sparrows, literally choked on her feelings. And now…

"Katya ..." - as gently and carefully as possible she turned to the invisible companion Klava.

"Not by phone, Klavochka," she answered, swallowing tears. - I'll tell you everything when I come. Good?

- Yes, yes, of course. - She wanted to ask something else, but Katya hung up the phone without saying goodbye.

Klava listened to the short beeps for several minutes.

Chapter 1

The carefree sparrow huddle was rigidly involved in the implacable struggle with the natural sounds of the waking up morning city. A whole cacophony of sounds burst into the open window, starting with the rustling of the foliage and ending with the whistles of the car horn. It seemed that even the atmosphere had changed dramatically, somehow energetically filled up, or something.

An agile ray of sunshine tickled the nostrils of a young man of seventeen reclining on the bed, with a shock of redheads twisted into tight pigtails of hair on his head. A great many of these braids, if not for their shade, looked like a kind of wild-growing shrub or, at worst, Italian spaghetti leaked into the colander holes. The guy slowly opened his eyes, dodging his face from direct light, raised himself on his elbows and, with the complete absence of any expression on his face, slightly hung his lean body from the bed. His gaze came across the dial of the alarm clock on the floor. The young man narrowed his eyes slightly, and his hand, emerging from under the terry cloth, rose up and hung in the air for a moment.

The wait was not too long. A bell-bell alarm almost at the same second filled the room with a joyful peal, notifying its owner about the need to leave the sweet and in all respects pleasant embrace of a warm bed and switch, as they say, to the waking mode. To the mechanism devoid of emotions, human weaknesses were completely inaccessible. However, as a thank you for fulfilling his direct duties, he took a crushing blow on his metal head with an open palm.

Satisfied with the results of the clash with the metal enemy, the guy with pigtails smiled insidiously and with bliss flashed on his face again laid his head on the pillow. Hand safely returned under a warm blanket. But the guy was not in a hurry to close his eyes. On the contrary, he blinked intensely several times, gaining a sense of reality, and then stretched sweetly. It can be seen, the young man's past dreams were colorful and cloudless. Could it have been otherwise at seventeen? But the next moment, the guy's face became wary, and the hand, so cunningly treated with the alarm clock, energetically rushed under the rug down to the abdomen. The young man winced and pulled back his fingers.

"Firs," he whispered barely audibly, obviously dissatisfied with the unforeseen reaction of the body. - Only this was not enough ...

The young owner of an exotic hairstyle sprung up and took a sitting position on the bed. Thoughts about rainbow dreams had disappeared irrevocably. But, most likely, they were the direct cause of the incident that happened to the young man. Looking around, the guy got up to his full height and ran barefoot to the door. Looked out into the common living room. The noise of pouring water and the clatter of dishes informed him that his dear aunt had already occupied the kitchen and the housekeeping was in full swing.

The young man very quickly, in three jumps, crossed the small-sized apartment, which was not distinguished by its rich and refined decoration, and disappeared into the bathroom. He critically assessed his reflection in the mirror and only after that he started hygienic procedures. He felt a little confused.

- Fedech, you woke up? - An elderly, stout woman came out of the kitchen and stopped in the center of the living room, casting a short glance at the open door of the teenager's room. - I have everything ready.

Fedechka, namely the name of this hippie young man, did not answer immediately. The woman even allowed herself to approach the bathroom and gently knock on the jamb with bent knuckles. Fedech nervously turned over his shoulder.

- I saw Aunt Klava! - he said as loudly and vigorously as possible, and added a little later with obvious displeasure: - And he asked for a thousand times, do not touch my jeans!

- It was necessary to wash, as "do not touch"?

Claudia returned to the living room. Her hard, by no means feminine tread testified only to the invincibility and firmness of her character. With all her appearance, the owner of this monastery caused involuntary respect for her person and unwillingness to once again enter into confrontation with such a stately woman.

- And why did you care? - Fedech continued to talk with her through the closed door, shouting over the sound of water. - Who makes the arrows on the jeans smooth down? What to go now?

The last question was purely rhetorical, nevertheless, a clear bewilderment was reflected on Claudia's face. She approached the chair on which in the morning she hung ironed jeans and a colorful nephew's shirt. Raised one leg. Smooth arrows on worn, worn jeans pleasantly pleased her eyes. The woman even smiled to herself and shrugged.

- Jeans are pants. On the pants should be arrows. - The summary was clear and not objectionable. - Very cultural look.

Fedechka did not hear her words. And not even so much because they were said too quietly, but because of a change in their own flow of thoughts. The guy's stern look attentively felt in the mirror the reflection of his face. Today was an important day, and Fedech very much wanted it to be safely formed.

Having sighed heavily, he turned off the water, dried himself with a towel and confidently left the apartment, that is, to put it not so pompously, the combined bathroom.

Wearing ironed pants with trendy arrows Fedechka did not become fundamentally. Despite the slanting, dissatisfied looks of his aunt, he defiantly donned a pair of fringed and lilac t-shirts. The dress under his hair was just right. Fedech even liked it. Throwing a sports backpack over his back, he left the apartment and, not very precisely whistling the melody of one of the modern hits, went outside. He boldly turned the corner of the house and almost tripped over the dog. The small light curly Cocker Spaniel, which at first moment was inspired by the young man and did not notice, raising his hind paw, defecated. Another careless Fedechkin step, and a tiny dog could easily tag his shoes.

The young man cursed softly and turned his disgruntled gaze on the owner of the shameless dog, a boy of fourteen, with blue eyes like a heavenly dome, eyes and a bright short haircut. He just spread his hands guiltily. Say what can I do? I always answer for myself, but the pet ...

- Hi, Finch. - Fedechka rounded the undersized cocker and approached the lad.

"Hi," he answered, not very cheerfully. - Do you do everything?

In the voice of the juvenile dog breeder, it seemed to Fedechka, a barely perceptible arrogance and a bit of neglect sounded through.

- Not. Tied up. - Hippie straightened his shoulders backpack. - Today - the results.

"I have already been accepted," said the interviewee proudly.

Now I understand why he behaved so arrogantly.

- Where?

- In medical school.

- So, you will be a nurse? - Fedech smiled.

- Why should a nurse? - Chaffinch whimsically puffed out his already plump lips. - I'll be a nurse!

Fedechka looked at him from head to toe. Seconds six to seven, not looking away from the interlocutor, thought about something else. Only after that, looking stealthily around, turned to Chaffinch, lowering his voice almost to a whisper:

- Then tell me, Chaffinch, as a future nurse ... Everyone has a dream?

- Pollutions? - he asked.

- Well.

- Not everyone. Goats do not have wet dreams.

- Why precisely goats? - Fedech even flustered from such an unexpected turn in the conversation.

Chaffinch chuckled and important, with the arrangement, emphasizing each word, explained:

- Because the basic instincts of goats are not burdened by any conventions - neither age, nor financial, nor these ... ethical.

Fedech pensively scratched his sharp chin with his fingers.

"So I'm not a goat," he said with a clever look.

- In a certain sense - not a goat. - Chaffinch shrugged. - And in all the others - another question.

- Do not be rude, young man.

Fedech straightened up, again proudly threw up his head, and his face was reflected on his face. At this moment, he was sure that today would bring him so passionately expected positive results. The young man was full of energy and optimism for the future. Condescendingly patting Chaffinch on the shoulder, he pushed him slightly to the side and continued his victorious march through the courtyard.

"Not a fluff," a very peaceful wish of the lad reached his back.

- Go to hell! - Fedechka did not even turn around, but answered with a smile.

Chaffinch spent his long look, waiting until a more senior comrade disappears around the next turn, and again turned his bored gaze in the direction of the Cocker Spaniel. The little dog, spinning round in place and entangled in its own leash, re-ran to the end of the building and famously lifted its hind paw up. A new vital process absorbed her head.

- Caligula! Stop pissing! - Chaffinch discontentedly raised his voice. - Where did you get so much urine?

The namesake of the legendary Roman emperor with obvious incomprehension turned his little face towards his master. The answer, expected by Chaffinch, was not heard out loud.

Alexander Moshkin, known in criminal circles under the panther Sancho, long ago accepted his partly advantageous and honorable position of the right hand of the eminent thief in law Laurus. Custody of an aging authority and melomanic attachment to classical opera music were two of the most important life criteria once, in youth, a desperate and successful thief. Sancho did not complain about his fate, and he would have been a sin. In his fifty or so years, he felt firm ground and confidence in the future. Confidence, of course, relative. For in the criminal world, full of everyday surprises and deadly life turns, you can not think of anything in advance. Moshkin knew this better than anyone else. However, now this balding and getting fat literally before our eyes, the lord did not talk like a dandy, like before. On the contrary, it seemed to Sancho that it was at this stage of life that his existence entered a calm and measured channel.

Sancho put a tray on the table, fished out surgical gloves from the right pocket of his wide trousers and, with special pedantry with short fat fingers, began to pull them onto his hairy arms. The morning preparations, which were made shortly before the moment the Laurus rested on the second floor of the Lavr mansion, should have been awakened, were a whole process for Sancho. Already in gloves, he took the crystal rosette from the sideboard with his right hand and hoisted it on the center of the tray. Left picked up a glass of orange juice. Soon a plate of porridge appeared on the tray, followed by a glass of hot tea with lemon, and only at the end Sancho poured some capsule-shaped pills into an empty rosette.

All the preparations of the homegrown "butler" took about fifteen minutes. Throughout this time, Sancho was also fascinated by the fact that he enjoyed the immortal work of the Italian composer Leoncavallo "Pagliacci". The player peacefully rested in the breast pocket of Moshkin's white shirt, and the miniature earpiece in Sancho's left ear aired the outgoing game.

In fairness it should be noted that music was for Alexander almost the only outlet in life. It was in her that Sancho found for himself an inner harmony and thanks to her could reach a state very close to Buddhist nirvana. Moshkin preferred the Italian classical opera. All the inhabitants of the luxurious mansion knew about this "butler" point, and therefore no one was surprised by the fact that he could be met with a player in the lobby or on the stairs at almost any time of the day.

The eyes of the comrade-in-arms Laurus were moistened, and he even imperceptibly wiped away the mean male tear. He looked over his shoulder, checking if anyone had noticed his weakness, and then, turning down the volume of the player, he picked up a silver tray. A teaspoon in a glass tinkled treacherously. Swung and outlet with pills.

With his head held high, Sancho proceeded from the kitchen through a row of rooms on the ground floor and stopped near the stairs. With a tenacious gaze he looked at the colorful figures of two short-haired brothers, frozen like marble sculptures, in two high leather armchairs. The boys, according to their status, were dressed in black stylish tail coats and butterflies, which entered into a very strong discord with their natural brutal facial expressions. In addition, both coat-cocks picturesquely bristled near the left armpit and testified to the presence of firearms in shoulder holsters. Skinheads honestly and faithfully carried the watch. Chef safety is paramount. Sancho smiled and knowingly shook his head in approval. He straightened the tray and walked up the stairs.

The second floor of a luxurious comfortable mansion met Lavrovsky henchman with the same coffin silence as the first. Despite his build, Sancho silently, catlike, moved forward toward his master's bedroom. Pleasant Italian music is still pleasing to the ear, calling in unison with the size snoring of the music lover himself.

Suddenly, the window curtain stirred from the right side of Sancho and immediately turned back vigorously. A ray of sunshine flashed in a silver tray. Moshkin shuddered nervously and turned around. The headset fell out of its usual place and hung at the level of a thick belly, swaying from side to side, like a pendulum.

- Essentuki, why are you making a fuss? - Evil hissed a big man, referring to the broad-shouldered, athletic man, dressed in an elegant double-breasted suit.

Sancho could not see the interlocutor's face, due to the fact that he was standing with his back to the light, and his face was lost in his own shadow.

"Zhuchkov is catching and eavesdropping," the head of the laurel security service retorted in a businesslike manner.

- At night, perhaps, "bugs" divorced? - Sancho shook his head with displeasure, thereby demonstrating a sincere disregard for the action. In his view, such a procedure had the right to exist only if the person is deadly bored and he has no idea where to put himself than to do from idleness.

- Routine prevention.

- Hush then you can catch?

"It's impossible," Essentuki chopped him off too roughly, but then, noticing obvious displeasure on the interlocutor's face and not wanting to engage in useless confrontation, changed his tone: "Why?"

"You wake up the laurels — they will kill you," warned athlete Sancho quite seriously. - He is afraid of sudden spills.

- Since when? - Essentuki narrowed his eyes in disbelief, reasonably assuming that Moshkin simply plays him off.

- Yes, I read an article in the newspaper about the astral body. - Sancho shrugged his sloping shoulders. - It is in a dream - away. Laurel and fears that his soul hovering somewhere on awakening will not have time to return to the physical body.

"Vo gives ..." Yessentuki grinned at his retard smile, exposing his naturally yellow teeth. It seems that the topic of the outlined conversation he was childishly interested in. - Hey, I wonder, but where is his soul hovering?

But Sancho, as it turned out, to lead discussions with a comrade was not located. Carefully adjusting the tray with dishes with his free hand, he turned his back to the interlocutor and made it clear to everyone that the time and place for the lengthy conversations were clearly unsuitable.

- How should I know? - He vaguely led the neck. - Said: somewhere.

- I see. - Essentuki leaned his back to the window sill. - New fads.

"It's not for us to discuss them with you."

Sancho looked at his interlocutor for the last time over his shoulder, muttered something else under his breath and, leaving the pledged chief of security service in splendid isolation, as majestically as before, walked to the snow-white double doors of the bedroom of his immediate boss Fyodor Pavlovich Lavrikov. He turned the gilded handle and squeezed sideways into the room. With his free hand, he returned the earpiece of his player to its original position.

However, a huge double bed of unquestioned authority appeared to the eyes of an ally completely empty. The blanket is thrown to the side, exposing the crumpled sheet. Sancho involuntarily gathered.

- Lavrusha! - gently, but at the same time, he called out with noticeable anxiety, making a couple of uncertain and cautious steps towards the bed. - Laurel!

Sancho slightly turned his head to the right, and at that very moment something firm rested against his stomach. At a subconscious level, Moshkin easily guessed that a foreign object was nothing but the deadly muzzle of a firearm. Already, Alexander has seen plenty of these toys in his life, learning to feel them both in the stomach and in other parts of the body.

- Muzzle to the wall, hands behind your head! Alive! - sounded a terrible cry at the very ear of the "butler".

Sancho still started, but rather out of surprise than for some other unworthy reason, and grabbed a silver tray danced in his palm with both hands. He barely noticeably tilted his head forward and squinted at the enemy who had taken him by surprise. And first of all, his gaze immediately snatched the oblong finger buried in the stomach with a massive signet strung on it. It turns out that the old woman is prorukha, as they say. Sancho noisily exhaled the air from the lungs and turned around on the so-called enemy with a displeased facial expression.

Laurel, according to his passport, was listed as Fyodor Pavlovich Lavrikov, a lean man with a pale face and thick gray hair, smiled happily in his mouth. His frankly amused minute confusion ally. The authority was barefoot and dressed only in a fluttering dressing gown. Despite his impressive years, Lavr was still very handsome. The wrinkles that have creased the face only emphasized the correctness and brightness of its features. In the eyes of a mischievous glitter, the back is straight, the figure is taut. Apparently, Laurus still watched himself.

- Jokes, however! - Sancho noisily put the tray on the table to the right of the boss, turned off the player and again turned his attention to Laurus, who was laughing heartily. - I almost dropped everything.

Laurel, extremely pleased with himself, moved to the window and gently sank into the leather chair. He threw his head back and locked his fingers into the lock, gently and with a certain degree of dignity putting them on his stomach. After a moment, with a familiar gesture, he reached for a pack of cigarettes, but immediately changed his mind. More than once he already caught himself thinking that smoking on an empty stomach before breakfast was the last thing. If it is impossible to get rid of this habit at all, then it is obviously necessary to introduce some restrictions. Fyodor Pavlovich pulled his hand back and reunited his fingers on his stomach, squinted gaily, focusing his eyes on his comrade-in-arms.

- Why are you so startled? - He hospitably shook his head in the direction of the next chair. - Sit down ... conscience is not clear?

Sancho ignored the question of the eminent thief in law, but he kindly accepted the offer to sit down, squeezing his overweight body into the narrow space between the two rigid armrests with noticeable difficulty. This difficult procedure for him Moshkin spent almost five minutes. Or so.

"Juice, then a little pudding, then pills, juice again, tea," he informed the authority dryly.

- Yes, I know these ... - waving his hand, Laurus spent three seconds looking for a suitable and more or less decent word, - ritual services!

"My conscience is clear, Laurel," thought it necessary to notify the chief of Sancho, returning to the original topic of the conversation that had begun, and he added with great weight: "Before you."

"But I haven't," Laurus retorted, sighing heavily. The former gaiety and complacent mood caused by a recent joke was erased from his face, as if by magic. Thoughts returned to something deeply intimate. - In front of.

With these words, he picked up a tray, put himself on his knees and the first thing he drank orange juice. Only after that the kingpin reached for a plate of porridge. Slowly earning jaws, Laurus stared out the window with a blank look. The expression of his face could only be described as sad thoughtfulness or melancholy.

"I don't consider myself in front of me," a colleague tried to distract him from gloomy thoughts. - Theme, in kind, not relevant. Why worry?

- Then! - Laurel turned his gaze to the massive, massive "butler" who was sitting next to him, and the pupils of his eyes flashed like in his youth. Daring and boyish. - I dreamed, Sancho, in the morning ... - he began in confidence, - horror! As if I died suddenly. At a flourishing age, Carlson died, one might say. And it means that someone from the deputies of the Lord God is committing to me ... uh ... a preliminary interrogation.

"The main thing is not to sign anything in such a situation," Sancho said. - Without a lawyer, they say, I will not say a word!

- Shut up better. - Laurel winced. He was not in the mood for jokes and took the essence of the matter very seriously. "And this means that this archangel tells me, or who he is there according to the position:" Well, "he says," Lavrik, I received vodka coupons and sugar coupons in the ninety-first year, but didn't buy it? "Can you imagine what a nightmare? He rode, he says everything you need!

- Who rode? Who!

- I! - Laurel poked his finger in the chest. - His grub rations - bzdyks!

- Yes, how so, Laurus? - Sancho leaned forward the whole body. - You never expected mercy from the state! Especially in the ninety-first! When it was?

- Well! In the last century it was. - The thief in law burned more and more, proving his case. - I told him the same thing ...

- Right evil is not enough! - Sancho slapped his round knee with annoyance. He was actively involved in the game proposed by Laurel. - You took everything with your own hands, with your head! There they have nothing to do, probably, - to pester an authoritative person with coupons! Found what to sew! Talona, ugh! ..

Laurel snapped his fingers up and pushed the plate away from him on a tray. Then he relocated the entire breakfast brought by Moshkin to a round table on the right of the chair. The meal was interrupted in the most ruthless way, but apparently this aspect worried Fyodor Pavlovich the least now. Say, not by bread alone, are a living man.

- Well! I am about the same archangel and declared. - He raised his voice even more. - Like, I wanted to die according to the law, it turns out - and died.

- And he?

- Who?

"Archangel," Sancho said tactfully. He was impatient to find out how this whole story ended in the dream of the chief. Alexander himself rarely could ever boast that sometimes the god Morpheus presents people for consideration.

But with Lavra already flew courage. He slowly picked up a glass of tea and stirred with sugar with a spoon, threw one of the pills Sancho brought into the open mouth, took two unhurried and small sips.

"Archangel," he continued, frowning slightly, "bore you steeper, his oppression:" You are bankrupt, "he says," for he lived shamelessly — he never bought any laundry detergent for coupons, nor sunflower oil. "

- I would stick it on his paw, and the whole conversation! - Moshkin advised with skill.

- There is no surprise, Sancho. - Laurel leaned back in his chair and slightly contiguous eyelids. The glass of tea was still trapped in his lean hand. - Will not work.

- Everywhere it turns out, so you know!

The last words of the comrade forced the thief in law to be thoughtful. For some time he even froze in a ridiculous pose and opened his mouth ridiculously. His whole appearance and, most importantly, a puzzled expression on his face seemed to be asking: "Why am I really so childishly mired and didn't do good to anyone with a generous gift?" conversation with the archangel. Weighed the pros and cons. Sancho was also silent, waiting for a logical continuation.

- Do not wait, but why poke? - unexpectedly exploded authority, annoyed at himself. - Why on earth so?

"To get unhooked," said Moshkin calmly.

Fascinated by the conversation with the boss, Sancho somehow even lost sight of the fact that Laurel stubbornly ignored the pills he brought. Only deign until take one and only. Only now, lowering the gaze of his honest and open eyes, Alexander noticed on the tray a cherished rosette. Sancho's eyebrows sternly gathered around the massive nose. In the careless at first glance, the interlocutor instantly woke up a strict and categorical mentor.

"The food additive is burning up," he strongly advised Laurus, but then, catching in his intonation too demanding notes, he politely added: "Please."

- She is from what? - With obvious reluctance, Laurus picked up another capsule with two fingers, but was in no hurry to send it to its destination.

- From the prostate.

- In terms of? - Laurel like a cockroach wiggled his gray mustache, as if sniffing at the questionable ingredient of nutrition.

- In the sense that it was written without problems. - Sancho lowered his voice just in case, fearing that such intimate problems of the boss would not be overheard by extraneous ears, and even glanced at the door.

Laurel sighed heavily and famously abandoned, finally, this unfortunate pill in his open mouth. This time, I found it advisable to drink the additive not with tea, but with orange juice. His prickly tenacious gaze intersected with an expressionless, absent gaze of a comrade.

- And there are no additives for remorse?

This time, outwardly, the absolutely good-natured and melancholic Sancho, as he always tried to look like lately, could not stand it. He even, as far as his dense complexion allowed, sprung up in a leather chair as if stung and rose to its full height on legs that were naturally crooked.

- I beg you - leave this attitude! Drop immediately! "Pangs"!

He confidently defiled himself to the exit from the bedroom, slightly opened the door and looked out into a wide corridor.

- Well - no one sees, hears. With the move would smell - weaker! - Sancho returned to the room, went behind the back of the Laurus's jaws working intensively and, bending down, spoke almost to the very ear of authority: - In fifty-something years old, there was already a ruin with Soviet inferiority complexes! He didn't buy the coupons ... "Pangs" ... Ugh!

Fyodor Pavlovich sharply threw up a sharp chin and slightly turned his head in the direction of Alexander's wrath.

"Talk, talk! .." said the famous thief sternly. - I read about the complexes! Fuck them, and not a ruin! - Laurel with a feeling portrayed the combination of two hands known to each and every one. - I still will drive about twenty years! - He vigorously threw a napkin with monograms onto the tray and, like an ally, also assumed a vertical position. - Where is the architect?

- What is the architect? - Sancho woozy curled his bulging pupils.

- To whom I ordered to build this house. They asked for his house! Cozy! "Laurel was already nervously running around the room from corner to corner, and after many years of working closely with him to get used to such rapid changes in the mood of his boss, Sancho only changed the position of his balding head, following the movements of the laurel body. - And what is he zahrenachil? A tomb of some thirty rooms, a palace of congresses with drafts! Who am I - Tutankhamen ?!

The laurel stopped at the door, sharply turned the gilded handle and stuck his head into the resulting opening.

- Oooo! He loudly proclaimed with a howl.

- What are you doing? - did not understand his actions and inadequate behavior of Sancho.

- Do you hear?

- What?

- Echo! How in the gorge! - Laurel closed the door and tiredly plopped down on a low curved sofa. - Where is this good for? Emptiness! There can be no echo in human housing! - Seconds five authority kept silence. - Who slipped him, architect?

"Hamlet," Sancho said laconically.

He was neatly packing the remains of a laurel breakfast on a tray.

- Hamlet? - Lavrikov frowned in disgust. - Against this Hamlet, my intuition has rebelled for a long time.

- Maybe what to do with it? - slowly, but knowingly suggested Sancho.

- With Hamlet?

"You can't do anything with Hamlet," Moshkin shook his head. - The only competent economic adviser in our team ... I'm talking about an architect. Punish, maybe an architect?

- Architect? - Laurel rubbed his fingers on his temples, and then sadly stared at his bare toes. An attack of uncontrolled aggression from authority subsided, and the thinking that is in perpetual chaotic ferment has already shifted to something else. - By itself! Just not now. From sleep, I wake up a little horrible, then remind me. - On the lips of Laurus, a cynical grin appeared, resembling the grin of a full-grown predator. Before, Sancho did not once see such an expression on Fyodor Pavlovich's face. And so he liked him the most. - We will punish the architect.

- In! - Ally grin in response. - It is quite another matter. The master has awakened.

Fully expressing his approval of the "correct", in his opinion, the mood of the boss Sancho did not allow the door to Fyodor Pavlovich's personal apartments, which had suddenly opened from a crushing blow, was not allowed. Loops creaked plaintively, nearly torn out of the joint.

Lavrikov quickly jumped off the couch, ready to personally repel the enemy's unexpected attack, and Moshkin, in turn, leaving the tray with the dishes to the mercy of fate, rushed to the eminent thief in law, snatching up his weapon as he went.

The first in the room flew Essentuki with a weapon at the ready. It was a real raging beast. He crashed to the floor, famously rolled over his head, and, crouching on one knee, sent a black, deadly muzzle to Sancho who was rushing towards him. The trunk of the recently imposing and seemingly awkward "butler" also shot up in the direction of the chief of security who had fallen off the coils. Smooth, polished steel was reflected in the morning rays of the rising sun. Another moment, and a whole code of his subordinates broke into the authority bedroom. Man six, at least. And all with cocked cocks, faces twisted with rage.

Sancho prepared to die heroically in the upcoming fight, but the very next moment Yessentuki, having understood the situation, lowered the gun.

- Laurel, how are you? - with the participation in the voice asked the faithful bodyguard.

- Whats up? - Fyodor Pavlovich was still in some confusion and honestly tried to grasp the essence of the question asked by Essentuki.

- shouted. - He slowly rose from his knees and, with a barely noticeable nod, commanded his Arkharovites to hang up. - "Ay" shouted.

The authority sighed with relief and, approaching the security chief, patted him on the shoulder in a friendly way.

- Fake call. - A smile lit up the face of Laurus. - A drill. Absorb.

- Got it. - Essentuki also allowed himself to happily stretch his lips. - Free guys. All take their seats.

The "guys" retreated in a flash, and the leader of the shock brigade again shrugged guiltily, hid under the Stechkin's extensive jacket, and, backing away, was the last to leave the bedroom. Carefully, as if relying on the door that was subjected to a senseless attack, will forgive him for his former mistreatment, he closed both doors behind him.

- Have you seen? - proudly asked Laurus Moshkin. - No one sleeps.

Sancho also disarmed.

- Commendable. - On his face again returned the missing expression, and he calmly moved to the left tray.

Chapter 2

- Yes, what is it! - Fedech fiercely and completely involuntarily, having nothing personal for his soul, pushed aside the short, pimply blond boy in huge glasses. - Skip it!

He resolutely got out of the dense crowd of different voices huddling around the stands with the lists hung five minutes ago. The old, built in Stalin times, the university building today resembled a disturbed anthill. However, it was also such on other days, but when there was also a crowd of applicants striving for knowledge to the usual permanent student body, you will certainly not get over it. If not trampled, then crushed.

Fedech famously threw his compact backpack onto his shoulder and, leaving behind him mired in his own hubbub, screaming and emotionally overwhelmed by the impressions of the youth, he confidently headed for the wide granite staircase leading to the second floor. Here are just offended pursed lips, like a small child, devoid of sweets before going to bed, entered into a bright discord with a not childishly determined look and glitter of blue eyes. The boy swiftly, like on wings, flew up the steps and also quickly, without slowing down the tempo taken as a basis, headed for the office with a door upholstered in red leatherette. Near the entrance to the necessary room he stopped and took a lot of air in his chest. The knock knocked on the wooden jamb with bent knuckles.

"Actually, it's dinner now," came a dissatisfied male voice from within.

However, Fedechka, as if not having heard the words of the interlocutor invisible for the time being, pushed the door away from him and stepped onto the threshold. In his heart he threw a real storm, requiring immediate release.

- And I want justice! - He said harshly, boldly gazing at the full mustache gentleman, who sat at a massive table near the window.

A man with gray temples and a huge, almost half-face, red-nosed cheekedly chewed the same impressive size as he, a cheese sandwich, and crumbs rolling down his thick mustache, fell onto a polished tabletop covered with numerous documents. Seeing who exactly had complained to his office with complaints, the representative of the university authority changed the indifferent and lean facial expression with a sarcastic smirk.

- But only? - He chuckled.

- Seven people scored the same score! - Grievance overwhelmed Fedya. - Passing!

The mustache man just for one moment interrupted his chaotic chewing process and said forcefully:

- With such a score, it was possible to take only five.

- Why not me? - The boy's pressure was impressive, but he didn't dare to take a couple of extra steps towards the massive table.

- Answer in the forehead? - all with the same malicious smile the opponent has taken an interest. - Without a protocol?

- Go ahead, no protocol.

A moderately well-fed red-nosed gentleman slowly sent the remaining piece of sandwich into a wide mouth, absolutely not trying to break the silence established in the office, then with deep satisfaction from the completed process alternately licked each finger on his right hand and wiped his trouser piece hidden under the table. Only after that he clasped his hands in the lock and put them straight in front of him. Skeptical about the hairstyle of his young companion.

- Who are your parents, young man? - followed by a simple question.

"Suppose ..." Fedechka looked down at the floor and gritted his teeth with annoyance. - Suppose there are no parents. Only aunt is.

- When there is an aunt - it's great. - It seemed that in the man's voice warm intonations flashed for a moment. "When there is no aunt ..." He shook his head vigorously, regaining his former aplomb and a sense of apparent superiority. - The only thing that can be done is preparatory courses. Without an interview, without exams and at a discount of fifty percent. Like an orphan.

- How many? - Fedechka again raised his eyes open.

The interlocutor smiled. Apparently wanting to emphasize in such a straightforward way all the weight of his further words, he took some printed paper from the tabletop in a businesslike way, briefly read it and put it on the other side of the table. Well, just the very employment!

- Approximately two hundred a month.

- What? - Intuition prompted the young man that he already knew the answer to the question.

"Well, not rubles, naturally," his counterpart justified his predictions.

- Without discount? - In a childish voice, undisguised hope slipped through.

- Not. - Mustache shook his head. - Two hundred - already at a discount.

In the conversation again hung a pause. The interlocutors carefully studied each other, gazing at them closely. Fedech bit his lip.

- It's funny! - without the slightest sign of any gaiety he said.

"Shall you laugh," this red-nosed corrupt official replied in unison.

But the boy no longer heard his words. Turning round abruptly, Fedechka left the office, and the last replica of the mustache drowned in the sound of a loudly slammed door.

And the boy no longer just descended the stairs, he literally went downstairs head over heels and, swiftly past the crowd that was still kicking around the booths with lists, rushed out into the street. The resolute and confident man and his actions the man disappeared, giving way to the vulnerable young man. Independently of his will and desires, large tears rolled down on Fedechka's eyes, and the resentment of all mankind that came to her throat stuck in her throat with an unpleasant clod. Now the guy most wanted to, spit on all the propriety and assessment of the people around him, just a childish tears.

The street met Fedechka with its familiar hum and carefree passers-by scurrying back and forth. The caressing summer sun, which by now already had time to warm up the pliable soil, for some time disappeared behind the clouds, as if sharing with the young Fyodor Rogin his not at all bright mood. Pedestrians cautiously began to glance at the dome of the sky, fearing that unwanted downpour would break out after dinner. Fedech stopped for a moment, noisily inhaling and exhaling the air with his mouth open. In such a simple and standard way, he expected to regain emotional inner balance. At this very second, his wandering eyes and snatched out her aunt in a multi-faced crowd.

Claudia crossed the roadway with enormous leaps and bounds, deftly dodging a private trader entering the corner on a broken antediluvian "six" and rushed towards her nephew. She noticed it even at that moment when Fedechka stepped on the porch of the university. A simple old-fashioned dress in green peas was neatly and with dignity on a woman, her open sandals were on her legs, her hair was pulled back, and the absence of any make-up on her face made her look more like a representative of a bygone era. But Claudia never sought to impress others, and therefore always based in clothing and her own external appearance on the inner spirit.

Her gaze was hopeful gaze stumbled upon the gloomy, almost weeping expression of the face of his nephew, and Claudia shook her head in dismay. Some words in this situation and was not required. The disappointing result was predicted without apparent difficulty. Rozgin felt a treacherous heart beat in her chest. She regarded Fyodor's failures as personal. Over the years, developed, one might say, maternal reflex.

However, the woman, having come close to Fedechka, still allowed herself to turn to the young man with a simple question:

- Well?

She tried to look her nephew in the eye, but he stood, looking down at the hot asphalt, and was in no hurry to share with the aunt the results of today's desperate foray. Fedech waved his hand vaguely and, instead of answering, was about to pass by Claudia, but she tenaciously grasped his elbow.

- Well, talk, talk as it is! - In the voice of a woman appeared harsh intonation.

- Ay! What to talk about? - An unpleasant lump again blocked the airways, but already a second later, Fedechka, taking himself in hand, attacked his only relative with obviously unreasonable claims: - Why did you come? What has come? I asked: stay at home!

- Do not yell! - Claudia had already pulled him up completely as a parent. - Corruption?

- What's the difference? - the young man frowned and already peacefully added: - Two hundred dollars ask for preparatory!

- In year? - Auntie asked naively.

Her words brought an involuntary smile on Fedechka's lips. However, sincere gaiety in him did not increase, but because this expression was more like a certain monkey grimace. Totally unnatural and even slightly repulsive.

- In a century! - he grinned. - In a month, aunt. Two hundred a month! Rummage in the bag.

For twenty seconds Claudia was silent, either mentally reducing her personal debit to the credit and wondering how much infinity is minus in the end, or comprehending some other aspects of the matter, but in the end her gaze became prickly and her lips tightened in a tight line. Such a metamorphosis, as Fededech already knew from personal experience, did not bode well for those against whom his aunt was directed. She stepped confidently towards the university building.

- I am in the middle of these customers!

This time the nephew had to stop and grab the woman by the hand.

"Brakes," he said softly, trying not to attract too much attention from passersby to his aunt. There is absolutely no need for them to know about any troubles there related to the fate of absolutely strangers.

But Claudia started up in earnest. Anger and righteous anger floated inside her and diligently tried to find a way out corresponding to the situation.

"I'll ... drown them! .. Two hundred! .." she raged. - They must pay you! For genius.

- Drop it. Do not embarrass yourself! - almost in a whisper doomed uttered Fedechka.

Realizing for himself that it was absolutely impossible to convince his aunt and it was not worth even joining with her in the discussion on this topic in the middle of the street, Rozgin abruptly turned and walked away. He already did not give a damn about what Claudius would throw out. Worse now will not be exact. But his act, oddly enough, brought a fruitful result.

- Fedechka! Wait! - Auntie rushed after him, forgetting about her recent threats against corrupt officials, and walked alongside her nephew. An attack of surging anger gradually receded into the background, but Claudia was still looking for an object to attack. - I told you: change your hair! With such a hairstyle will not take anyone! Nowhere!

Fedech smiled bitterly in response.

- I have to change Baska, aunt! - he declared with feeling.

- Do not kill you, Fedechka. - Claudia suddenly clearly understood that her reproaches to her nephew are now, to put it mildly, inappropriate. The guy was already a chore. She even scolded herself for such egoistic behavior, and her thoughts immediately turned to a different course. - I'll think of something.

- Bank robbing? - the young man asked with undisguised irony.

But Claudia did not catch his intonation. She was already completely immersed in an adventurous idea that had seized her headlong.

"The bank is not a bank, but ..." The woman stopped in the middle of the street, not paying attention to the fact that her nephew had already rapidly gone forward. - Why not?..

- Ay, do not pass by! - the Caucasian shouted at the whole market with a huge hooked nose, more like an eagle's beak. - Why are you leaving, dear? Look at what the goods! Tomato - lovely! Appetizing and ruddy, like a female ...

The comic of the situation was also in the fact that a true native of the mountains with a similar proposal, using eloquent comparisons of his tomatoes with feminine charms, addressed exactly to the girl. To which she, only sniffing contemptuously, walked by, not honoring with her attention the goods of the mustache and the unshaven trader.

On the whole territory of the market, however, just as on the ground in front of it, it was extremely rare to see people with Slavic appearance behind the counters. For the most part, it was the Oriental characters that prevailed here, whatever type of product was offered for the purchaser's view.

Out of breath from the brisk walk, Claudia passed a number of food stalls and went deep into the very center of the shopping complex. Pushing the people elbows, she, like a locomotive, sweeping away everything in its path, quickly reached the sector of household chemicals. Behind the counter with various washing powders and other washing-cleaning products, like many others, a Caucasian with pitch-black hair and a wide mustache settled down. True, he did not strive to create advertising for his product and did not invite potential buyers passing by with guttural cries based on the fact that Losk laundry detergent, for example, surpasses the most seductive female buttocks in its structure.

The mountaineer smoked a cigarette, carelessly shaking off the ashes under his feet, and he looked indifferently at the bazaar happening around the market.

Claudia stopped in front of him, but the conversation did not hurry. Firstly, due to the fact that she could not catch her breath from the unusually fast pace for her, and secondly, because the thoughts of the woman at the moment were too far from household chemicals and everything that is somehow connected with her . The Caucasian frowned sternly.

- Why are you frozen, Claudia? - He asked strictly, catching up to the voice as much as possible dissatisfied intonations. - Get in the place, please.

The woman continued to be silent, and even the thoughtful look of her gray eyes was directed not at her interlocutor, but somewhere behind him. The pause, formed after the appeal of the Caucasian to the venerable lady Claudia Rozgina, frankly delayed. Coming from the sunny warm countries frowned even more. In addition, he managed to notice with what sarcastic smiles the merchants of the neighboring tents gaze at him. Already they better than anyone else, were already known for his difficult relationship with Rozgina.

- Hey! Sorry, of course. - Caucasian raised his tone. "But who has a paid employee?" Are you with me or am I with you? I was three hours late, and now you think. What do you think you are?

"Duma," said Claudia simply. Her, on the contrary, was not at all interested in the close glances of those around her. Or she just did not notice them.

- State?

- No, private. - She finally managed to focus on the main idea. - I can not today, Rusik. In another place is necessary. Subtract today from the salary, you're kind.

- I'm angry. - On the dark face of the Caucasians, a fierce expression appeared. - I'm scary when angry!

"One day," Claudia asked pitifully.

- I'll just fire you! - The representative of the solar countries, whom the interlocutor called none other than Rusik, sighed heavily. - Why do I need your chemical and technological education, when there are so many unemployed khokhlushek?

"Just one day," Claudia said.

- Khokhlushku take on powders! - threatened Rusik.

"Khokhlushki are illegal," the woman gently informed him. - I really need to.

Rusik grinned wryly in wide mustaches the color of a raven's wing.

- In one place?

"Yeah," Claudia didn't argue with him. - Do not be angry.

A Caucasian, a bit tedious for Claudia, thought about something, while continuing to frown theatrically, then threw a cigarette butt on the ground, took it with the tip of an orange shoe and tenaciously stared at the chemical face of the graduate. Claudia cute as she could, smiled at the employer. Rusik grunted loudly.

- But mind you! He warned gravely. - This place will be the last straw that will fill the cup of my patience! Get out of sight! - He vaguely waved his hairy hands. "And tomorrow at eight."

Claudia coquettishly doused herself, somewhat vulgarly bummed with big eyes, and at the end she also winked playfully at the Caucasians with her left eye.

"You are good, Rusik," she said with feeling.

- I know myself.

Her words, paradoxically, caused the Caucasian to be embarrassed. Young, about twenty-five years old, the mountaineer himself was sometimes afraid to admit to himself that this good, as they say, woman in her body often enough caused him to have acute sexual desire with her appetizing forms. Perhaps this was one of the main reasons why Rusik kept Claudius in his submission, turning a blind eye to her periodic forteli.

A Caucasian with a greasy look followed her stately figure. Claudia was just as quickly removed now along the trays, as before she was approaching him. Soon a simple little dress with green peas disappeared among the noisy crowd, and Rusik lost sight of her. He again sighed heavily, fished a pack of cigarettes from a wide pocket of his trousers and plunged into another nicotine-narcotic dope.

And Klava had already completely forgotten about her secret admirer, whose feelings she, like any normal woman, naturally, could not have guessed, and completely switched her consciousness to the upcoming business planned by her. Claudia was in a hurry. She herself could not explain why. After all, in the end, a few minutes, which she spends on a forced road, by and large will not decide anything, but the woman was afraid that she would internally burn out and a little later she would not dare to act so reckless.

She reached her apartment in a crowded trolleybus, and then walked a couple of blocks more. Her breathing, which was unaccustomed to such intensive walks, was completely lost, and Claudia hardly managed to climb the stairs to the necessary floor. I turned the key in the lock and stepped over the threshold. In the dim hallway stopped, listened. Apparently, there was no one in their house with Fedechka.

- Fedechka! - She called for greater certainty.

Nobody answered her call. Consequently, his nephew, who was upset by today's not very pleasant events, was walking somewhere in the city, engaging in self-flagellation based on his own insolvency. Klava shook her head hard. But on the other hand, she was glad that she did not find Fyodor at home. Now she was absolutely useless for meetings with a tribe. Memories of days gone by swept Rozgin.

For the sake of justice, it is worth noting that this simple Russian woman had lived like a machine for many years. She has never thought about herself personally. And this crazy jump on potholes and potholes of life began for her, oddly enough, even in her adolescence.

At that time, Rozgin could well have called herself pretty and not only lovers of magnificent forms stared at her. On the contrary, Klava was a slim, neat girl in all respects. All her thoughts were initially aimed at meeting a worthy young man, getting married, and having children. In short, to achieve what, according to the majority of the fairer sex, is the ultimate dream. But fate decreed otherwise.

Claudia and her younger sister Katya lost their parents early. Father died suddenly when Klava was eleven, and then his mother passed away from a severe and incurable disease. The eldest of the sisters has just turned eighteen, and Kate is fourteen. That's when Klava put a cross on herself. In the literal sense of the word. Realizing that she is the only one whom the sister can now rely on, Rozgina the elder entirely devoted herself to Kate. Forgetting about the coveted husband and children, Claudia went to work in order to feed herself and her sister. After all, Kate needed to learn.

Numerous admirers, from whom at first there was no peace, resolved themselves, eventually disappearing altogether. In the absence of a personal life, Klava stopped following her appearance. Sports and diet have become elements of unauthorized luxury. Where else to find time for it?

As for Kati, despite the decent education she received, she was not as serious as her older sister. Of course, it was also impossible to call her broken, but, unlike Klava, Rozgina Jr. could more often be found in the company of her friends and young people. Katya dreamed of getting married. Partly also in order to rid the sister of a burden in her face. However, the personal tragedy that happened in Catherine's life crossed out her plans for marriage. Pleasant compensation was the birth of the son of Fyodor. A child born out of wedlock. But Katya never even thought about having an abortion. She even categorically rejected all even the slightest hint of this unworthy topic in her understanding. About who is the father of Fedya, Kate told only her sister. Claudia understood and did not condemn. But worries in the family of Rozhiny increased. Katya has changed. Maternity is a serious thing. But even greater responsibility for the fate of two close people fell on Claudia's shoulders. Life rolled along the channel marked by fate.

Fedech grew. Two sisters managed not only to adequately educate him, but also to instill in the boy the most positive qualities. Financial aspects continued to be desired. But the child was not demanding.

Despite the absence of men as the fundamental pillar of existence, neither Klava nor Katia murmured life. They were already accustomed to this state of affairs and were quite happy in this small, but belonging only to them, now three, little world.

Then Katya died. Ruthless disease, which does not stop neither age categories, nor social status, nor the nature of the person affected by this ailment. Her death, of course, was a new serious test for Claudia. Both moral and physical. Mental experiences associated with the loss of a loved one, mixed with worries with the further fate of Fedechki. Now Klava had to become everything for the boy. The only loved one. Yes, and she was well aware that, except for her, Fedor no one. Katya always dreamed that the fate of her son was not like her own. Young Rozgin, unlike their sisters, was supposed to receive a prestigious higher education. The boy's abilities for this were abundant. The case remained for small. Help him push, so to speak. And now Claudia had to do it.

By and large, for a woman, little has changed. All the same concern for your neighbor, all the same self-sacrifice. First, the sister, then she is the same, only with her son, and directly Fedechka. This was the very life of inertia. And now, looking back, Claudia could realize that she could not achieve absolutely anything definite for herself. Could, but did not realize. For she had absolutely no time to think about it. And life is almost gone.

And again a new problem appeared on the horizon. The late sister's global dream was in jeopardy. Despite the phenomenal, as it seemed to Claudia, Fedechkina ability, stubbornly refused to take him to university. Required either money or communication. For some reason, before such a thought did not occur to Rosgina.

There was an urgent need to do something. And Claudia knew what it was. There was simply no alternative. Otherwise - the collapse. The collapse of all hope.

Quickly getting rid of her worn sandals, the woman energetically hid in the room and moved straight to the double wardrobe. Pulling a chair, Claudia climbed on him, which is why the old representative of old furniture squeaked pitifully, and reached out with her hands to the canary-colored suitcase that was peacefully resting at the top, pressed down by two colleagues as old as he. Claudia abruptly pulled the wicker handle. Once, secondly, thirdly, and only from the fifth in a row of an attempt she managed to achieve the desired result. The canary suitcase slipped out from under the brethren, but the woman failed to keep him. Having shot up a layer of age-old dust to the ceiling, the bulk of the luggage flew to the floor, almost dropping its liberator from the chair. With a thud, the suitcase fell to the floor, rolled over its axis and swung open.

As young, Claudia jumped off after the suitcase and crouched beside him. The contents of the family heirloom were in a chaotic mess, and the woman had to sort through a bunch of different junk in the form of paper that had turned yellow with years, various small jewelry boxes, pieces of cloth, and many other things, before gazing out of all this chaos. The one that Klava so diligently and tried to find. Almost from the bottom of the suitcase, she fished her black lacquer handbag into the light of day, which was previously fashionable to call theatrical. The layer of dust covering this very bag would have caused envy and respect from anyone.

"It seems to be here," Claudia whispered, moving her lips barely noticeably.

She flipped the metal clasp and peered into the bag. Her predictions were justified by one hundred percent.

To the gray steel gates of a massive mansion, surrounded by a high fence of unpainted concrete slabs around the perimeter, a dark-purple foreign car slowly drove. The black peephole of the video camera, located to the right of the entrance, turned on the calling sound of a car horn. Hamlet, a burning brunet with brown eyes and a square jaw, who had nothing to do with the legendary Shakespearean hero, merrily waved his hand to the lens, leaning out of the salon right on the half-body. An invisible opponent, located somewhere on the territory behind a special monitor, easily recognized the guest who had arrived at the mansion, and therefore the gate, powered by a simple mechanism, smoothly drove off to the side, letting the car into the yard.

Hamlet took a quick glance at the wrist of his left hand, where the expensive Rolex casually dangled. But Hamlet rarely paid attention to such trifles as monetary expenses. With financial issues, he was always on "you" and could literally make a fortune out of thin air, which is why he was considered an indispensable person in certain criminal circles. And Hamlet himself, it should be noted, knew his worth.

He turned the car in the center of the courtyard and got out of the cozy leather interior. He flicked an alarm stick and turned around with his well-groomed face to the front porch. Thirty-year-old financial adviser Laurus adorned with stylish, light-colored trousers, a pink shirt with a single-colored long tie, and dark smoky glasses that hid the Caucasian's narrow eyes from nature. Hamlet's legs were shod in black pointed shoes. With his right hand, the guest pressed to the torso a chic leather briefcase with documents brought with him.

Hamlet climbed onto the porch with a confident gait, nodded affably to two gorilla-like guards at the entrance, and disappeared behind the doors of the mansion. No one met a Caucasian, but he, incidentally, didn't really need it. The location of the rooms in the house of Fyodor Pavlovich he already knew so well.

Lavra was already informed by internal telephone of the arrival of the financial adviser, but the thief in law rather sluggishly met the guest in the same bedroom, where a couple of hours ago after breakfast he was left in proud solitude by faithful Sancho. The lawyer did not even consider it necessary to change his clothes, still flaunted a pair of slippers in his bare feet and a dressing-gown. From time to time Laurus was attacked by some kind of laziness, and he could not help it. Even the fight stopped. For what? Everything will pass and so, by itself.

As soon as Hamlet crossed the threshold of the authority bedroom, he immediately turned his attention to Lavrikov's bored face. It turns out that the conversation will not be easy. The thief did not like the topic that the adviser had thrown to him for reflection the day before. Hamlet took off his glasses and squinted. Nothing. He also had a trump ace up his sleeve, reserved for the final chord. Today he will use it. And there will be nothing to cover the Lavra. Yes, and the desire of his like does not arise.

"Hello, Laurel," the Caucasian said as energetically and naturally as possible, settling down in an easy chair, without an invitation. He attached the briefcase with documents on the armrest, covering it with his right hand.

- Hi Hi. - The thief in law did not deign to rise from the bed, but, on the contrary, picked up both his legs. He picked up a nail file and focused on studying his fingers. - What's new, Hamlet? Is everything calm in the Danish kingdom?

The Caucasian smiled tightly, showing that he fully appreciated the boss's humor, but he immediately put a serious expression on his face.

"I would like to return to our conversation yesterday, Laurus," said Hamlet softly, but with some pressure. - It would be desirable to hear your decision. From the first, so to speak.

- Wait. - Laurel proceeded to polish the nails, not looking at the interlocutor. - Do not drive horses. Explain to me how a simple idiot, fuck us this plant?

- How the fuck ?! - The financial adviser was a little confused. It seemed to him that this question was not even negotiable. - Very fucking! Just a minute.

He got up from the chair and walked to the switched on computer modestly tucked in on a low table by the window.

- Here. - Hamlet quickly ran his thin fingers on the keyboard, like a real hacker. - Will now be!

After some short actions, he turned a flat crystal monitor screen to the Lavra. On display, the authority was offered a scheme of urban development with a red rectangle blinking on it almost in the center. The forefinger of Hamlet with a well-groomed, like a woman's, fingernail picturefully stuck into this most notorious square.

- Here - we, yes! - He rattled, turning around to the Lavra. - And here we are, and here, and here! And in the middle - this donut hole, this plant! Here we are not! No one is here! - Emotions overwhelmed the horseman.

- What does it produce, a factory? - Lavrikov asked sluggishly, flexing an unlit cigarette with his fingers. The thief in law still cherished a dream in his soul to reduce his need for smoking to a minimum.

- What's the difference? - Hamlet frowned. - In a pinch, each shop is thousands of square meters of retail space! And the fact is that the dowel was abandoned about his bankruptcy and the introduction of his external manager.

This was the trump ace, carefully kept by Caucasians for a suitable occasion. Such a case has come, and the reaction of Laurus, expected by the interlocutor, was not long in coming. The authority swallowed the bait with a hook, like a starving stupid minnow.

- Dowel? - In the voice of Fyodor Pavlovich, genuine interest finally appeared. He had gotten all the way, a lazy expression had flown from his face, and the cigarette, just like the nail file before, had been thrown out of uselessness on an unclosed veil.

- And how! - Hamlet returned to the chair and picked up the expensive briefcase dropped from the floor. - It turns out - around us, and in the middle - he! This is a blatant expansion, Laurel!

- Dowel bummed. - Lavrikov sprained his feet on the floor and rose from the bed.

- And how! - Financial Advisor frankly exulted. - It will turn out, Dowel - like any other Kaliningrad in the Baltic environment.

- What? - did not get the idea of laurel.

- Dowel - Kaliningrad allegedly. Kenigsberg Dowel!

- Dowel - Koenigsberg ?! - indignantly repeated the thief in law. His long legs had already begun to pace the room energetically.

- Well!

- And we? - The gray head turned towards the financial adviser.

Hamlet smiled brightly.

- And we - like the Baltic, it turns out - he concluded.

Lavrikov stopped near the monitor turned on, silently peered into the bright yellow image with a blinking red square and rocked monotonously on his toes for several minutes. Thinking over something. What kind of thoughts were overwhelmed at the moment by a major criminal authority, Hamlet would not have taken it upon himself to predict. All that he hoped for was that these very thoughts were moving in the direction he needed, the economist at Laurels. He silently waited for the decisions of the big boss. Finally, Laurus unexpectedly stopped his movements and abruptly pressed his right fist to the open left palm.

"It does not come out," he said with a ferocious grin, and his high forehead was cut through by several majestic relief wrinkles. - What are we to the devil Balts? If the Balts. - He turned over his shoulder and carefully gazed at the swarthy face of his financial adviser. - We are Russian, Hamlet Oganesovich.

A moment of confusion was reflected on the adviser's face. He could not understand: whether Laurus deliberately makes fun of him and sarcastically raises the question of nationality, or whether authority is so carried away by reasoning that he utters phrases on autopilot, mechanically. However, Hamlet would not be the very Hamlet, which he was, if in an instant he did not control himself.

"Of course they are Russians," he did not argue, yet still in some confusion at such unexpected pressure from the boss. According to the Caucasians, Lavr clearly overplayed his emotions.

- Therefore, Dubel is on-kas, not his external manager! - meanwhile continued to rant authority, poking a crooked kishish almost in the nose of the hushed and dumbfounded Hamlet. - We have our own - if you want external, you want - internal ...

- In bulk all right? - cautiously asked a Caucasian, fearing another outbreak of groundless rage Fedor Pavlovich.

- Yes! - Laurel stepped to the window and pulled wide the heavy curtains. The bedroom immediately became noticeably brighter, which further breathed energy into the owner of these apartments. He proudly straightened and pushed his chest wheel. - You'll give up the dowel, he will grab the entire passbook! - the eminent thief did not let up. - There is a question of principle! - It seemed that Lavrikov only now noticed Hamlet peacefully sitting in the chair and said no longer in faceless space, but directly in the interlocutor's eyes: - You must act, act! What are you doing? Get up, run.

"I'll run now." - Caucasian vigorously jumped to his feet and almost on the fly picked up his fashionable leather briefcase. - But ... Price? What is the price?

Laurel shoved his hands deep into the pockets of his wide-brimmed dressing gown and swung his toes several times. Automatically he caught himself thinking that another ugly habit had stuck to him.

"In matters of principle, I don't stand behind the price," he said, and immediately a new wave of aggression swept through his mind. "Heh ... Dowel! .. Who is Dowel ?! A puppy with milky incisors! .. I used to pin such dowels into the wall of the bucket with a finger.

Laurel thought for a second, then tiredly plopped down in a chair where his financial adviser was still so seated, and snapped his finger in the air. From experience, Hamlet knew that Fyodor Pavlovich usually focuses in such a way on the attention of others to an idea that has suddenly matured in his head. The Caucasian himself, as a rule, was afraid of these accents. With Laurel, everyone was supposed to keep their ears open. You never know what kind of trick he will throw out in the next moment. Hamlet tensed, as before waiting for a crushing blow to the jaw, and a stone mask appeared on his face. Intuition did not disappoint the native of the mountains.

- I'll warn Essentuki! - Lavrikov said weightily, and his tenacious fingers instantly fished out a miniature cell phone box from his pocket. The authority has rejected the panel lid. - I will not even soil myself! Let him feel it ...

Hamlet jumped to the boss and somewhat familiarly laid his hand on his right shoulder. Laurel squinted a disgruntled look, and the Caucasian, feeling that he had enough in his familiarity with the lawyer, abruptly drew his hairy brush, retreated two steps back and shook his head in dismay. Fyodor Pavlovich raised his left eyebrow in surprise, trying to understand exactly what the still silent protest of the economic adviser was based on.

- What? - with frank disdain he stared at the Caucasian. - Any problems?

- Not. - Hamlet nervously swallowed and immediately added hastily, without taking his brown eyes from Laurus' finger hanging above the telephone buttons, with the look that this very finger was preparing to take off an atomic bomb anywhere in the United States of America. - Yessentuki is not necessary! First you need to try macroeconomic methods, and then we'll see.

Thief in law slammed compact phone.

- sure? - just in case he asked briefly.

- One hundred percent. - Hamlet nodded.

The little black box again disappeared into a spacious pocket, and the authority itself gradually began to calm down, leaving the storm raised by the Caucasians themselves. His head, with already thoroughly graying hair, lay back limply, safely meeting the high leather headrest. Laurel adjoined the eyelids and several times with the noise exhaled from the lungs accumulated air. Hamlet hesitantly stalked around, not knowing how he should do in this situation. Either quietly retire, without straining the boss with his presence, or be sympathetic to inquire about Fyodor Pavlovich's well-being.

Laurel opened his eyes.

- Are you still here? - asked in an ordinary everyday voice, as if it was not he who was burning up and splashing saliva in different directions a couple of minutes ago.

"I'm leaving, I'm leaving," the Caucasian began to fuss.

"But keep in mind," Lavrikov threw after him, the Highlander's barely hairy brush lay on the gilded door-handle. - If macroeconomic fails ... Then right up to the war!

- Of course. - Hamlet smiled tightly, turning over his shoulder, and already the next second disappeared through the door.

- Dowel! - again grunted Laurus, left in splendid isolation.

And Hamlet, fully and completely satisfied with the outcome of today's talks with the boss, and in particular with the achieved result, slowly descended the stairs with a sugary smile on his lips, passing an impressive cordon of guys from the lethal Essentuki brigade, and smoothed his hair curling at the back of his neck with shaggy fives. He put smoky glasses on his nose and went outside, exposing the already sunburnt face to the hot sunshine. The day could be considered successful. A Caucasian fished a car key chain out of his pocket, and his foreign car squeaked with joy, freeing himself from the alarm lock. Hamlet freely settled in the cabin and set both hands on the wheel. For a minute, he probably sat motionless, after which he resolutely started up, as if returning from the world of dreams to the vital reality, and playfully turned the key in the ignition under the steering column. The engine responded to his call with a soft, monotonous rumble.

Chapter 3

For about twenty minutes, Claudia looked hopelessly and with pronounced vexation on the concrete fence around the perimeter of the wide courtyard, in the center of which stood a country mansion. She also carefully studied the steel gates, located directly in front of her, and a video camera at the top, which, probably, also with no less interest looked at her black eye as an uninvited guest in an old-fashioned attire. Local technicians have not yet seen such persons. But this woman did not care. Much more worried about her was the sad moment that she would hardly be able to penetrate the territory without hindrance, as she had planned it initially, still heading here. But, you can say, the last money spent on a taxi. And why did she, fool, decided that without any hindrances she could achieve an audience with Lavrikov?

Claudia was about to turn around in disappointment and move on foot towards the city, without achieving the desired result, when suddenly the steel gates drove off to the side, releasing a dark lilac automobile of foreign production. Klava did not understand the brands of a foreign manufacturer, and she didn't need it. She just clearly realized at that moment that she simply wouldn't have another chance like this one. The woman rushed forward very quickly for her build, and Hamlet, who was leaving the territory, had to press the brake pedal sharply on the floor in order not to knock down the crazy pedestrian.

Claudia, like an enraged fury, stormed into the courtyard with a voluminous white bag over her shoulder and rushed vigorously to the high porch of the mansion. However, the local guard was not asleep. One of the Mordovortov in a black double-breasted suit and with short cropped blond hair literally in two giant leaps jumped to the cheeky person and abruptly intercepted her arm above the elbow.

- Stop, aunt! - His terrible cry sounded Claudia in the ear. And in the back already poked a shortened barrel machine. - Where?

Claudia turned over her shoulder. In addition to the aforementioned willy-nosed men in a suit, another type of medium build, with big brown eyes, like large bowls, joined their warm company. He was dressed in camouflage from head to foot, and the machine gun, the barrel of which Claudia felt with her spine, also belonged to him. From the concrete gatehouse near the very gates, the third arkharovets rushed swiftly, waving their arms. This arsenal was completely killer. "AKM".

- Bag! - he shouted at the whole yard, and Claudia felt that the young boy, about twenty years old and more, had the intention of knocking a woman down by all means, pushing her down on the ground and taking the dangerous, in his opinion, burden.

Claudia abruptly pulled her hand out of the blond's tenacious fingers and jumped aside. However, she, as she could, took the fighting stance. This position, she has repeatedly seen on television in the steep Hollywood action movies. With the help of this simple trick, Rozgin, naturally, did not hope to repel Fyodor Pavlovich Lavrikov's most powerful and professional protection, but in any case, there was a chance that this stance would cause some confusion in their ranks.

- I'll give you a bag now! She bravely yelled back. - Papers there, not a bomb! Remove the barrel!

The desired effect of its action is not produced. Camouflage and did not think to fulfill her request, continuing to direct the weapon in the direction of a harmless woman. He was holding her as a sub-gun, but he was not in a hurry to open fire. The vibrations affected his tanned, clean-shaven face. Meanwhile, the AKM owner jumped close to Claudia and, together with a guy in a dark suit, made a desperate attempt to seize the alleged terrorist in the ring and withdraw the questionable inspection from her dubious baggage store.

- Arms! - Claudia screamed, eerily dropping up her bag as a means of defense. - Do not paw!

Having described a semicircle in the air, the burden with documents was beautifully imprinted exactly on the top of a short-haired blond. The camouflage smiled wryly. Hamlet, still in the car near the gate, also looked at the events taking place in the courtyard with interest. The aunt was a desperate special, capable of causing genuine admiration. At this moment, the front door of the mansion opened, and a new character, still unknown to Claudia, flew off the porch. It was the head of security service Essentuki.

- Stop screaming!

He quickly walked towards the scene. There was no jacket on Essentuki, only a snow-white shirt in a barely noticeable section and a thin fashionable tie slightly weakened in a knot. As a result of this circumstance, the shoulder holster with the "stachkin" tightly squeezed into it was on public display. But Claudius was not intimidated by such trifles.

- Who are you, madam?

He stopped directly in front of the persistent visitor and spread his legs wide apart, like a real granite monument. But at the same time, Essentuki tried to look like gallantry and courtesy itself. Unlike his henchmen, he was aware that she was only a woman and, despite the belligerent behavior of this person, she could hardly present a real threat.

"To Lavrikov for me," Claudia replied with her natural dignity, dropping her formidable weapon.

Essentuki waved his hand briefly, and two of the recent opponents of the woman who arrived arrived at the gate gate. Having lost interest in what is happening, Hamlet also left the territory. Next to the security guard, there was only a blond in a double-breasted suit, and he stayed away from the guest talking to the boss at a respectful distance. To receive a new biting blow to the shaved head did not smile at him.

"Regarding the issue?" The security chief continued to try in the meantime.

- By personal.

Essentuki nodded knowingly and fastened on his face a stupid smile on duty.

"Mr. Lavrikov works on charity on Thursdays from two to five," he politely informed the person in the old-fashioned dress. - By appointment. There, in the booth, sign up and - all the best, madam ...

"By the way, I'm a maid," Claudia sniffed contemptuously.

- It is to blame. - Essentuki frankly blurred.

- And not for begging! - In the voice of a woman came true true natural dignity. - Are you a caretaker?

- Something like that. - The pressure of the woman finally confused the interlocutor.

"So take this one." - Claudia pressed the bag to her chest and with a quick movement undid the sewn "zipper". I launched my right hand into the dark leather interior.

- What? - Essentuki's watchfulness appeared in his eyes.

- What you need! Wait, get it now ...

Under the watchful, intense eyes of the guard, a woman spent about two minutes, probably rummaging through the contents of her bag, until she had taken out an old photograph of God with lightly cut edges. Carefully smoothed it with a plump palm and only after that stretched out to the bewildered Essentuki. Silently he took the picture and, for some reason, turned doubtfully on the blond subordinate. He only looked to the side, not wanting later to bear any responsibility for the decision of the chief. Yessentuki turned the photo and carefully looked at the image. The youthful, trimmed man in the picture seemed to him vaguely familiar, but there was no absolute certainty. And where could he see him? The colorless glass eyes of the security chief again went up to the woman standing in front of him.

"Until I let you in, I won't leave," Claudia said more than weightily, noticing the serious hesitations on the face of her counterpart. - Though shoot from all your howitzers!

Yessentuki frowned. It seems he had no choice.

Laurel studied for a long time and thoroughly a snapshot that had turned yellow over the years, setting up horn-rimmed glasses on the bridge of his nose in a businesslike manner. After the report of Essentuki, he expressed genuine interest in meeting the newly arrived person. Now Claudia was modestly sitting right in front of him, snuggling on the edge of a high-backed chair. The authority took her in his office and for this purpose even deigned to dress in trousers and a light shirt with short sleeves. Moreover, Laurel brought his shaggy hair in relative order and, in a fashionable fashion, brushed it back and wet his temples.

Unlike the head of his own security service, the thief in the law easily recognized in the male representative in the picture himself, who only looked much younger. But besides this, the photograph also had a pretty girl with a radiant smile, which Laurus himself gently hugged her waist against the background of subtropical Black Sea plants. Captured events clearly related to some holiday season, but when exactly this happened, Fyodor Pavlovich could not remember. He could not remember the girl he hugged, although, as a true connoisseur of feminine beauty, he could not help but recognize the shedding of completely forgotten lady charm.

Laurel finally raised his eyes and gazed at Claire, who had fallen silent over his glasses. She, on the contrary, avoided looking at the owner of the apartments, devoting all her attention to the modest smoothing of the calico dress in her lap. Honestly, she could not even imagine that this visit would be so painful and awkward for her.

- It's me. - Fedor Pavlovich slowly lowered the picture on the tabletop in front of him. "Fifteen years ago."

"Eighteen," Claudia corrected mechanically, without raising her head.

- May be…

Silently, Lavr continued to stare at the guest sitting in front of him with a tenacious gaze. He sincerely hoped that the woman would still deign to explain to him the purpose of today's visit, but Claudia, too, was in no hurry to break the silence established in the office. The dialogue frankly did not develop. Authority could not stand the first:

"But it's not near you." - In his short phrase managed to fit several emotional intonations at once. On the one hand, Lavr was sure of what he was saying, but then a little doubt flashed, and as a result, a hidden hope sounded in his voice, mixed with the fear that a woman who arrived at the mansion could be his old passion.

- Next - my sister. - The woman's answer made Laurel sigh with obvious relief. - Katya. The youngest. Katerina Rozina.

- Ugh, what a sullen last name. - Fyodor Pavlovich openly smiled and threw one more sidelong glance at the picture before his eyes. - I do not remember. All, dear, with whom I ... smiled for a couple, it is impossible to keep in memory.

Laurel himself liked how floridly he put it. And he did not seem to offend anyone with a harsh word. Intelligently so sounded, politely, but with some irony.

"A smiling young man, however," Claudia shook her head.

- That was, that was. - With a satisfied expression on his face and a lecherous smile on his lips, Laurus leaned back on the high back of the chair. Memories of stormy youth pleasantly touched the soul. Not in vain, therefore, lived. - Loved to fool around pre-love-deino!

- "Loved" - in the past tense the word, - Claudius cooled his nostalgic mood, returning the graying man to the harsh reality. - And now? Pills?

Her words and an ironic smirk made Laurus instantly grow ridiculous.

- Careful, woman! - He leaned the body forward.

"Don't twitch yourself, he asked for rudeness himself," Klava said more peacefully. - She died almost three years ago. Tumor.

- Who? - The main thread of the conversation was lost.

"Sister," Claudia explained. - Katya. Died.

- Yes? - No shadow of condolence or, at worst, human participation flashed on the stern, wrinkled face of authority. - I sympathize ... People are mortal. And I know this much better than you.

"I know something else, Lavrikov," Claudia continued, ignoring his purely philosophical maxim. - You then seduced the girl in Sochas ...

"In Sochi," Lavr interrupted her.

- What?

"In Sochi," he repeated forcefully. - Sochi is not leaning.

- Yes, I do not care if Sochi is inclined or not inclined! - suddenly the woman got angry and significantly raised her voice. - Katyushka once in her life received a trade union ticket from a hosiery factory. For the victory in socialist competition received. And I, fool, let her alone. You on pleasure.

- ABOUT! I can guarantee. - Slightly chapped lips Laurel touched another smirk of the serpent-tempter. "Your sister was not disappointed." And ... - He frowned. - No, first name is last name. But something related to the hosiery industry ... I vaguely recall this ... Because it's ridiculous. It crashed ... There were no socks, but the industry was there. - Sukhonko laughing, the authority suddenly vigorously rose from the table, squinted suspiciously and came close to the visitor. "But why all the sweet talk about the last century?"

"Katya gave birth to you, Lavrikov," Claudia said toughly, emphasizing on almost every word.

The expected response from this message was not followed. The view of Laurus has not changed at all. Complete calmness and indifference to what is happening. This time, however, he did not struggle with temptation and, bringing the ashtray closer, lit a cigarette. According to the old camp habit, Fyodor Pavlovich preferred to use strong cigarettes. All he managed to do was switch from the truly thieving cigarettes "Belomorkanal" to something more decent and civilized. A cloud of thick smoke shot up under the high ceiling, and a moment later it dissolved there. Laurel cleared his throat.

- Yes? - indifferently asked the thief in law after a pause.

- Yes.

- Interesting.

Claudia's eyes filled with treacherous tears. Deep in her heart, she expected a slightly different reception in this mansion. More soulful or something. Or at least more affable.

- No matter how they broke it in the trade union, an abortion was not given. - A sad phrase completed a heavy sigh. - Has given birth.

- Boy or girl? - The undisguised sarcasm of the kingpin acted on Claudia in a depressing way.

"Boy," she said softly. - Fedor Fedorovich Rozgin. In the metric opposite dad stands.

Laurel smacked his tongue and went back to his desk.

- What to do? - He crossed his arms over his chest, imitating Chernyshevsky and only slightly distorting the question that tormented the writer. - A dash, it is a dash.

"We raised him together, child." - Claudia did not hear him, completely immersed inside her soul. - Now I am alone.

- Well done. - Laurel pursed his lips. "In our time, to raise a child alone is a big, very big feat ..." After a short pause, authority again rapidly approached the guest and already hung over her formidable golden eagle. Fyodor Pavlovich's eyes froze. - Just something late you blackened up with such foolishness. Or sent someone taught?

Claudia looked down at her sandals and shook her head sadly.

"Katya was afraid of this," she said, breathing heavily.

- What?

- You! - Slightly pushing back on an oak chair, as if pulling away from the Laurel breathing in her face, the woman rose to her feet. The growth of Claudius was approximately equal with Lavrikov.

"Why fear me?" - The lawyer stepped back a couple of steps. - I - not Kashchey.

"I was afraid that you could ruin a child because of your criminal laws. - Claudia's words were scathing, loud, like hammer blows on an anvil. She regained her habitual aplomb, knowing full well how stupid and absurd her decision was to come to this house. She counted on humanity! Funny But now there was nothing to lose. Although there is an opportunity to speak out. The good thing is the interlocutor that is needed. - And the kid did not say a sound. Thoughts did not even appear to you.

"So, she, at the seduced and abandoned, did not have," Laurus interrupted rudely. - And you - announced?

"And I wouldn't go for anything," the woman said firmly. - Only Fedechka is a genius. And he was not accepted to the university - with a passing grade, but without the father-mother. Two hundred dollars a month is required for preparatory courses. Wherever you spit - the mafia is everywhere!

For a moment, Lavra thought that Claudia was really going to spit on the tiled floors of his private apartments.

- Two hundred is a problem? - The authority, in astonishment, raised its left eyebrow in relief and fished it out of its mouth.

Claudia smiled bitterly. She perfectly understood that she and the wealthy man sitting in front of her had completely different ideas about large and small amounts. The fact that she considered two hundred dollars a fabulous sum, to possess which was something from the field of unscientific fantasy, did not mean that for Laurus. Fyodor Pavlovich, according to Rozhina, could even spend so much on things completely unnecessary for a day. The woman involuntarily fixed her absent-minded gaze on her own knees and it is not known why she put on a modest chintz dress, acquired by God knows what year.

- Where can I get them, when the entire salary is half the least pulling ?! - With sad irony in relation to herself, she said. - And the child should be fed growing, and his computer eats money on the first-th.

Lavrikov unexpectedly started and, returning to the ashtray for a moment, put out his cigarette, having smoked it, probably less than half. With a tenacious gaze he gave the confused face of the lady, who had come to visit without invitation.

- Computer, you say? - For the first time during a lengthy conversation in Fyodor Pavlovich's voice a keen interest appeared.

- Computer ... Okay. - Claudia waved her hand and, turning abruptly, headed for the exit. - I can see by a smirk, in vain I thought of it - to ask. You are right. - Her huge palm rested firmly on the door handle. - A dash, it is a dash.

But in the soul of Laurus something has already interconnected, so to speak.

- Wait a minute. - The authority caught up with her and intercepted the brush that had already fallen down. - Do not jump. Photo where?

"On your desk," Rozgin shrugged. - Forgot?

- No, not that. - Laurel returned to his desk, grabbed the picture and approached Claudia with him. - Take this one. The boy. And the phone is home.

- Home to you to anything. - The alignment of forces has changed, and the woman no longer felt in herself the former insecurity. The atmosphere of the richly furnished room ceased to act depressingly on Claudia. And the unexpectedly changed behavior of the apartment owner played a role. Roszina even allowed herself to stand up and proudly throw up her head. - At home, we do not need help. So I wrote the institute, the faculty of economics. "She took a resort photo from Laurus's hands, in which the crime boss was depicted in an embrace with her sister, and instead of her, she put a folded four-page sheet in the palm of a thief. - If you want to help with your studies, it's good. No, God is your judge.

But it was not so easy to contradict Fyodor Pavlovich, to dictate and impose the rules of the game. The next second, the woman's hand was captured by his tenacious, thin fingers.

- Photo come on! - evil hiss Laurus, flashing eyes. - I see - the bag is full, the entire archive, come, dragged. And God will not judge me, but you, if this is a setup. And - no sound, sister! I live with the crown and I want to die with her ...

Their faces came together in close proximity to each other, and for about five seconds, probably both were snorting heavily. Claudia's wide nostrils flared dangerously. That and look, the smoke will fall down.

- Loosen the claw. - The pupils of the woman, too, unkindly flashed with undisguised challenge. - I'll leave without eyes! - She swung her free hand shortly, and Lavrikov involuntarily recoiled. - Scared, of course! "And yet she opened her purse and looked inside. "Dracula ... Thrifty thunderstorms." On! The fingers grabbed one of the photos of Fedechka, fished it out, and handed it to the other person.

After that, Claudia turned the doorknob and, without saying a word to the owner, left the office. Even to utter the elementary words of farewell, the woman considered superfluous.

"Not a woman, BTR," Fedor Pavlovich grumbled, and, clutching a precious trophy in his hands, won back with such difficulty and stress on the nervous system, he returned to his desk.

Coming down from the second floor of the Lavrovsky mansion along a wide staircase, Claudia almost face to face faced Sancho ascending. True to his invariable perseverance, Moshkin, being alone with himself, rarely did without the traditional headphones of a compact player inserted for the intended purpose. While enjoying the classical operatic music of great composers of all ages and centuries, Sancho was filled with powerful inner energy and at the same time rested with his soul. But, noticing the monumental figure of Klava, who was marching towards him, Sancho stopped dead in the middle of the staircase, and his narrow eyes, by nature, began to rapidly grow in size.

Heart pounding in his chest, sending an involuntary impulse to the head. The hand mechanically freed the ears from the two miniature circles closing them. For a moment, all the music of the world ceased to exist for Alexander, muffled by the new masterpiece that appeared before him. Hitherto unknown feelings of Sancho visited his soul and mind. He nervously swallowed the closure of his throat and even blinked at the necessary moment when he should have stepped aside to let the lady through.

- Watch out. I will touch, - Claudia loudly proclaimed, whose plans obviously did not include stopping the started descent.

Already at the last second, Moshkin managed to squeeze into the railing, pick up his beer belly and straighten his shoulders for greater solidity. Claudia promptly walked past him, not even deigning a passing glance. Only when she was at the foot of the stairs, she turned briefly over her shoulder and contemptuously threw a phrase unfavorable to the inhabitants of the mansion:

- Raspberries!

"Well, why is it so ... right away," said his faithful associate of the famous thief in law, discouraged, but the woman did not hear his dull attempt to justify himself before a stately stranger. Sancho has never felt so undeservedly offended, insulted to the depths of the soul.

The front door slammed shut, and Claudia again appeared before the gaze of the Arkhar fighters who had been trying to join the hand-to-hand fighting with her not so long ago. Essentuki promptly separated from the common mass of thugs and stepped towards the guest.

- Girl! - he said prudently, remembering how Klava offendedly reacted to the pompous treatment of "Madame". "There is an order to take you home."

He bent in a gallant bow, and then pointedly pointed out with his hand at a crowed jeep huddled near a steel gate with headlights on. Now Essentuki reminded his guise of a guilty cab driver, who diligently tries to atone for past mistakes and curry favor with the lady. His appearance was very comical, but none of his direct subordinates allowed himself a rash smile.

- To the subway, boy. - Claudia condescendingly put her huge hand on his broad, pumped shoulder. - On the subway will be a hundred times faster. There are less traffic jams.

The icy snake grin for a moment touched the narrow lips of the security chief, but he immediately picked himself up and gently said:

- As you say. - Essentuki stepped aside, passing the woman forward. - I beg…

Claudia confidently walked to the jeep and climbed with difficulty to the salon. The driver was already in place, and a second later the front passenger seat took Essentuki.

"Let's go," he said shortly.

The best way to get rid of sad thoughts, as well as to wash off the irritation and feeling of an unjust resentment, Fedechka determined for himself the opportunity to swim in the cool, caressing body exhausted by the summer heat of the water. To this end, he arrived at noon on the beach of the Academic ponds, instead of going home or somewhere else. People on the beach, despite the weekday, was also plenty. However, what is there to be surprised. Summer is a holiday season, and everyone, if he or she does, seeks, if not to the resort, to the Black and Mediterranean seas, then closer to the waters for sure.

With confident movements, Fyodor Rozgin threw off his clothes, folded his shorts and a T-shirt next to his backpack, and merrily ran towards the weak waves rolling on the beach, wrinkling painfully at every contact of his bare feet with hot beach sand.

The pond, located on the edge of the Timiryazevsky Forest Park, baptized Academic, occupied a very impressive space. And underwater springs allowed to keep the water relative cool. So the local youth in the hot summer vacation here was the most favorite place.

Fedech, with a run, plopped down into the water, splashing at the same time a fountain of splashes sitting on the beach, like him, lovers soak up near the pond. The puny youthful body quickly went to the depth, and the boy emerged after a couple of minutes already almost in the very center of the reservoir. The accumulated internal bitterness only forced with every second to increase the speed of the span of long, like oars, hands. Fedech moved energetically across the pond to its opposite bank, lined with concrete slabs.

The nervous state gradually began to release the body, yielding its rightful place to physical fatigue. Rozgin, breathing heavily, set foot on firm ground, happily put his face to the scorching sunshine and sank on warm plates drained by the summer heat.

- tired?

Suddenly, a hoarse, slightly cracked voice sounded, making the young man shudder and turn his head sharply to the right.

A few steps away he squatted a dirty homeless man with a shaggy beard and the same uncombed hair. There was a long cloak and heavy galoshes on the wanderer. In the summer it is rare to meet someone in a similar dress. The eye of a man dressed apparently not in season was practically invisible due to the bushy eyebrows hanging over the centuries. A tiny cigarette butt was smoking in his bum's teeth, it was hardly burning his lips.

"Look at me," said this strange type hoarsely, with dry and sunken lips. - Look carefully, kid ... You know what I could be?

Fedechka remained silent, not engaging in controversy imposed on him.

- Do not you know. I could become a member member. Academician could! And become? Look at me! - The bum endured a heavy pause, after which he finally pulled out a chinarik from his mouth and threw it under his feet. He crushed the big overshoot with a toe, and a light breeze, immediately picking up the remains of tobacco, dispelled them in space. - Do not get tired! No, no, no! Shendz is guarding us.

The bum proudly threw up his chin, and only now the young man managed to make out his eyes. These were the inflamed pupils of a sick person.

Fedech jumped to his feet, frightened, and, no longer turning in the direction of the unpleasant type, rushed into the blue water. He didn't have time to rest and recover his confused breathing. But unconsciously, he wanted as soon as possible to be away from the shore. Turning to a more gentle swimming style, the guy headed for the other side. Already in the center of the pond, Fedech did allow himself to turn around. There was no longer a gloomy, bearded bum on concrete slabs. Or maybe it seemed? Overheated in the sunshine, here and zhahnul heatstroke.

Rozgin, exhausted by two long heats, slightly reeling when walking, stepped onto the sandy shore. Not at all embarrassed by prying eyes, he famously got rid of wet swimming trunks and dressed in shorts and a T-shirt. An item of clothing that became unnecessary, he shoved it into a side pocket of a backpack, and only after that, throwing a simple luggage on his shoulder, he walked away. The mood has not improved at all.

By the time the lunch meal was taken, when Sancho, the executive and loyal to the schedule he had planned, had crossed the threshold of the Lavra's office with a tray, FedorPavlovich was seated at his desk with a gloomy expression on his desk looked at the polaroid picture left to him by Claudia. Laurus's dry fingers were thrown into a thick head of hair, his eyes slightly clouded. The photograph in full growth depicted Fedechka, who proudly flaunted the abundance of his red, tightly braided braids. Next to the guy, as in that old picture with figurally trimmed edges, where there was a young Laurus, there was a girl unknown to the authority. The young people smiled happily and openly looked into the future with confident, full of life eyes.

Laurel sighed heavily, and at the same moment a round tray brought by his comrade fell heavily next to the picture. The authority slowly raised its head and only now noticed the arrival of Sancho.

"Time," Moshkin announced laconically, nodding at the dishes he brought. - And waiting in the waiting room. Magnum, Nedorezok from Cyprus returned, Kosya is nervous. About five people gathered. - Informing the boss of the upcoming plans, he deeply stuck his little finger in the ear and several times vigorously turned it around its axis.

The appearance of Sancho, as it usually happened, pulled Laurus out of the pool of gloomy thoughts. He stretched sweetly and turned his full attention to the contents of the tray. Problems are problems, and you should never forget about the digestive process.

- Are these human names? - sadly grinning, said Fedor Pavlovich.
- Oh, what it is.

"Such names ..." Laurel methodically knit a personalized napkin around his neck and gently straighten the edges. - They hide bad karma.

- What? - Sancho looked at him incredulously.

Fyodor Pavlovich considered it expedient to clarify a deep thought:

- In the next incarnation, the Underbite will be an outcast in a pack of hyenas. Magnum ... - Authority thought for a second, without ceasing to chew. - Magnum will be born in a family of drug addicts. But not ours, but Latin American drug addicts. And he will die in a shelter as a baby. - Fantasy, nourished with taken calories, played out in earnest. Laurel bore.

His sayings made Sancho grunt loudly in complete bewilderment.

- Right Wang number two, e-my! - He said, not without a share of admiration. - And who will you be in the next incarnation?

- I? - Laurel raised his eyes to a flat white ceiling. - Better not ask. I probably will lobster. Or lobster.

- By whom? - Sancho pulled closer chair, which recently sat Claudia, and with great pleasure settled on it.

"Well, with such an imported crab," Lavrikov explained. - Which carrion eats and marches along the bottom of the ocean for some unknown reason.

"Jolly perspective," Sancho smacked his lips and immediately added, noting how lost in extrasensory thoughts about the transmigration of souls, Laurus was distracted from his main occupation: "Eat! This is not carrion.

- This is worse. - Authority sluggishly mixed with a spoon a watery mess of ingredients unknown to science. The proposed food did not cause any signs of healthy human appetite. - This is again a mess.

"Not porridge, but pudding," Sancho muttered discontentedly, ridiculously sipping his huge nose, like boiled up potatoes, in the direction of the laurel plate. - In the morning from semolina pudding was. Now - from oatmeal. Fractional power. Little by little, but often. Put so.

- Who is supposed to? - Fedor Pavlovich disdainfully sent another batch of oatmeal pudding into his mouth.

- Doctor. - Moshkin gently but persistently pushed the rosette with the capsules to the Lavra. "Little red ones from an ulcer," he explained at the same time.

- Why pudding?

- So there was something to add.

- What to add?

- Capsules! - patiently informed the associate of his immediate boss. It was not the first time when Lavrikov started a conversation on this topic, and Alexander had nothing to do but to heroically put up with these oddities. - Nutritional supplements! That is, to add them to something, you first need to eat something!

"Logical," grinned authority. - Sancho, do you know how your supplements differ from drugs?

"I know," he said firmly.

- Well, what? - Laurel looked at him. - What?

- The price. They are expensive because they are natural, ecological. They should be drunk more often and much longer than any pyramidone or aspirin, for example. Aspirin drank - walk. And these - day by day, day by day, for months, for years! Only then will the effect come out.

"Or the donkey will die," said Lavr, gloomily, issuing his own resume.

- Not understood. - Foggy philosophical thought did not reach Sanchev's level of consciousness.

"There is nothing to understand," Lavrikov waved his hand. - Fool our brother. Oh, and make a fool! - He picked up one pill from the rosette, turned on the spinning chair to the wide-open window and began to carefully examine the capsule in the light, gazing at it from under the squinted left eyelid. - Who releases?

- Americans.

- It seems to me ... - Laurel leaned back in his chair and curled his lips in a contemptuous grin, - these Americans - domestic spill. They put the shop somewhere in Verbilki and drive foolishness from chamomile flowers mixed with birch sawdust. - The thief in the law neatly put the red pill in place. - Tell Hamlet to get help. I am interested in such supplements. Let her take a look - who, whence ... And you take a closer look.

- For what? - Sancho often blinked his eyes from confusion. Abrupt races on topics so inherent to the Laurel, he never managed to comprehend. As the saying goes, what is allowed to Jupiter is not allowed to the bull. But Moshkin was not afraid to never show in public, and even more so before the boss himself, his own short-sightedness.

Laurel laid aside a silver spoon and, picking up a picture taken a few minutes ago from the table top, handed it to Sancho. He carefully took the photo, with a look that seemed to be offered to hold on to the young lady's bare leg at the society ball.

"By the kid," said the authority shortly, and paused, waiting for Alexander's reaction.

For about a minute, he probably turned a picture in his hands with an expression of complete concern on his face, he even tried to turn him upside down a couple of times, and at the end of the fight he scratched his sparse hair at the back of his head. In his eyes, once again raised on Lavrikov, there was an even greater confusion than before acquaintance with the photo. Sancho felt himself a complete idiot this second.

- Where is the kid here? He finally asked. - Here are a couple of girls.

Fyodor Pavlovich pointedly twisted his finger at his temple.

"The one with the pigtails is a kid," he said heavily, as if he were talking to a mental patient. - Can you mentally remove the pigtails? Or shove a finger with my finger, if mentally fails! - on the move he made a sensible offer.

- It turns out mentally! - Sancho was angry. - And with a finger - here you are, - squeezed!

He really did what the lawyer advised him, and a happy smile instantly lit up Alexander's round face. He removed his finger, after a second pressed him to the picture.

"True, kid," he said happily.

Moshkin liked playing with a finger, and he did this amusing procedure four more times, until Laurel fished out a new photo from under the newspaper lying on the edge of the table and gave it to the "butler".

"Now compare with this," the legitimate said with a smile. - With fatherlessness.

The new picture, proposed by Sancho, was old and faded, with very noticeable yellow divorces, but you could easily see two boys of seventeen or so in it, famously worn on the back of their caps of the sixties . Laurel leaned over the table and pointed his finger at the right okhlamon with mischievous eyes.

"I," he said proudly. "Only just from the colony came out for minors ... Free then there were preparatory courses," he concluded, turning to himself.

Sancho stared at one photo or another. Similar smiles. Similar cheekbones

- Well? - hurried colleague Lavrikov. - give a magnifier?

- Do not need a magnifying glass. - Sancho lowered his gaze and, after a short pause, depressedly shook his head. - Ah-ah-ah ... Lavrusha ...

- What is "Lavrusha"? - The thief in law sprung up from his chair and walked around the table around the perimeter. - What are you whining?

- Even if it is. - Moshkin's face became obscenely harsh. - It is impossible, Laurel! In no case! Well you - the last of the Mohicans! Classic thief! A quarter century as crowned! With a reputation for spotless! Not like the current sheluponi! - With every word spoken, Sancho's face was increasingly filled with blood. He was really nervous. - I have now clearly inside the bell zinknul: "danger"!

- You dink, - grinned Laurus. - And who is the decree for me?

- Law! - Sancho raised up his index finger.

"I myself am a lawyer."

"But you cannot, like these ..." Not finding the right word, Moshkin shook his head vaguely. - With titles purchased. Old people are offended. Here, sorry, - he habitually smacked his tongue, - smacks of impeachment.

- Bored! - Fedor Pavlovich jokingly weighed a light cuff to his comrade. - "Impeachment"! Say more "sequestration"! I'm not a jerk, Sancho. I just pretend to them. - He walked to the door and looked out into the corridor. - We will not give a reason for any swallowing. And all of them, not impeachment! - A rolled-up stick poked under the very nose of Moshkin, but after a moment, Laurus turned to a serious tone: - Bring the fraternity to the evening, all the magnums and undercuts there ... Sickly! The fact is still to be established, and not to head it off ahead of time! Veli Essentuki - let him harness. Small departure.

Even without bothering to ask where exactly the thief in law was going to leave at an inopportune hour, Sancho dejectedly rose from his chair and slowly wandered towards the door. Already from the threshold, he turned around once and, nodding at the cooled lunch, in a disgruntled tone reminded:

- Eat porridge.

"This is pudding," said Laurus mockingly.

However, as soon as the door closed behind Alexander, Lavrikov, naturally, did not even remember about any pudding. He quickly returned to the table, sat down in a chair and pulled the telephone unit towards him. From memory I dialed the number he needed and turned on the speakerphone. Waiting for the connection nervously drummed his fingers on the tabletop. After several long beeps, he heard a still cold, computer-synthesized female voice.

- Good day. You have reached the reception of the Deputy Minister of Health ...

"I know," grumbled authority.

- ... please, dictate a message, complaint or suggestion and your contact phone number to the answering machine. We will contact you.

"Yeah," grinned Laurus. - Invented noodles on the ears of workers. - He leaned toward the phone and sternly said, turning to the invisible opponent: - Hey, honey! Lavrikov on the wire. Come on, quickly pick up the phone and contact me with a citizen of the head!

"Honey" did not make the client repeat the request twice. In the dynamics there was a pair of deaf clicks, then a piece of music, and as a result a lively male voice said cheerfully:

- Fedor Palych? Glad to hear that!

Laurel decidedly picked up the phone, and the process was loud, the communication was automatically interrupted for his entire office.

"Hi, Lenya," he said with a noticeable laziness in a tiny speaker. - I'm fine, what are our years. Are you healthy? Well, thank God. I have a question ... of an applied nature. - Lavrikov endured a short pause. - Now, I heard paternity can be established under a microscope? What is the analysis? - He picked up a pen from the table. - dictate, write. Des ... wuxi ... srebo ... how? Nucleic ... Yeah, I get it. Acid. It would have immediately said - DNA. - Laurel diligently put all this on paper. "Where does her DNA come from?" Does it hurt? Yep Then, not in the service, but in friendship, Lenya, find me quickly a good specialist in this profile. And so that he immediately, while I was going to change clothes, called here. And for his office I will buy some cool gadget, which he won't ask for to your death. - Laurel grinned crookedly. - Yes, I'm waiting. Only without idle talk, so that instead of the gadget of an overseas coffin in a red sitchik not to receive. Just kidding Thank you dear.

Authority did not say goodbye. The handset just took up its original position, and the Lavra's gaze again focused on two photographs lying on the table. The more he looked at two different images, the more he became convinced of the identity of their content. In other words, Fyodor Pavlovich at the moment was inclined to believe in what the "BTR woman" told him.

Chapter 4

- Where, Laurel? - Essentuki cautiously bent over the open window of the black old-fashioned "Seagull", in the cabin of which the eminent kingpin conveniently located himself in the unchanging society of Sancho, committed to him like a dog.

Fyodor Pavlovich was already dressed in a lilac double-breasted suit, fashionable shoes and a solid-colored tie, matched with taste to all other wardrobe. Sancho was wearing a black tuxedo with a bow tie. His loose fleshy neck with great difficulty fit in a narrow collar of a shirt, which is why Moshkin felt not very comfortable, but, as they say, the situation obliged.

Behind the "Seagull", a black jeep escort stumbled behind the wheel of a shaven-headed boy with green eyes. On the green-eyed cheek there was a barely noticeable scar, which slightly tightened its youthful skin along the edges. The guy meekly waited for the results of the negotiations with Essentuki with the big boss.

He idly smoked a cigarette, occasionally clicking his thumb carelessly dropping a column of ash on the tip of an open window into an open window. An ordinary action movie by and large did not care where to go and for what purpose. He tried once again not to delve into such subtleties of his specific, but already routine work. As they say, more expensive. You know less - you live longer.

Contrary to the expectations of the pessimistic part of the population, torrential rain in the afternoon did not break out. The clouds cleared safely, the sun's rays, re-entered into their legitimate law for the season, caressed the green tops of trees. And all of the above had a very beneficial impression on Fyodor Pavlovich, despite the fact that he still had to do today.

- First - to the medical school. - Laurer's hand dived into the inside pocket of a stylish jacket and pulled out two folded sheets of paper to the light of day. First, he handed Essentuki one of them and immediately added the second to the first. - Then - here in this institution. Higher education ... Academic day we have today.

He grinned cheerfully and with a boyish enthusiasm poked his elbow into the hushed Sancho's shoulder. He did not respond to such a vivid manifestation of friendly affection on the part of the boss. He defiantly continued to keep a gloomy expression on his face, letting Lavr know how personally he did not like all these undertakings with extra-marital children. Moshkin very seldom could have kept his lean mine for a long time and sulked at Lavra like a mouse on a rump, but today he clearly decided to surpass himself in this matter. Laurel felt this and deliberately izgalyalsya over his entourage.

"Let's do an academic," Yessentuki smiled in response. "Sometimes useful ..."

The head of the security service, in a military way, spun on his heels and strode toward the jeep with the green-eyed kid at the wheel. He briefly gave him and his two other subordinates the necessary instructions, and only then returned to the "Seagull" and promptly dived into the cool cabin, sitting in the front seat next to the driver. Motor vehicles rumbled for a call, and the jeep was the first to leave the territory of the mansion through the prudently open gates. Already after him, the Seagull, driven by a curly-headed type with a drooping mustache, dressed in a French jacket with an incredibly high stand, also moved.

Laurel, with a contented smile on his lips, leaned back in his seat and turned his head to the side of today's excessively silent comrade.

- What are you sniffing ?! - At such moments, it gave him great pleasure to mock Moshkin. - Do not create, please, a negative aura in the cabin!

"What aura," he muttered discontentedly, without turning his head towards the authority, "when he had sinusitis tortured."

- Blow your nose then! - advised Lavrikov. - Humanity has learned to use the atomic bomb! A handkerchief - in any!

Sancho sniffed and got even bigger. Out of spite to the authority, he snarled even louder, but after a couple of minutes, drawing attention to the fact that Fyodor Pavlovich unexpectedly lost interest in his person, he stopped making wasted. He leaned toward Lavrikov as low as possible and, barely opening the corners of his own plump lips, whispered into his ear:

- Hear?

- BUT?

- The wave was raised, but suddenly everything is crap? - In the voice of Sancho, she shone an unmistakable hope.

It became extremely clear to Lavrikov that it was this very thought that occupied the consciousness of a faithful ally in the last few minutes. Moshkin fastened as best he could and diligently kept himself from the temptation to speak with authority, but purely human weaknesses eventually did prevail.

- A wave rolls. Because of someone else's.

Laurel thought for a moment and even scratched his pointed chin with the fingers of his right hand. He himself thought about this opportunity, and, to be honest, he didn't very much pleased him. Over the past few hours, Fyodor Pavlovich was beginning to get used to the idea that he had an heir. And this thought more and more impressed him.

"Even if he is a stranger," the authority said, "justice must triumph, Sancho!" I am not a dog that is shaken up, to turn up the muzzle from triumphant mayhem!

Moshkin fell silent again, feeling the mood of the lawyer alien to him. Cramped inside the car was filled with loud opposition sap.

On the threshold of the university, where Fyodor Rozgin was unsuccessfully seeking justice a few hours ago, three men stepped out. A broad-shouldered pink-cheeked ambal with huge, like Cheburashka, ears, a man with a lower sprout, a wedge with a beard and a neck, swollen due to unsuccessfully transferred in childhood mumps, and a green-eyed kid with a scar on his left cheek. The Trinity with all its appearance showed the gloss and external solidity. The left elbows loosely adhered to the hulls, which indicated the presence of firearms under the dark open jackets. But the young policeman, sadly trampled in the empty lobby of the university, did not immediately pay due attention to this weighty argument of the arrivals. With a formidable expression on his face, he stepped forward and barred the way for Cheburashka, who was marching ahead.

- Where are you young people? - he said.

- Ay, move over. - Lop-eared, with a scornful grin, pushed him away with his hand and, without slowing down his pace, headed for the stairs. Two other brothers and did not even vogrovtsa honored with a passing glance.

The guy, perplexed and with a certain degree of fear, squinted at their backs, and then turned his gaze back to the front door. Laurus himself appeared in the doorway in proud loneliness. But escort authority was not required. It was enough to look at his majestic, proud posture, his chin raised high and his squinted eyes willed to understand that the true master of life had arrived.

Instinctively, on a subconscious level, the young vohrovets also felt this moment. As a result, he not only moved aside, as he wisely advised him to do this rosy-cheeked ambal, but also decided to pay Laura honor just in case of fire. The guy saluted shortly. Fyodor Pavlovich casually nodded in response and went on. Trinity brave guys from the team Yessentuki already waiting for him near the leather door with a red sign on it: "The CHAIRMAN of the RECEPTION COMMISSION." Laurel silently stopped.

For guys, this fact sounded like a team to action. The victim of a child from a pig mate kicked the door and first flew into the room. Two of his accomplices rushed after him.

A plump, dyed blonde in a strict steel-colored suit, watering flowers from the carafe standing on the windows of the office, shuddered in surprise and turned her curly head toward the uninvited visitors who broke into her apartments in such a brazen manner. She had already opened her mouth in order to rebel against such a blatant act of impudent people, but they completely ignored the hostess's presence, silently went around the office around the perimeter and finally stopped at the entrance. The blonde was literally in shock. Lopouhy squeezed his head into the doorway and said, addressing someone in the hallway:

- Clean.

Laurel, with his hands in his trouser pockets, slowly crossed the threshold. He looked around the room indifferently and shook his head slightly, inwardly agreeing with some kind of own thoughts known to him.

"Free," he said briefly to the zealous old man.

They retreated from the room in a flash, carefully closing the door behind them. A lady in a steel suit shook her head, regaining a sense of lost reality and spraying raised shoulders with dandruff. Her perfectly plucked eyebrows, which obviously spent more than one hour of painstaking work on perfecting, sternly converged near the nose.

- Citizen! Are you illiterate ?! - She pounced with reasonable, in her opinion, claims. - Reception by personal ...

- Shut up! - abruptly cut off her authority.

After that, he went to the desk of the ladies and, freely settled in an empty chair, threw his legs. He took out a pack of cigarettes from the inside pocket of his jacket, fished out one and slowly put it in his mouth. The lighter clicked, and Laurel was shrouded in a puff of smoke, waved his hand to disperse the smog.

- Why is there no rector on the spot? - He asked peremptorily.

His shameless behavior embarrassed a woman, and she suddenly found herself in her sticking to stutter. However, before this, it was not found.

"R-rector in Paris," she murmured. "On the line ... of sharing ..."

- Exchange dollars for francs? - Fyodor Pavlovich openly smiled, showing his teeth to the interlocutor.

- I am not responsible for the rector! - She put the carafe on the windowsill. - I ... I listen to you!

- No, I'm listening to you, young lady. - Laurel inhaled deeply and, throwing back his head, released a powerful stream of smoke at the ceiling.

Such an inexplicable behavior of a strange visitor finally finished off the university lady. It was absolutely impossible to understand what exactly they wanted from her. Shaky female nerves could not bear the pressure exerted on them.

- What's the matter, finally ?! - she asked loudly after a short pause, during which she sincerely tried to comprehend the train of thought of the interlocutor. - Stop ... hypnotize! I do not understand!

- Now you will understand, - the thief in law has assured her, simply switching from a woman to "you". - Take a piece of paper from me. Here it is. - He fished out a sheet from the side pocket of his jacket and rightly stretched it to the woman with two fingers. - Request a case. And call this boy this very second. To apologize. Like, a mistake turned out with enrollment. I set tasks available? Or explain more popular? - Laurel frowned, feeling in the interlocutor hesitations. At the same time, he narrowed his left eye, protecting it from acrid tobacco smoke.

In the meantime, the lady, as if in a trance, approached the man sitting in the chair and, with an unsteady hand, intercepting the sheet offered to them, stared blankly at what was written. Being by nature not a stupid woman, now she is fully aware of what is being sought of her. High-ranking petitioners have repeatedly appeared in the university building with similar requests.

"It's not necessary to be popular," she said sluggishly. - All d-available.

"Good girl," Laurus praised her with feeling and took another deep drag. - Everything is available. Education - including. Unless, of course, a man deserves it. Of education.

- Of course. - In the sky-blue eyes of the pompous Madame, there appeared a genuine interest in this confident lord. She turned on all her charm and sang with a velvet voice: "To tea?" Coffee? Lemonade cold?

Laurel slowly left the cozy arms of the chair he occupied. He stepped up to the desk of the office mistress and put out a cigarette in a crystal ashtray. Smiled.

- Not. - He shook his head. - I'll go to the dining room to eat fractional. Kashki eat rice. An ulcer, - the authority has explained. - It seems to be nonsense, but it can kill.

"Of course," the woman agreed again. - With an ulcer jokes are bad.

- Oh, bad jokes. But we are not joking. - Eyes of authority flashed with excitement. It suddenly woke up a long slumbering heartthrob. - We are with you - people are serious. Is not it?

The greasy gaze froze on the deep neckline of a women's jacket, which with difficulty kept the immense bust in captivity. The lady skillfully caught his gaze. Hips swung vulgarly, and the overweight with a share of some exotic and coquetry bent over the polished table top.

- Of course! - Blue eyes dimmed dull languishing.

- Hello. - Nat rose from a narrow bench in the courtyard and pulled down her overly short little skirt. - Are you home?

The girl had already been waiting for more than an hour at the entrance of the return of Fedeks, who was walking around somewhere. It should be noted that to date, Nata had very serious and desperate plans. And they dealt directly with the person of Fedor Rozgin. However, it was not difficult to guess about this by just one type of girl. She thoroughly embellished herself, although in general she did it not very skillfully, put on the very skirt that was mentioned above, and added a white T-shirt with luring sign "I want you" to it. This already spoke of many things, and Fedech, who stopped near the girl, naturally, could not help but guess about the ideas and desires that were wandering about in a flighty head. Not otherwise, Natusia set out to say goodbye to her orderly virginity today. There was simply no other explanation.

- Home. - Fedechka clearly realized that he, unfortunately, has a completely different mood today. - Why not call?

- I've phoned. You were not at home. - Nat coquettishly smiled, shooting eyes. - You're hiding.

- I sunbathed - justified the guy.

- Today is a bad sun. - The girl frankly hesitated, apparently not daring to move on to the topic that was painful for her. - And yet, Fedechka, I want some certainty. Or we are with you or not. There are other options, but I'm losing time.

Rozgin sighed heavily and pulled the access door out of the peeling handle.

- Come in. - He stepped aside, letting Nata go ahead, but the next second, concern showed on his face. - Stop! No aunt?

- No one. - The girl shook her head.

"Come in," Fedechka repeated with noticeable relief.

A pause frankly inhibited and began to act on the girl's nerves. Fedechka was always on his mind, and today, even more so, he looked very strange. From the two-cassette cage located on the shelf, a pleasantly slow, slow song delivered by Nata flowed smoothly and melodiously, but even this fact could not stir the guy who was in prostration. He sat on the floor, cross-legged in Turkish, and automatically made unhurried journeys with the index finger of his right hand over the bare female leg. At first, his hand rolled down to the miniature Nathina's foot, then just as slowly rose up to the pointed knee. And this process has been going on for half an hour. The girl could not stand it. Her hand gently lay on the shaggy Fedechku head with numerous pigtails and slightly patted it.

- Hello! Speak - Nat did not manage to hide the notes of the irritation that slid in her voice.

- What? - Fedech hardly got out of the state of complete weightlessness.

- Hang, Fedechka? The girl asked mockingly, identifying her lover with the computer.

- Not. - He also smiled, appreciating the humor. - Search for the desired program.

- And what options? For example, is it scary to raise a hand higher?

Nata, not without a call, threw her legs on the leg, which is why her already short skirt turned into a completely symbolic loincloth. Even Fedeka, who had not yet thought of anything related to sex issues, could not help but notice the beauty that had opened up to his eyes. Nata really had something to look at. He frantically swallowed the spit that had come running and buried his forehead in the slender left calf.

- You decided to surrender? - just in case he specified, although the answer was already obvious.

- It's boring to live without love. - The girl left the direct topic of conversation, touched by her boyfriend. - All people are like people, and we have with you - two years already.

- And then who prodinamil in May? - Rozgin was even offended by such an undeserved accusation.

Nata smiled wryly. She perfectly remembered the incident about which Fedech made a speech. Her May rejection of physical intimacy was planned in advance. Thus, the girl hoped to stir up Rozgin, to force him to move to more decisive offensive actions. However, this did not happen. Female calculation was not justified. Now it is time to change the ineffective tactics.

- So when it was! - Nat slyly squinted.

- What, really do not mind? - Fedech suspiciously narrowed one eye, as if checking if it smacks of another trick here. - matured?

- Yes. - The girl threw up her chin, parading a thin, swan neck with a miniature mole above the right collarbone. - In the relationship of the sexes should be certainty.

- Put the bird, right? Said Fedech sarcastically.

"Complete the stage," the young coquette corrected him with a smile.

Her fingers, which continued to wander in a man's exotic head of hair, squeezed a few braids painfully and pulled them up. Nat called the man to action. But this attitude did not like the representative of the opposite sex. He jerked his head away too sharply and sprung to his feet. Nata with complete misunderstanding of what is happening now looked at the guy from the bottom up.

- No, do not! - Fedech spoke dryly, but, noticing the dramatic changes in the girlfriend's face, he added much softer: - The aunt can break in. It's unpleasant when you are snooping ... "He paused for a second or two. - Then - the army.

- What then? - I did not understand the girl.

- Well ... Service in the armed forces. - The gaze of his blue eyes turned to the shabby palace on the floor. - I have nothing to repose, and you will not wait.

- Of course I can't wait. - Nat did not deny the obvious.

It slightly jarred Fedechku.

- Why? - Despite the fact that Rozgin expected exactly such an answer from her, he nevertheless expected that the verdict would not be so severe and unequivocal. As they say, hope dies last.

- Because then - a pension, then - a nursing home! - Nat rolled her eyes to the ceiling, very vividly imagining such a sad picture of the future to come. - Do you, perhaps, physiological development lags behind the brain?

"Intellectual," Fedechka gently corrected.

- Lags behind, then? - this bitchy person has maliciously been twisted.

- All type-top. - The guy proudly rolled his chest with a wheel and two steps closer to the young beauty sitting on the sofa. - Hypersexuality. You can check.

- I see. - She shrugged. - So what then?

"The setting ..." the guy admitted with a sigh. - I ... I remember this sofa as much as myself. Upholstery ... She's all rubbed on my memory!

Nata sniffed contemptuously and with a graceful gesture threw a blond curl from her forehead. I rate myself in the mirror located to the right. I straightened the topic with the calling message and was satisfied.

"There is a bed," she said gravely.

- What are you? - Her proposal frankly scared Fedechku. - Auntie!

- Mat! - did not lag behind Nat.

- Dusty rug!

He himself was well aware that he was looking for non-existent reasons for which the girl's planned event could be postponed for today. It was hard to explain why he did it. Either the mood was really not right, or the boy was just afraid to try something new, hitherto unknown. Intentionally distracting his girlfriend from himself, he quickly ran to her, grabbed her wrist and, energetically pulling on herself, made her rise from the failed sofa.

- Let's go to the entrance! - he whispered passionately, knowing full well that he would receive a one hundred percent refusal to his offer. "The top floor is dead." No one walks. In one apartment, the grandmother is deaf, from the other everything is at the dacha from April to October. It's cool there, let's go! - He was breathing heavily, imitating impetuous desire. - Let's go to! And the hatch in the attic. The lock is not locked!

Nata, frightened, pulled her hand out of his un youthful tenacious fingers. She recoiled back and almost fell down, bumping into a round armrest.

- You are absolutely crazy, Fedechka, yes ?! - she screamed wildly and twisted her finger at the temple. - "In the attic"! Then the basement is better! Tell me honestly: you do not love me and you do not want! All excuses are some silly!

Yes, you can not fool a woman. They have, as you can see, the internal flair is very developed. But Fedechka could not admit the true causes. He himself did not know them. The usual lack of a suitable attitude, and nothing more. In his head completely different thoughts were swum, far from lust.

- Yes I want to! - he said as seriously as possible. - Feel!

- Then why bother troubles with the upholstery of the sofa? - Nata squinted in the direction of Fedechkogo groin, but did not proceed to action. Watch out.

- Does not understand! - Fedor shook his head hard.

"I don't understand," she said. - What is the matter then?

The guy had to answer something, but a more or less intelligent and plausible explanation in his head was not ripe. Fortunately, the situation was saved by a telephone set unexpectedly chirping on the coffee table in the hallway. Fedechka smiled and, with a shrug of guilt, retreated from the room. Nat heard him pick up the phone and spoke in a low voice:

- Yes? .. Yes, I ... Of course. I'm already on my way.

At this conversation and ended. The handset neatly returned to the telephone, and Fedechka, with a strange grin on his lips, again appeared before the girl in the doorway.

- What's the matter? He asked, returning to the interrupted conversation. - In the hat business, Nat! .. Well, I persuaded! Let's fall on the children's couch, to hell with him, with a sofa! Quickly! .. If a girl asks ...

He famously jumped toward her like a giant bloodsucking spider, hugged him with long hands and made a silly attempt to throw the girl on the sofa.

- Figushki! - Nat rested with both hands in the chest of the gentleman and pushed him. - I do not want more! I do not want, leave me alone, pervert! ..

At peak times, an impressive number of vehicles always accumulated on the central avenues. The people traditionally hurried to their cozy inhabited nests, leaving the workplaces that had got tired in eight hours. This happened every day without any major changes. While still at work, a person builds ambitious plans about how to spend this evening, to realize their legitimate right to rest. Sometimes, of course, not all these plans are destined to come true, but it is necessary to strive towards them. For some, it is quite convenient to fall apart in a chair in front of the TV and enjoy the communication with the blue screen, for someone it is much more pleasant to break away to the full extent, for example in a bar or a nightclub. The third one dreams of just spending the evening with the family. To each his own.

Laurel with genuine interest watched this anthill that came into a chaotic movement, sitting in the back seat of its antediluvian "Seagull". Next to him, there was still a loyal Sancho, who continually straightened his fingers with an excessively tight stand of his shirt, unpleasantly rubbing an Adam apple. More than anything, he now wanted to get rid of this tight vestment and put his exhausted body into a spacious home-made T-shirt.

In the front passenger seat, next to the driver, the Seagull was sitting with a cigarette in his teeth, Yessentuki. He culturally smoked his stinking "Camel" in an open side window. Unlike Moshkin, the head of the security service did not feel any discomfort from the standard formal clothes for him and at the moment he was suffering only from inaction. Their academic day, as Lavrikov deigned to say a few hours ago, frankly delayed. All planned actions have already been successfully completed, but for some reason only known to him, the thief in law was in no hurry to give the green light to return to the mansion. Both the "Seagull" and the black jeep of authority support still pressed against the curb near the university building.

"Nah," Sancho said weakly, resuming the conversation interrupted a few minutes ago. - I would not go with Dyubel on b azar.

At the same time, he once again pulled a tight stand on his neck and took a deep breath. The official part of the day had already been completed, but for some reason Moshkin was in no hurry to get rid of the tie he hated.

- And who goes? - Laurel did not look at an ally. The look of his tired eyes was directed out of the "Seagull" window.

- You.

"I am not going," Fyodor Pavlovich rejected this maxim. - He came. Rumbles.

- How? - An interest appeared in Moshkin's voice, and he tried to look into the interlocutor's eyes. The attempt was unsuccessful.

"It's a long time to explain," Lavrikov said casually, taking the white handkerchief from his jacket's chest and putting it to his forehead. Despite the built-in air conditioning in the cabin and open windows, it did not become cooler in the cramped space. - Ask Hamlet.

"Hamlet is hysterical," Sancho made his non-medical diagnosis, but there was more than enough confidence in the voice of the indisputable rightness of words. Then he scratched his head with his fingers and added anxiously: "And Dubel is a beast."

- Is the dowel a beast? - Yessentuki, who had remained silent until that moment, intervened in the conversation. His lips curled in a contemptuous grin. - Dowel is not a beast. Ponterer!

"And do you keep your mouth shut," Moshkin grumbled discontentedly. - You just have to shoot.

The security chief released another thin stream of smoke through the window and flicked a cigarette butt out with a flick of his thumb. Chinarik, having described an exotic pirouette in the air, ran into a roadside curb with sparks.

- Sometimes useful. - Essentuki turned his head to the passengers in the back seat. - The boys lose their shape.

At the same time, he nodded expressively toward the driver, who stood in a strict jacket, which stood as a marble statue. He did not react at all, continuing to stare stupidly at the lane in front of his eyes. The guy could easily earn money in Madame Tussauds wax museum as one of the exhibits.

"Hold the boys for now," Laurus said emphatically. "He, I mean Dyubel, called and invited me to the" cellar "for lunch ... or lunch. - On the face of authority reflected thoughtfulness. - How to? - However, he did not practice linguistic exercises for a long time and returned to the main topic of conversation: - One on one, without any accompaniment, without firing. I will go.

- And I? - Essentuki leaned back in his seat, twisting his whole body.

The thief in law monotonously shook his graying head.

"You have an assignment," he reminded his first bodyguard.

Essentuki cautiously shook his tongue, however, noticing that the boss didn't react to this, turned around on the leather seat even more refinedly and snatched Sancho's eyes, looked expectantly at him, hoping for the necessary support. But Moshkin just shrugged and pouted his lips. Say what can I do? He really did have a conversation with Lavr on this matter, but Alexander did not succeed in achieving any positive result. However, he knew perfectly well: if the boss, as they say, rests on a horn, no one can convince him. The stubbornness of Fyodor Pavlovich was not to occupy.

"You are risking, Lavr," he ventured, however, on the confusion of Yessentuki, without receiving adequate support from Moshkin.

- I said! - severely cut Lavrikov, stopping further attempts by the security chief to reach his consciousness. - Dowel, of course, young one, but - sane. In the open does not even farts, afraid ...

There was a tense pause in the cabin of the Seagull. It became extremely clear to all that the authority had uttered its last word, from which it would not back down. It is not in its rules. Sancho defiantly turned away in the opposite direction, and Essentuki's hand mechanically reached for a pack of cigarettes lying on the dashboard for a new batch of nicotine and tar.

I did not have time to smoke the bruiser. Lavrikov's worn and tattooed brush squeezed his shoulder to the pain in the very second that Yessentuki had already flicked a lighter. The hand froze in the air, and the unlit cigarette, having broken off from the lower lip, fell somewhere under its feet. The bodyguard turned around. The gaze of the unexpectedly illuminated Laurel eyes was directed toward the university porch. The authority has all leaned forward, almost falling out of the body in the open window. The handkerchief promptly darted into its chest pocket.

Essentuki followed his dazed gaze and already personally saw an awkward skinny guy with a downhole hairstyle on his head, who hastily climbed up the steps. His numerous, tightly woven pigtails fluttered in the wind. Honestly, the security chief did not immediately manage to determine the gender of the potential entrant.

- Essentuki, look! - With each second, the fingers of Laurus pressed harder on the shoulder of the bodyguard. He gritted his teeth, but did not dare express displeasure. - See? Short, difficult to confuse ...

- Well. - Essentuki really was sure that he would hardly confuse this youth with someone else.

"When you are free, you will take it and bring it to these ... to geneticists-energetics," he said weightily to authority and, for greater convincingness, explained: "Where have you gone already."

"Well," Essentuki gritted his teeth.

Laurel removed his hand from his shoulder, and he finally sighed with relief. The shaggy lad disappeared into the building, and there was no longer any sense in staring in that direction. The bodyguard turned back to the thief in law.

"Only so that he would not guess where and why," Lavrikov continued to instruct him.

- Chop off, then?

A joyful smile lit up the usually stern and gloomy face of Essentuki. The big man has already managed to thoroughly miss the assault. Deep down, he even feared that his trained muscles would atrophy due to long downtime. And then suddenly the boss gives him a real chance to break away. Not on Dubela, really, but on a little boy, but this is better than nothing. Warm up, so to speak, charging.

- Careful! - Fedor Pavlovich fighting spirit cooled him down. He severely moved his eyebrows to the bridge of his nose, and this instantly made Yessentuki shove his radiant smile to hell. - Without injury for the child's psyche. And heads, by itself, - the thief in law added.

- Mask ethereal amiss? - sadly asked the bodyguard.

Laurus thought for a second and nodded approvingly.

- Sort of. But ... - He raised his index finger again. - Neatly.

"We'll do it," the big man assured him. After that, he often-often blinked with big eyes, scratched his chin and, fidgeting on a leather chair, cautiously asked: - It's to blame, of course. Shaggy this - someone's son? - Essentuki frantically swallowed running saliva and lowered his eyes. - What kind of event is planned?

Laurel silently looked at the wide face of the bodyguard for several minutes. It was necessary to answer something, but the problem was that the eminent thief did not trust one hundred percent to his assistant, as, for example, Moshkin. With all his desire, he could not utter the whole truth out loud. Sancho squinted at the boss, and Fyodor Pavlovich noticed this.

"The paradox is, Essentuki," the authority said with constellation, "that we are all sons." - He crooked grin. - It happens - and daughter. Regardless of the activities.

Sancho turned to the window, hiding the mocking expression of his face. Laurel, on the contrary, seriously pursed his lips.

- Do you understand? - The question was addressed to Yessentuki.

- Well. - He nodded uncertainly in response. Philosophy and everything else that somehow mated with her were not for him.

- Then do it. - Lavrikov leaned back in his seat.

The bodyguard slowly left the cabin "Chaika" rather cramped for his build, giving the driver the necessary instructions, in his opinion, and strode toward the front of the standing jeep. There, he was eagerly awaited by the gallant trinity, which ensured the safety of the Lavrovsky visit to the university building. Essentuki sat in the front seat. In the rearview mirror, he was pleased to note that the boss's car started off smoothly, turned on the roadway, and rushed through the city center in the direction of the Lavrovsky mansion. Essentuki took a quick glance at the clock, then at the college porch.

The expectations of the left brigade Laurel were not too long. Joyful and happily smiling Fedech appeared on the threshold of the institution about ten minutes later. He looked as if the most desirable miracle in his life had happened. Swinging his backpack in the air, he crossed the high porch in three strides and found himself on the sidewalk.

"Kul, start the engine," Essentuki ordered shortly. - Ushan, you are with me.

After that, he energetically opened the door and went out. Following him from the cabin of the jeep came a lop-eared type in a strict suit. Fedech was already cheerfully pushing in their direction. Essentuki looked around. His right hand was casually laid behind his back. The engine of the jeep gently purred.

Chapter 5

Claudia swiftly crossed the old courtyard, formed by several monolithic high-rise buildings, in the center of which there was still some kind of a playground. Local kids were happy even to what they had. It was much preferable to play among the remains of slides, swings and the only horizontal bar on the whole yard without a crossbar, but in the fresh air rather than in stuffy apartments.

The woman stopped near the mentioned horizontal bar and, breathing heavily, looked around. Never in her life had her face expressed such a sacred horror. A confused look finally focused on a low roofless gazebo. Claudia continued to cross in that direction.

As she was informed by friendly acquaintances on the phone, Fedechka reclined on one of the benches cut by a penknife, ridiculously twisting his left leg under him. Hands dangled limply along the body, head thrown back. Claudia scaredly pressed her own mouth with her hand, warning a cry of horror, but already a second later, on the measured, heaving Fedechkin stomach, she realized that the boy was only sleeping in a serene sleep.

- Lord! She said softly, and approached the body of her nephew.

Her heavy heavy hand grabbed the guy's shoulder and vigorously shook her a couple of times so that Fyodor almost fell on the plank floor. With her impressive build, the Rozgina could, if desired, be very strong.

- Fedya! - She screamed almost a bass at the top of her voice. - Fedor! Fedechka! - Not reaching the expected result, Claudia, briefly waving, slapped the young man smack in the face. Blow it turned out that it is necessary. The woman obviously didn't calculate her own strength, and on the delicate youthful skin a red imprint of a weighty five appeared at once. - Get up, brute! Sprawled, a parasite! - Her eyes were filled with tears that were already uncontrollable. - My disgrace ... Neighbors say, but I did not believe ... Get up, you bastard!

The aunt slapped him across the face once more, but this time slightly diminishing his strength. This action was positive. Fedech barely untied his heavy eyelids, lifted his head with a tight bench, and after a brief effort, he managed to focus his muddy, wandering, like a drug addict, glance at the woman bending over him.

- A? - stupidly he said in a deaf voice.

- Bae! - Claudia mimicked him with her unaccountable anger inside her. - Are you obsessed with anya, or what? Vodka get drunk? Breathe! "She brought her round, wrinkled face to her nephew's lips in places.

Rozgin winced painfully, confidently pushed his aunt away and took a sitting position on the bench. Dark circles went before my eyes, and the fulcrum was rapidly leaving from under the feet. Never had a guy felt so overwhelmed. Even on that memorable morning, when he actually tasted alcohol for the first time. Rather, its action after a short sleep.

"Auntie, don't yell," he asked pitifully. - Without you noggin - smithereens.

- Why is that ?! - Claudia slyly grinned and, having lowered, at last, the sonorous timbres of her voice, quickly whispered: - Let's go home quickly !!! People looking out of the windows! Circus!..

- Yes, wait. - Fedech felt he could not get up on his feet without losing his balance. He weakly felt his own limbs.

- What to hang out? - a strict aunt started up on the new one. - Saw good. You roll like a homeless pissed off!

The boy timidly lowered his frightened look. For greater certainty, he even felt his hand.

"No, I'm dry," he said, puzzled, lifting his head to Claudius again. The face lit up with a happy smile. "I was accepted at the institute after all ..." Doubt lingered in the eyes of the young man. - Or not? Dreamed? .. No, not a dream.

The face of the aunt was petrified. She sat down beside her nephew on a bench and looked into his face.

- So accepted or not?

- Wait ... - Fedech again rubbed his temples, reminded of the plight of another attack of dull pain. Thoughts were confused in his head, unable to form the usual slim order ... "I tried to seduce Nata ..." he began memories from afar. - It was.

- What happened? - Claudia swallowed frightened stuck in her throat.

- There was nothing with Nata yet. - The guy casually waved his hand. - Then, at the crucial moment, they called.

- From where?

- From the admissions office. - Fedor nodded confidently. - Called. They said "the error came out," and I - in the list. I remember exactly ... Then I moved to the trolleybus stop. Next - a car like ... A man got out, started talking and ... - No matter how hard he tried to strain his brains, he could not remember anything more. - Nothing further. How cut off.

Claudia straightened her back, and her pupils narrowed. An unexpected guess came to her mind. She simply did not find any other explanation for what her nephew had just confusedly and confusedly told her. Auntie callous palm gently covered the young man's slender fingers. It seems like cheering.

- A machine? - She asked with genuine interest. - What car?

Fedechka sighed heavily. The brain gradually began to clear up, and the sense of reality gracefully burst into his mind. The events of this evening acquired noticeable outlines.

- Jeep, it seems. - The voice of the young man was not so deaf and impersonal as a few minutes ago. - Cool car ... what's the difference? - He stared at his aunt curiously.

- Black jeep? - just in case Claudia specified, ignoring the last question of the nephew. I asked only for pro forma. The answer was so obvious.

"Jeeps are almost all black, aunts," the teenager spoke with skill.

"Don't tell me," the woman's lips parted in a mysterious smile. Thoughts she already soared somewhere far away, but the palm still lay on the oblong fingers of her nephew. - Black to black discord.

- It does not happen.

"But it happened so," Claudia said automatically.

- What happened? - From her vague sayings, Fedechka once again felt himself in some unreal dimension. He clearly realized at that moment that one of the two people sitting now on a bench in a broken arbor in the middle of the courtyard was crazy. But who exactly? I really wanted to hope that it was not him.

"I don't know yet," Claudia replied thoughtfully, which further alarmed Fedor, who was worried about her aunt's well-being.

He vigorously snapped his fingers in front of her face, trying to bring the woman back from the world of dreams to the sinful earth.

- Hey, wake up! - the young man said loudly. - Did you, by any chance, not smoke anasha, Aunt Klav?

But this question of his remained unanswered. Rozgin simply did not hear him.

Lavr studied the appearance of a young man sitting in front of him at a round table under a white tablecloth with a charming smile, thanks to which everyone around him could appreciate his snow-white, even teeth, with an attentive gaze from under his gloomy eyebrows. This type also had marvelous almond-shaped eyes, resembling a sea wave, pointed chin, and straight nose. A dandy polosochka of a thin sparse antennae flaunted over the upper lip, and it was clear from everything that the guy was used to taking care of them daily. "Pontyarschik", as Essentuki quite accurately and aptly put it. But on the other hand, Fyodor Pavlovich perfectly knew that it was precisely this type of modern man, who also had weighty capital behind him, but not quite legally obtained, but most of all attracted people of the opposite sex. Surely Dubel, namely, he was the man with whom Laurus had dinner today in a basement restaurant on the outskirts of the capital, in brides and fans, he was rummaging about like that. However, as far as Lavrikov was aware, the young crime boss did not hide his numerous victories on amorous soil. On the contrary, on occasion, he always tried to tell about them to society, which, in the opinion of Dubel himself, added weight to him. Reputation is the basis of all great victories. added him weight. Reputation is the basis of all great victories. added him weight. Reputation is the basis of all great victories.

In addition to the two of them, at that hour there was not a single visitor at Iguana. The restaurant's management has prudently started warning about this issue, knowing full well what guests will come to their establishment today. The light in the room also did not turn on, in the semi-gloomy basement only two candles were burning, which were central to the table of the two negotiating parties. The huge long shadows of Laurel and Dowel stretched along the entire perimeter of the restaurant, creating an ominous sight by their sight. Flames fluctuating from light drafts reflected in the pupils of the interlocutors.

"I won't learn how to put a fork in my left hand," Lavrikov said with a good-natured smile on his face, trying to look as careless as possible when dealing with an uneasy person. - More comfortable on the right. Then you can help with the left bread.

Before him was a deep plate with cabbage leaves, and the main course was carrots seasoned with sour cream. In front of his opponent, on the contrary, a whole heap of spicy meat dishes rose, and Dubel ate them with incredible bliss, without worrying at all about the harmful effects on the digestive tract. On the contrary, with mockery and a certain degree of superiority he gazed at the eminent kingpin who, as he knew, suffers from an ulcer.

- Do you know how to make chopsticks? - the young authority sarcastically asked.

He initially took as a basis for such a policy. To belittle Lavrikov, thereby accomplishing what is called an extension from above.

- Not where! - Laurel pretended not to notice the interlocutor's obvious sarcasm. - Yes, and why chopsticks?

"Sometimes it's necessary," Dubel continued to sneer. - Suddenly at the reception - Asian cuisine.

Laurel contemptuously twisted and picked up another cabbage leaf with a fork, sent it into his mouth and diligently earned his jaws, chewing vegetarian food with a crunch. For a few brief moments, there was a pause in the conversation.

- I have seen such tricks in a coffin. - This time in the voice of Fyodor Pavlovich metallic notes sounded. - Any tricks, even with European cuisine.

- Sorry, but you yourself - a typical product of Asian cuisine.

Dowel frankly provoked the opponent, and a visionary, experienced Monastery in such matters was easy to calculate his possible moves. So, instead of flaming up, as he would have done in any other, similar situation, Fyodor Pavlovich restrained himself, put the fork aside and concentrated all his attention on the signature seal. Such a process often helped him calm the rebellious nervous system. Today's case was no exception.

"Just a moment," Lavrikov said softly, but coldly. - Are we talking about food or about me?

"For now, about food," Dubel answered with an obvious challenge.

- So here. - Laurel left a signet in peace and folded his hands on the table. - About food. It is necessary to eat comfortably, Dowel, and not as ... fashion model on the scene. Surely you need to eat. Thoughtfully.

A young but defiant by nature representative of a new generation of thieves instinctively felt that he was politely put in place. Unobtrusive, but confident hand. In the depths of his soul, Dubel could not help but respect and not admire Laurus. For many people of the criminal circle, Fyodor Pavlovich was a role model. And for this Dubel did not like him the most. He quietly gritted his teeth, looking for a decent answer to the laurel tirade, but he did not manage to do that.

A waiter in a black dress suit with a butterfly under a white collar silently approached the table of authorities and carefully placed a plate with mashed potatoes and a pair of some gray, inconspicuous cutlets in front of an elderly thief. Without a word, he quietly retreated into the twilight that surrounded the two warring parties.

Dubel squinted at the set dish and winced in disgust.

- But what are you eating, Laurel? He asked casually.

- Cabbage. - The authority again grabbed the fork with his left hand and turned his gaze to his plate.

- Not this. - Opponent leaned forward with his body and reluctantly nodded at the special order just delivered by the waiter. - It.

"These are steam cutlets, Dubelk," Fyodor Pavlovich gently cooed, as if speaking not with his eternal irreconcilable enemy, but with a beloved relative who had complained from the province.

Only a man who knew Lavra well enough would have managed to catch a hidden threat in his intonations. The behavior of the criminal authority was like the actions of a highly experienced panther preparing for a decisive and deadly leap for the victim.

- The view from them, I'm sorry, disgusting. - By Dubel returned his usual impudent manner of behavior. - Diet?

"She, the forerunner ..." Laurel shook his head. - I spoil your appetite?

"No, my appetite is fine," he grinned. - It is very difficult to spoil my appetite.

- But probably? - Laurel squinted.

- I do not advise trying.

This already looked like a direct threat, all the more so considering how intonation Dubel spoke the last words. But Lavrikov again pretended that nothing super-special had happened, but the usual humorous conversation continues.

- And if? .. - Now he provoked the young one.

- expensive will rise.

The calculation of the eminent thief justified one hundred percent. Dowel wound up. It was not difficult to determine this fact. Even in the dim light of faint candles Fyodor Pavlovich noticed how the face of the interlocutor had gone brown spots of indignation, his lips pursed in a tight line, and permafrost appeared in his eyes.

- I see. - Laurel for the species dropped speed, but confidently went on the offensive with regards to the topic for which today's meeting was taking place. "I know your appetites, Dowel." But, dear, you have your table, I have mine. Why carry someone else's food?

Dubel smiled broadly and openly, but the lawyer's experienced gaze could not help but notice what kind of expression lurks behind this mask thrown over his face. The scumbag felt like a fish in water. Finally, their conversation went in the right direction, in his opinion.

"I want to take an unowned dish," the spicy lover said slowly, with the arrangement. - Inedible dish. And managed to invest in it thoroughly. And your ... Prince of Denmark began to stir up the water this morning.

"Hamlet acts on my command," said Lavr, his interlocutor, dryly chopped off the effusions. - And someone invested or did not invest - do not care. The dish lies to the left of the highway. And your pastures are on the right.

"It depends on what to turn your back on," Dubel said biliously.

There was an ominous pause in the conversation. Laurel was reaching for his constant signet, but changed his mind. I sent a portion of carrots in my mouth, diligently, chewed without haste, and with a prickly look I rested in the face of the interlocutor.

"I give free advice," he said icily. - The main thing is not to turn your back on my legitimate interests. And your dream will be undisturbed. And the back is whole.

The words were spoken by a man who knew what he was talking about, and confusion and confusion were reflected in the dowel's green eyes. He had already regretted that he had so zealously begun to go too far. Laurel becomes dangerous if angry, just like a lion awakened at the wrong time. And many knew about it, who was familiar with the eminent thief.

"This is such a trifle, Laurus," said the young dude conciliatoryly.

- Especially! - Lavrikov smiled sweetly, as if it wasn't he who poured biting words a second ago. - Drink wine and forget. Stone - also a trifle. But you can slip on it and break the neck.

Instead of red wine, preferred by Dubel, prestige of a prestige of wine shouted a glass of mineral water. Summoning raised him above the table. Dim light reflected in the crystal faces. Conversation of two bigwigs of the shadow business reached its climax. All decent words were spoken, the interests of the parties clarified one hundred percent. The case remained for small. For those who take what action.

"Your health, Dubel," loudly and, as it seemed to his opponent, Fyodor Pavlovich too proclaimed too theatrically.

"Your health, Laurus," he nevertheless responded, raising a glass of amber liquid.

But drink "pontyarschik" did not. On the contrary, he abruptly tilted his capacity with expensive wine, pouring the contents onto a snow-white tablecloth, and at the same time did not take his searching glance from Fyodor Pavlovich. The same indifferently looked at the plumes of Dubel with a lean facial expression. To the last drop of wine rolled down the glass edge on the table, after which the young thief with a flourish threw his glass on the floor. The sound of broken dishes caught the attention of the attendants. But Dubel didn't care. He rose sharply to his full height and swiftly strode toward the exit of the restaurant. At Lavra never turned around. Mood arrogant young change every second.

Lavrikov shook his head. He doesn't seem to have anger or hatred towards Dubel. The lawyer, perhaps, expected a similar trick.

"Kind of cultural," he said gruffly, moving away from the table so that the wine spilled by Dubel would not fall on his snow-white trousers. - A nasvinyachil ...

The waiter was already running to the thief in law with a rag at the ready. Laurel squinted at the steam cutlets, the appearance of which in fact did not cause the slightest appetite.

- Ugh! - with displeasure led nose prestige. - Indeed, an abomination ...

Knocking the wheels on the curved rails, the tram slowly drove to a halt, and for a long time the doors, which had not been oiled, were creaking aside with a creak. The expecting people, angrily shoving each other with their elbows and pushing on a high footboard, began to pile tightly into the metal womb. A particularly high-spirited old woman of about sixty-five or so was the most aggressive towards others, and just retribution did not slow down to catch up with her in a couple of seconds. A tall, lean man with a black "diplomat" - "soap box" tried to go around the elderly lady, but instead, driven by the crowd from behind, very noticeably pushed his grandmother in the back. The woman stumbled on the steps, fell, and this circumstance eventually formed an even greater crowd on the approaches to the tram.

Laurel looked around, straightened his bright stylish jacket, and, waiting for all the others to stay in the cabin, quickly jumped onto the back footboard before closing the doors.

Saconously watching him from the black "Seagull", Sancho shook his balding head in frustration and, addressing the driver, quietly said:

- Touch it!

He obediently started the engine, and the old-fashioned car rushed after the tram knocking on the rails, not overtaking him, but not lagging behind. Sancho fished the player out of his shirt pocket, unwound the headphones and attached them to his ears. Fat finger deeply pressed the play button. The hearing was pleasingly admired by the incomparable duet of Gilda and the duke The last time Moshkin listened to this very musical piece when, unexpectedly, he unexpectedly met his own love on the stairs of the Laurel mansion. Yes, here he was finally visited by this great and dimensionless feeling. Sancho did not doubt this for a second. Claudia stubbornly did not go out of his head. The image of this stately lady pursued Alexander the rest of the day. And now, having covered his eyelids, he imagined the solid figure of a woman. Fairy tale! The poet's dream!

Moshkin opened his eyes against his will. The need to be on guard all the time and not to lose sight of the tram in which, spitting on all the rules of established safety, Lavrikov sat down, did not allow Sancho to fully relax.

And Fyodor Pavlovich, meanwhile, being in the very hustle of the tram hustle, unobtrusively slipped his eyes around the passengers surrounding him, asked the price and began to confidently make his way into the center of the car. From all sides, the authority of the thieves angrily hissed, expressing the utmost displeasure of his highly brazen actions. The obese gentleman chosen by Laurel in mirrored sunglasses and a spacious light jacket was already located in close proximity. The thief made some more short gestures and rounded the fat man.

- Let me ...

Laurel lightly touched the men, and thin, thin fingers quickly dived into the back pocket of his pants. Authority movements were precise, deft, natural. And most importantly - completely invisible to others. Including for the victim himself. For the entire operation, Lavrikov took no more than two seconds. He did not even reset the pre-selected pace of movement on the car. The obese gentleman in mirror glasses was left behind, and Laurel was already clutching his thick, tight wallet in his hands. A happy smile lit up the lawyer's face. He turned the loot in his hands, as if sensing its full significance, and then casually tossed himself under his feet.

- This is not you lopatnichek dropped?

He gently touched the shoulder of the man he had cleaned, while he himself squatted vigorously and again picked up his leather wallet. He rose to his full height, showing the fat man his "find". The man's hand jerked to his back pocket and caught only the void. He raised his glasses on his forehead, gazing in amazement at an honest man. Being a sensible man and having spent his entire adult life in a barbarous country called Russia, the man was struck completely on the spot inexplicable from the point of view of logic, but a noble act of an unfamiliar passenger.

- Yours or not? - Lavr continued to pry with all the same disarming smile on his face.

- My! - reluctantly nodded fat. - Thank you! .. Wow! ..

"We need to," Lavrikov strictly scolded him, like a teacher of a student at fault. - More careful than that.

Without adding another word, Lavr turned and reached the door closest to him just at the moment the tram was stopped.

The doors with the same unpleasant screech opened, and the authority jumped off the steps to the smooth asphalt. His mood was elevated. Whistling an unpretentious tune under his nose, he approached the Seagull parked by the side of the road and, pulling the door to himself, slipped into the salon. Sancho took off his headphones, turned off the player and estimated Laurus's blooming physiognomy as an extremely grave condition of a mentally ill person. But Fyodor Pavlovich was not embarrassed by such trifles. In addition, he was in a very gracious mood.

The driver smoothly touched the Seagull from the spot, and the car began to rapidly pick up speed. Laurel leaned back in his seat and pointedly raised his splayed hand. Lovingly examined his hand from all sides.

- Fingers ... - he sang affectionately.
- What are "fingers"? - Sancho glanced in his direction.
- Imagine still working. - Laurel proudly demonstrated to the comrade-in-arms each finger individually, and then played them in the air. - Fingers-boys ... Palchichushechki! .. As in the most carefree youth.

Moshkin looked at the boss not only with sympathy, but, frankly, with genuine anxiety. He was already thinking that he should get a cell phone out of his pocket and consult with some sensible doctor right now. Sancho stared intently at the pupils of Laurus, and they also seemed to him not quite healthy.

- Lavrusha, you dogs did not bite? - he asked sympathetically.
- what are the dogs? - The words of Alexander, who was sitting next to him, shamelessly pulled the thief in law out of euphoria.
- Mad.
- Not. - Laurel frowned. - What's the matter?
- Why do you need it? - Moshkin gently nodded at the hands of authority.

Lavrikov laughed heartily. He just now fully caught the train of thought of his faithful assistant.

"It's just that," he said happily. "For the feeling ... Well ... That I still live!" Participated in life. - Laurel reached into the inside pocket of his jacket for cigarettes. - And the nerves discharged. Feel better, you know ...

"I imagine," Sancho said grimly. - Where are we now?

Laurel reflected on this topic for a few seconds. Mood required something special. Any unusual trick. Something like that! And the original, to his view, the decision immediately matured in my head.

- I want a new car! - on the exhale said authority.
- Finally! - Now Sancho joyfully grinned.

He had long hinted to the chief that it would be time to change the antediluvian mode of transport. And now the day "X" has come. Well, how not to rejoice here?

Tightly compressed lips in a thin single line, Dubel, who is also Victor Grotsky, rushed at breakneck speed along a deserted country highway towards the red disk of the sun setting on the horizon. Grotsky slowly put a cigarette in his mouth, flicked a lighter, lighting a cigarette. Acrid tobacco smoke pleasantly filled the lungs. With true delight, Dubel energetically inhaled several times in a row, after which the cigarette, which had not had time to fade to half, tumbling in the air, flew to the side of the road. Victor tapped the gas pedal to the ground, the speed increased with every second and eventually managed to reach the maximum mark on the speedometer. Dubel sharply hit the brakes. The car with a wild tire whistle went skidding on hot asphalt, turning ninety degrees. She carried it into the oncoming lane, but Grotsky immediately immediately spun the wheel,

The pause in this crazy and, in the opinion of a sane person, completely unreasonable game did not last long. Having made a few turns on the spot, the "Audi" again fell off the spot, but this time in the opposite direction. The stunt of the dowel was repeated with amazing accuracy. Even the distance covered was the same plus or minus a couple of centimeters.

In such an exotic and idiotic way, Victor usually dumped the tension that had accumulated inside. In my heart, everything gurgled after a restaurant meeting with Fyodor Lavrikov, and the body demanded an additional adrenaline rush. The dowel's green eyes were still lifelessly frozen without expression. On a naturally strong neck, swollen nipples were clearly visible.

The blow to the brakes, the squeal of the tires, the U-turn, the feeling of a furious speed again, the blow to the brakes again ... And so on to infinity, or rather, until Grotsky himself thought it necessary to stop these crazy throwings. He noisily released the air accumulated in the lungs and with a stone smile on his lips reached for cigarettes. This time he lit up quietly, without nerves, and leaned back in his seat. Now he felt like a complete man.

After pulling thick smoke out of the window for five to six minutes, Dubel gently squeezed the clutch and turned his silver car toward the city. After a couple of kilometers, I moved off the main line and smoothly turned onto the service platform. Victor was already waiting here.

Near the dark-lilac "BMW" impatiently shifted from one foot to the other Hamlet. There were no smoky glasses on the Caucasians, the shirt collar was loosened, the tie slid slightly to the side. Leaning on the open door of his car, Hamlet smoked a cigarette, every now and then throwing nervous glances at the Rolex dangling on his left wrist.

Grotsky stopped his car at some distance and blinked his headlights only once. It was a conditional signal. Hamlet fussily locked the "BMW", put it on the alarm and went to the arrived Dybel. The Caucasian looked alarmed. From the internal aplomb, with which Hamlet drove earlier to the mansion Laurus, not a trace remains. Now he was more like a petty crook than a confident financier. The dowel did not even get out of the cabin, showing frank disregard for the representative of the southern country.

- Well? - sluggishly threw Victor, picking a match in his teeth, as soon as the Lavrov economic adviser reached the lowered side window.

- There is information? - Hamlet leaned toward the interlocutor and briefly ran a hand through his blue-black hair. From time to time he nervously glanced over his shoulder, checking whether there were any unwanted witnesses in the vicinity of his secret meeting with a representative of the opposing side.

"It is," answered Grotsky lazily. - You answer the case.

Caucasian's swarthy face lit up with a happy smile. He proudly threw up his sharp chin and showed Dubel an eagle profile.

"In the case, yes," he said with dignity. - He pecked, Dubel. Fuse. Laurel has a crush! - The joy of a corrupt financial adviser was genuine. - As a child is small, naive! Honestly!

However, Victor continued frowning with displeasure. He clearly did not share the emotions that covered the head from the sun's edges. In addition, Dowel on a subconscious level did not leave mistrust. After all, it could be a trap, arranged by a major criminal authority. Caution is never superfluous.

"It seemed to me differently," he uttered, getting rid of the chewed match and instead inserting a cigarette in his teeth.

The fashionable, jewel-encrusted lighter clicked, and the orange flame reflected in Grotsky's pupils. Thick smoke cheekily crashed into the nose of Hamlet.

- How? - scared asked that, ignoring another demonstration of neglect.

- And so. - Dubel did not even turn his head in his direction, intently savoring tobacco smoke. - Not so naive.

- See you? - Caught Caucasians.

Victor nodded silently, this made Hamlet even more anxious and fussing. His hooked fingers randomly fermented in space, looking for a use for themselves. For some reason, he even took out his sunglasses from his breast pocket and put them on his forehead. He bent even lower to the open window "Audi" and quickly whispered:

- Do not see each other. Oh, do not. Everything is necessary through me. - Hamlet chattering, like a machine gun, swallowing the end of some words. - God forbid, Laurel rest. - He again zoiziratsya on the sides. - And the money come on. Prepaid expense. The risk is so terrible ...

Another stream of smoke was released in the face of the Caucasian. He coughed and waved five in front of his nose. Grotsky smiled contemptuously, watching his nervous manipulations. Hamlet, at last, overcame his inner fear of the man sitting in the salon and, as severely as possible, frowned his brows over the bridge of his nose.

- We agreed so? - However, the Caucasian didn't succeed in adding as much metal to the voice as we would like. The protest came out somehow vyalenky, unconvincing. - Yes? .. Quiet, peaceful.

"So, so," Victor responded, much softer, and his sinewy hand promptly dived into the back pocket of his pants.

Hamlet tensed. He knew very well that anything could be expected from this type. Even the most unforeseen meanness. And instead of money, to see a weapon in his fingers aimed at the forehead - and even more so. But Dubel behaved honestly, gentlemanly. He fished out a weighty purse and uncovered it. So it will pay. This not only calmed the Caucasians, but also returned to him a good state of mind.

"Let's go for lunch, Dubel," he offered in a friendly way from the bottom of his heart. "Here, in a glass, hashs do — stunned! - Hamlet nodded toward a roadside cafe on the right side of the highway. - This is Zhorik point.

- I know. - The dowel slowly peeled off several banknotes and handed them to the Caucasians through the open window. - But I'm full.

Money in an instant disappeared into Hamlet's hairy hands and disappeared. As if dissolved between the fingers. Where the nimble Caucasians had attached them so quickly, for Grotsky it remained a complete mystery.

- Listen. - Hamlet continued his attempts to establish friendly relations with Victor. - You and I did not greet at the meeting ...

"Good-bye, Hamlet," he interrupted. - There will be news - immediately report. It is important that he got. I slipped on a bone, "Dowel added with a grin.

- Which bone, huh?

- Kiwi on the bone.

With these words, Grotsky raised the side window, fencing off the interlocutor, and started the engine. Hamlet shrugged his shoulders dearly and had already moved back, when the thief of the new formation again activated the glass unit and stuck the short-cropped crown into the resulting window opening. In the thickened twilight, in the complete absence of the moon, Victor's face was not visible on the blackened sky. Only the glowing tip of a lit cigarette glowed.

- Hamlet! - Dyubel called his informer.

He quickly turned around.

- What?

- Why did you come to me? - In the voice of Grotsky sounded genuine interest.

The Caucasian thought and confided for a second with an ingratiating smile on his lips:

- Out of fear. I'm afraid of him. A tyrant, a ram ... Always afraid. With no reason. - Hamlet again held a slight pause. - Often dreams of Laurus killing me. With a smile ... I do not work against him, - he admitted. - Against your fear ...

Dubel, having restrainedly listening to such revelations, which, in his opinion, seemed more like a bullshit, turned away contemptuously, and the silver "Audi" started off. Victor rushed towards the city, and Lavrovsky, a frightened financier, looked at the noses of his fashionable shoes for a long time, shifting his weight from one foot to the other. It was lousy at heart, but the advance payment compensated in some way for this internal discomfort.

The long-awaited moon rolled out from behind the clouds and painted the sky dome in pale blue tones.

Chapter 6

The ground floor of the former Sytin publishing house has long been turned into a showroom at the Trinity Motors showroom, and it was here, as many knew, that there was the largest choice of vehicles for any, even the most pretentious customer taste. New owners of the premises launched a business fairly quickly. The benefit of the demand for vehicles has never fallen, therefore, and in the near future it was possible not to worry.

Lavrovskaya "The Seagull" sedately drove up to the central entrance just before the closing of the salon, and the stylish shoes of prestige, lacquered and polished to a shine, confidently stepped onto dry asphalt, long since longing for a fertile rain. Following the boss, Sancho got out of the car. The player rested peacefully in the breast pocket of his shirt, waiting in the wings, and Moshkin lightly and monotonously wound a thin cord of headphones on the index finger of his right hand.

Together they headed to the right building. Lavrikov's mood was still upbeat and complacent, which made him even with a certain degree of sympathy gazing at the gloomy and focused faces of the passers-by who, in their evening affairs, were seeking an uninterrupted dense stream. A young consultant at the Trinity Motors dealership with a pimply pale pink face moved cautiously towards the customers, having determined the financial viability of these gentlemen with an experienced eye in two seconds. He bowed in a respectful, but shallow bow. Kept the appropriate brand.

- Will you help us pick something up? - Lavr addressed him with a smile.

- Yes of course. - The boy nodded vigorously pumpkin head. - Come on in.

Fyodor Pavlovich, without any hesitation, followed the warning youngster into the interior of the room, and Sancho, having picked up a convenient moment, quickly put on the headphones and turned on the tape in his player. The aria from "Rigoletto" made him close his eyes and smack his tongue from aesthetic pleasure. He completely immersed himself, only from time to time monotonously shaking his head, like a real music lover immersed in trance.

- What's this? - The little finger of Laurus almost immediately poked into one of the cars he liked.

The authority never liked to indulge in a long and methodical choice. He had long ago based on the postulate that a person takes the only right decision for himself only in the first five seconds. In addition, Fyodor Pavlovich thought that this supernovae of some foreign car itself looked at it with round faramii, which was literally asking for the hands of a potential owner. The car was low, squat, but stylish. It seemed to Lavra that it would be very prestigious to drive around on such a miracle of technology.

A young consultant responded to the interest of the client instantly. Affected by the experience of working with such people. He energetically opened the driver's door and pressed the black button, dropping the tinted glass.

"Sit down," he suggested to the thief in the law. - You will understand everything without words!

The young man's face glowed with such pride that he himself had invented this type of transport or, at a minimum, was personally acquainted with the owner of the manufacturing company. In the eyes of Lavrikov, on the contrary, there was a clear doubt. He turned to Sancho, confused, but his gaze came only at the adjacent eyelids of his comrade. Moshkin was already mentally far away. He hovered under the clouds, to which his delicate and naturally delicate soul was sent by a musical classic. Sancho reveled in this divine state of weightlessness and complete detachment from all worldly things. Laurel sighed heavily, realizing that in the near future, waiting for moral support from this type is just as stupid as hoping for providence.

A stout seller pimply did not let up.

"Please sit down," he said urgently. - Do not be afraid…

Laurel grinned crookedly at the corners of his lips. The communication style of this novice is still, but, apparently, he already managed to fill his hand and the language on the sales manager's clients to Fyodor Pavlovich quite amusing.

"I haven't been afraid to sit down for a long time," he uttered, looking askance at the boy, but, following his advice, he still climbed into the cozy and comfortable salon of the car.

"I mean ..." the young man perished, but he was not allowed to finish the excuse by the professional qualities and direct duties of a consultant. - Feel?

His eyes lit up with fire. It seemed to the guy that the mere contact with the comfortable soft seat of the wonder-car should have caused a condition close to ecstasy in the buyer. If he was offered such a car and, of course, he would have had the means to purchase it, the guy would have taken the car without thinking. And these moneybags are also made!

- What you need to feel? - did not understand Lavrikov and even slid a confused look around.

"The degree of comfort and convenience," said the young man, in all appearances, a phrase memorized in advance. - Feel? - He repeated with a barely perceptible amount of pressure.

Fyodor Pavlovich comically twisted his backside on the seat and happily bared his teeth in a smile.

- Well ... Soft ass. I feel, - he said.

"Soft is not the right word!" - Brightened, like a brand new ruble, a consultant at Trinity Motors. - Here, take a look at the panel ...

And here he began to pour with technical characteristics that were incomprehensible to Laurus, with accompanying enthusiasm, accompanying his endless idle talk about what and where is located. From the words of pimply lad it turned out that the authority was now sitting in the most sophisticated and fashionable car that civilized humanity had ever seen. And it was with these words that the young man expressed himself. A whole stream of model merits fell upon a blurred and instantly darkened Laurus, the end and edge of which was not visible. A short, yellow man's finger from nicotine with nails nibbled along the edges also rapidly dashed around the dashboard, bumping it in one button, then in another. Fyodor Pavlovich, who at first tried to keep track of at least these chaotic movements, frustratedly abandoned this empty occupation and, without waiting for the end of the cognitive conversation,

- How much? - gloomily asked the thief in law.

- What?

A direct client question caught the dealership consultant by surprise. He blinked, trying to concentrate. The youngster, apparently, hardly came out of a state of complete euphoria, caused by his own praises of the offered goods.

- How much is the thing, I ask? - gloomy repeated Lavrikov.

The consultant in one breath blurted out more than a worthy figure and immediately rushed to add in a trusting tone:

- Just.

- Just?

The eyebrows of authority surged in amazement. Honestly, he expected to meet the sum of three times smaller than the one mentioned. Fyodor Pavlovich never had the reputation of being stingy, but always referred to himself as extremely economical people. He didn't like to scatter money on trifles, moreover, he always complained about the insolent state, zealously robbing the people in love with him. Every time, when faced with the injustices of life and the attempts of such well-made pimply boys to inflate their neighbor, Laurus was extremely indignant. In his opinion, it was a godless trampling of one of the commandments he revered: "Do not fool." Violation of others, he could somehow justify for himself. But not this one.

The thief in law got out of the cabin and angrily slammed the door. From the former complacency not a trace remains. At this point no climbing pockets will help.

- Yes, but for this money you get ... - the consultant rushed into a new attack. - You can say the embodiment of your dreams!

But Laurel no longer responded to his fervent infusions. The face of authority darkened, the hands slid under the jacket, into the pockets of the trousers, and the naturally thin lips closed in a solid line.

"They spoiled the mood," he muttered gruffly, and then fixed his stern gaze on the pimply and even paler face than at the moment they were with Sancho coming, the face of a young man. - First, young man, how do you or who else know my dreams?

"But ...

He was completely taken aback, confused, and Laurel, not accepting his weak babble as an attempt to justify himself, continued:

- Secondly, how can even the most miserable dream be realized in stamped iron and wires? - The thief in law squinted suspiciously.

"I assure you," this time the boy found the appropriate words from the stock of home-made preparations, "this model is really looking to the future!" By all measures!

"So be it," the thief in law did not argue with him, realizing the futility of these futile attempts. - The question is different. Where do I personally go? .. In all respects ... - Lavrikov endured a theatrical pause. - Do you know?

- Personally you? - The guy frantically swallowed saliva running down his throat. - No, how can I know ...

Authority sadly shook his graying head. Both hands simultaneously jumped out of his trouser pockets, and Laurel gently swung on his heels. All the universal pain of suffering humanity is reflected in its wrinkled, sallow face.

"I don't know either," he said sadly.

The young consultant had nothing to do in this situation, except to helplessly shrug. He was not given to comprehend all the oddities of the laurel consciousness, and he, in general, by and large did not intend to take any steps in this direction. Every person is a blacksmith of his own happiness. And even more such strange types as this gray-haired snob. They themselves do not know what they want!

Laurel turned and walked to the exit, putting a cigarette in his mouth as he went.

- Sancho! - A dry brush appealingly lay on the shoulder of a comrade in Nirvana and slightly shook him.

Moshkin instantly, as if on cue, stopped recording Italian classical music, clicking the stop button on the player, took a miniature speaker out of his ear and looked up at Laurus. Fyodor Pavlovich was skeptical of Alexander's sentimentality, and he, sensing what weakness he allowed himself to allow, drenched his eyelids with the back of his hand and quickly rushed to the exit after the boss.

- We will not buy a car? - He asked disappointedly, gaining prestige already at the glass doors.

"We won't," said Fyodor Pavlovich shortly, flicking a lighter.

- Why?

- Bullshit. - The argument in the mouth of Laurus was weighty.

Sancho nodded knowingly and, turning round, politely addressed the young salon consultant:

- Thank you for the excursion. And do not worry. - Moshkin lowered his voice to a confidential whisper. - He is in this business - not a belmes ...

- Sancho! - evil Lavrikov hissed, catching his last sentence.

He instantly painted a frightened expression on his face and retreated through the door. Following him, towards the city already shrouded in evening twilight, Laurus also stepped into the city. After the sun set over the horizon, the air soaked with stuffiness became a little cooler. In addition, he was stirred by a light unobtrusive breeze. The heat is a little bit. Fyodor Pavlovich let out a thick puff of smoke into space, lifted his head up, peering for some reason into the still dull stars scattered across the sky.

The driver of the "Seagull" patiently waited for the owners, standing in the fresh air and happily grinding a cigarette. Noticing the approaching figures of Lavrikov and Moshkin, he threw the cigarette butt to the side, walked around the car around the perimeter and opened the back door. However, the authority was in no hurry to get into the cramped and hot salon "Chaika". He continued to stand two steps away from him and breathed in the evening coolness. The view of the starry sky more than anything else, set up the Laurus in a philosophical manner. The old thief threw a cigarette, having managed to make two or three puffs under his feet from the strength and gently dabbed it with the toe of his boot.

- Ha! He tells me about dreams! - Fedor Pavlovich said gruffly, as usual, trying to hide his nervousness. - Anecdote! ..

"You yourself wanted to take a new one," Sancho reminded him, carefully stuffing the cord from the headphones into the breast pocket of his shirt. Experience prompted Alexander, that the boss would not give him the opportunity to enjoy the Italian classics. - He decided to go buy.

- Yes, I wanted a new one! - discontentedly growled thief in law. - But I wanted just that! - He nodded at an old "Seagull" parked at the side of the road with a non-leader from the Essentuki brigade standing still near him. - Twenty years ago, I really dreamed of this. And my dream came true. Everything! - The right fist of Laurus was boldly imprinted in the open left palm. - "Dream" is no more.

He took a couple of unhurried steps toward the sidewalk and froze again. Sancho poked his potato nose into his back. Laurel turned his face to him and, putting his hand on Alexander's shoulder in a friendly way, said bitterly in his voice:

- It ended, probably dreams. - He dejectedly laid his head on his chest. - Poorly.

"They ran out, they didn't run out," Sancho responded with a frank request for philosophical intonations. - But, to be honest, they are already laughing at your car.

- Who? - Laurus asked bitterly, and his eyes flashed unkindly.

Moshkin shrugged vaguely:

- All and sundry. Should you turn away.

- Let them try to laugh in the face! - Laurel with a withering gaze threw his faithful comrade-in-arms from head to toe, as if he was the very villain who ape and mocks him in the back of the head. - And then I'll see who was the last one to giggle.

"Yes, it's embarrassing, Laurel, in fact, on such a clunker ..." Alexander sniffed contemptuously and wanted to add something offensive in the same style, but Lavrikov abruptly cut him off:

- Aren't you ashamed in my garage for a "six" to be broken down?

The blow was, as they say, not in the eyebrow, but in the eye. Moshkin even seemed to shrink in size. Skukozhilsya all and frightened zoazira around, as if he publicly tried to slander, accusing him of something supreme. He lowered his voice to a whisper and lowered his gaze to make a sound of his excuse:

- Well ... I am on the post of "six" ... Sorry for the old woman. - Thoughts in his head chaotically replaced each other. - Running around. Not to the dump ... Suddenly, it is still useful.

His spontaneous attempts at self-rehabilitation did not suit the eminent thief in law. He only gave up his hand with annoyance, as if making it clear that there were already enough discussions on empty and non-binding topics, and finally sat down in the backseat of his car. The driver dutifully waited until the cabin placed his overweight body and Sancho, after which he returned to his rightful place behind the wheel of the Chaika.

- Maybe to another store roll up? - In the depths of his soul, Moshkin still hoped that the antediluvian Lavrovskaya dream would still get a legal resignation today. - To "Saab", for example?

- No, - Lavrikov frowned. - Do not roll. I changed my mind.

"You changed your mind, and we never bought anything," Moshkin said reasonably.

- Well, let's buy, - indifferently declared authority.

The driver silently sat behind the wheel, not daring to intervene in the debates in the back seat and waiting for him to finally be given the command. By and large, he did not care in which direction to turn the steering wheel. To "Saab" or in a country mansion. It would be an appropriate order.

- car? - Moshkin specified.

- Not. Tie. Or better wallet. - Laurel feverishly sought in his own mind that he could really be useful in everyday life. - No, my umbrella broke. Such a good was an umbrella, reliable.

Sancho laughed heartily. He even had tears in his eyes again. But this time not from tenderness, but on the basis of extreme gaiety.

"He died of old age, Laurus," he said with difficulty, unable to restrain the cramping movements. - In the spring the umbrella would have turned seven years old! Consider the anniversary. If the age of the umbrella counted on the dog, and then compare with the human ... It will be ... Exactly. Anniversary. As many as seven years. Very round date.

- So let's buy a new umbrella without any dog-hair! - The thief in law is not at all offended by Alexander's attacks. He himself realized that he was somewhat overdone in terms of savings. Yes, most likely, and this was not the case. Just all hands did not reach. "Are there special ... these ... umbrella boutiques?"

- Hardly. "Sancho wiped away the tears with his hand again, but the smile still played on his full lips. - Umbrella is a companion product, not the main one.

- But why? - Lavrikov unexpectedly broke into a wild cry, which was a lot of concern for Moshkin sitting next to him. - Why does someone decide for me where the main thing is, and where is the accompanying one ?! - Immediately feeling that the surplus was enough in emotions, Fyodor Pavlovich sighed heavily and calmly turned to Sancho, who was terrified by his fit, said: - Excuse me ...

However, the short word could not affect the overall impression that had already formed in Alexander's eyes. He cautiously, with a certain degree of fear, touched the authority's shoulder with the index finger and immediately pulled his hand back. I waited for the reaction. Laurel, frowning, was silent.

- What's happening with you? - seriously asked Sancho.

This time in his voice there was no irony, no complaints about Lavr. Only sincere friendly participation. Fyodor Pavlovich began to resemble the insane marazmatik. Not all the time, of course. Sancho understood this perfectly well. But these periodic uncontrollable outbursts of aggression ... It was worth talking heart to heart, anyway. Worse from this will not be.

- I do not know. - Lavrikov shook his head, and then several times vigorously shook his hands, forcing himself to relieve the accumulated tension. - I think about tests all the time. About DNA. How are they - our tests?

"The analyzes are being analyzed," Sancho grumbled discontentedly, realizing that the essence of Lavrov's problem was in the subject that Moshkin did not enjoy as much as he liked. It was not worth, perhaps, start a conversation. - No need for DNA.

But Alexander also subconsciously felt how Fedor Pavlovich was drawn to this issue. And now this constant nervousness.

"Don't," Lavrikov agreed with him and tried to depict a kind of sincere smile on his face. It turned out not very natural. - Let's buy ice cream! He unexpectedly suggested. - Creme brulee for fifteen kopecks. Be sure to briquette! And - home! ..

- Good. - Sancho gave the same, finally, a short follow-up to the driver, and the stagnant "Seagull", happily purring, started off.

The departure of the car Lavrikova through the glass dealership watched with interest pimply fellow consultant. An obvious annoyance appeared on his face, and to calm his own soul he twisted his finger at his temple, mentally addressing this gesture to a strange gentleman in a white suit, after which he also casually spat on the floor of the Trinity Motors car dealership. The evening at the young man turned out to be unsuccessful.

One motley site gave way to another, but this lesson, which had been lasting for more than one hour, could hardly bore a kid who was looking for all the new and new interesting information on the Internet. The World Wide Web stubbornly refused to let Fedechk who was stuck in her networks. However, he himself did not seek this.

Claudia only occasionally looked askance at him, and then returned to her usual evening pastime, consisting entirely of watching television series. The benefit of their case in abundance twisted through many channels. Naturally, the woman gave the greatest preference to the Ments, where the personality of the legendary Casanova in the brilliant performance of Lykova had long troubled the minds and souls of the weaker sex of humanity. Claudia, however, did not feel ardent feelings for Captain Kazantsev, but she fully enjoyed the interesting plot and the magnificent play of young actors.

Fedech also remained indifferent to such a meaningless, in his view, occupation and did not want to stare at the TV screen. He preferred to communicate with the monitor screen, which occupied more than half of his desk. Having bent in an unnatural posture and risking to make money on this business of scoliosis, he selflessly clicked a compact mouse, nestled on a mat specially reserved for it.

- Fedechka, you even called Nate. - Taking advantage of the advertising pause, Claudia turned down the sound of the TV and half turned to her nephew. - She called. Walked That you look after the girl, you forget. - She tried to add some weighty argument to what was just said, but she didn't decide which one. - Can not be so.

- Why walk when there is no money? - the young man growled with displeasure, not looking up from his extraordinary occupation.

Claudia sniffed contemptuously.

- Romantic relationships can be built without money. - She herself was confident in the spoken words.

"Yes, of course," said Fyodor Rozgin skeptically. - No money, no pants. Right?

- You have pants, Fedechka. Do not exaggerate, be kind.

The woman again turned her gaze to the TV screen, but some unpleasant aftertaste that appeared in the shower, did not allow her to focus on the ongoing broadcast of the series. Claudia hesitantly glanced at the back of her nephew, mentally rehearsing her next question, but, having failed to put it together, she turned to the guy at random:

- Fedechka ...

- What else? - displeased the guy. He managed to find on the Internet something interesting that completely absorbed all his attention and consciousness. Distracted by empty conversations now clearly did not want to.

- Do you need me, Fedya? - with difficulty squeezed out a woman.

- In terms of? - The unexpectedness of her question made Rozgin straighten up, turn on her hard chair and gaze intently at her aunt with a curious glance.

Anyway, the site will not run away, and Claudia's strange behavior has lately been fueling boyish curiosity in the boy.

- In a sense - in general. In principle, - bent his incomprehensible line Rozgin. - Do I need you next?

- Stupid question! - Fedechka declared gloomily. - How can I say that I do not need my own aunt?

"Honestly, you can," said Claudia warmly.

- Honestly? - Fedech jokingly portrayed on the face of extreme thoughtfulness. Say, before answering this question with absolute certainty, you should carefully weigh the pros and cons.

- Well?

"Needed," he replied after a pause.

- What for? - Claudia continued to seriously try, the more she threw her nephew into confusion.

"Well ... Lunch there, dinner ..." Fedech was confused. - ironed jeans. It is necessary for someone to get annoyed.

- And annoyed?

"And then," he even snapped his tongue.

- Right. - Claudia sadly lowered her head to a heavily heaving chest.

Another attempt by Fedor to turn into an incomprehensible and very strange conversation for him was not a success. Today, the aunt was clearly not in himself. Something inexplicable happened to her, but she was not going to share her experiences.

"You have no personal life because of me."

- And you have no. - Fedechka already all turned on the chair and leaned the body forward. Locked fingers hung between your knees. - Because of me.

His not-so-serious words still caused a timid smile on the female lips. Perhaps for the first time, Claudia realized that she was not a child, but a fully formed young man.

"I drove my own without stopping," she honestly admitted. "You have been my personal life ... But then mental agonies will begin."

- What? - I did not understand the guy.

- Female egoism. You can't keep a boy by the skirt for a long time, the women from the neighboring tents told me. It can have a destructive effect on your psyche.

Fedech mischievously laughed, rose to his full height, and marched to the sofa, on which his aunt modestly huddled. He tenderly embraced her by the shoulders and settled down beside him, putting his legs under him. His shaggy head came into contact with Claudia's hairstyle that had been drawn into the ponytail on the back of the head.

"I have an iron psyche, Klav's aunts," he admitted to her in a fit of kindred feelings. - You never know what the women in the tents say. Better tell me ... - This time, the boy hesitated with a question for a moment. - When mom was ... Well, have you ever truly been happy? Only not at all, but specifically. Because of something?

- Because of you. - Claudia with genuine love and affection gazed at the grown up child.

- No, not that! - Fedor shook his head, and several of his tight braids tickled his aunt's face.

- Because of something else? - The woman became thoughtful.

- Well! - hurried her Fedechka. - Specifically!

- Specifically? She suddenly smiled happily at the memory of days gone by. - Yes! Once were exactly. A year after your birth - for sure. Then there were no diapers. I used to wash diapers from old pillowcases, and my mother went to Semenovskaya for the liver.

- What for? - the young man blinked in surprise.

"Behind the liver," repeated Claudia. - Your hemoglobin has dropped, and the doctor has written a prescription, according to which a kilo of beef liver was released once a week in a special Diet store.

- Darkness! - rozgin twisted. - And you lived like that?

He was genuinely outraged by the Soviet way of life. He was hard to imagine how it all happened then.

"We lived normally," Claudia assured him, and again switched to the memories of many years ago. - And so, it means, once instead of the liver, they suddenly gave us a hundred grams of weighted black caviar in such a paper waxed cup. Shelf life, it is clear that the distributor has expired, spawn and thrown to protect motherhood and childhood. Kate came back with this cup, put it on the table in the kitchen, scooped up a spoon of eggs. They glittered in the light, shimmered oily with so all the colors of the rainbow - just like some black diamonds. We were very happy. Highly. Specifically happy. - The eyes of my aunt involuntarily moistened.

- And I? - Fedor became interested.

Claudia was silent for a while, recalling those bright events in their lives.

"You spat out the first batch," she laughed. - You are not used to such food.

"I did the right thing," Rozgin summarized with a smile too.

The guy wanted to show as much tenderness as possible, and he awkwardly shook the aunt's hand on his lap. Unfortunately, deeply moved by her revelations, he was no longer capable of anything more.

This morning, as well as the previous one, was extremely sunny. Bright and warm rays impudently penetrated through the gaps in heavy portieres, claiming to be their right in the room. Laurel slowly opened his eyelids, sweetly stretched and threw aside a light blanket. The lean and sinewy body of authority was filled with numerous symbolic tattoos, made at different times and for different purposes. Each of them always reminded Fyodor Pavlovich of an event that somehow influenced its future existence. Tattoos were part of his story. A person who is knowledgeable and well versed in the thieves' symbols would have been able to read his entire biography at one glance at the body of a lawyer, starting with the first short term spent on the youngster and ending with the honorary moment of coronation. The owners of these masterpieces of fine art themselves often said that tattoos for a prisoner are more important than a passport. Present, so to speak, in expanded form where necessary and without further ado won a place for himself under the sun. Honor and respect. Of course, it happened and so that were applied to the body and offensive, stigmatizing tattoo. In this case, the life of such a person and in the wild proceeded accordingly. As humiliated and insulted. Hiding received in the zone of art was forbidden, and it was impossible. Got it - be nice, wear what you expect. In this case, the life of such a person and in the wild proceeded accordingly. As humiliated and insulted. Hiding received in the zone of art was forbidden, and it was impossible. Got it - be nice, wear what you expect. In this case, the life of such a person and in the wild proceeded accordingly. As humiliated and insulted. Hiding received in the zone of art was forbidden, and it was impossible. Got it - be nice, wear what you expect.

Lavrikov sat up on the bed and made several circular movements with his head, flexing the numbed cervical vertebrae. After that, he picked up a dressing gown from the back, casually threw it over his shoulders and rose to his full height. Feet quickly dived in slippers. Laurel yawned. The night he had today was restless. I hardly forced myself to fall asleep, and then I reviewed a whole gamut of nightmarish dreams based on any kind of devilry that could only fit into the head of a normal person.

The authority approached the window and pulled back the curtains. Sunlight entrenched in impatience burst into his apartment vigorously, filling up space. Laurel heartily tried to depict a friendly smile on his face, turned to a new day, but he had only a painful grimace. He felt his cheekbones and stared thoughtfully at the high-rise new buildings seen in the distant morning haze. There, in the city, life was already seething and boiling.

Sensitive by nature, Lavrikov's ear instantly caught barely noticeable breathing behind his back. The authority turned sharply. On the threshold with the same tray in his hands Sancho stopped. Only this time, instead of breakfast, he delivered some form, lonely attached to a silver surface. The look of a devoted comrade was very sad, if not to say - mourning. Laurel involuntarily cautioned, and the middle-aged heart was already pounding wildly in the chest. It has long been Fedor Pavlovich not experienced such a rapid and huge release of adrenaline in the blood.

The thief in law broke away from the window sill and quickly stepped towards Moshkin. Then he stopped in indecision. Thin, like a pianist, fingers nervously ran through the hair.

- What? - Said Laurus in one breath.

Sancho carefully studied the non-standard behavior of the boss from under his frowning eyebrows and was deliberately silent, not answering his question. He was not even in a hurry to go into the depth of the bedroom, as he usually did.

- Stop making fun, Sancho! - Lavrikov jumped to him like a giant kangaroo, and unkindly flashed his eyes, drilling his nose to his comrade in arms. He feared to lower his gaze on the silver tray with a blank.

Moshkin cleared his throat.

"The doctor has come to dawn," he said weakly. - All night, he says, his team worked.

- Which doctor? - the authority reacted vividly.

- Yesterday's. - Sancho dejectedly bowed his head. - Who have you been and kosmatenky where they drove. From the genetic office of the doctor.

Laurel held out his hand in the direction of the tray, but then abruptly pulled it back, as if it was scalding with boiling water. His right eyelid involuntarily twitched, and the thief in law pressed him with his finger. Then he quickly turned and headed for his crumpled bed. He sat down on the bed and tightened the belt of his dressing gown.

"Give him money," the authority said shortly.

- Already gave.

- Enough? - Feodor Pavlovich did not let up.

Sancho grinned wickedly.

- He was quite pleased. Only about some kind of unit recalled. You promised him the unit?

- Promised. - Laurel nodded grimly. - It later...

In the bedroom illuminated by mischievous sunshine a tense pause again hung. Fyodor Pavlovich could not decide at all, and Moshkin did not even think to rush him. Say, you need it, and take an interest. Alexander, if he wanted, could be a very stubborn and stubborn comrade. Lavrikov put up with this, knowing full well about a bunch of other assistant merits. The gaze of authority running around, still focused on the elevated axis and froze tensely. To delay the decisive moment further did not make sense. Anyway, sooner or later you will have to touch upon a painful topic.

- And what does he write, doctor?

In the eyes of Laurus, there was confusion and genuine fright before the coming verdict. He was never so nervous at the trial. And then suddenly - just the same! Panicked! Like a boy. It is ridiculous, but at the same time, it seemed to the eminent lawyer, very reasonably.

Sancho broke off, finally, from the threshold, walked over to the wide bed of authority and attached his wide ass with Lavrikov. Tray placed in the center between himself and the owner of the apartment, folded hands on his knees.

"Read it yourself," he said grimly.

- But you read it? - Fyodor Pavlovich's palms were sweating treacherously, but he decided to seize the folded form with his fingers, delivered from an early morning to the efficient doctor.

"I read," answered Moshkin honestly. - See - the envelope is torn.

- I see. Could and be more careful to tear. The edges are completely uneven on the break. - Laurel fished out a sheet of paper from an envelope, but could not overpower himself and look into its contents. - So that?

Sancho understood perfectly well that simply without receiving the desired answer, he would not be left behind. The authority tortures him with Gestap torture using sophisticated methods, rather than decide to read the results of genetic examination. Moshkin sighed heavily and said gravely:

- The object "X" is ninety-nine and hell knows how many hundredths of a percent is the father of the object "Yp".

- Wait, Sancho! - Laurel threw the sheet on the bed, and he sprang up to his feet. Ran to the window, for some reason looked out onto the street and came back again. But he did not sit down anymore. - What is the "X-game"?

"Well, X is you," Alexander patiently explained, diligently portraying on his face the obvious displeasure of his duties and the need to talk on an unpleasant topic. - He himself asked to conspire.

- I?! - Hands of authority nervously shook.

- Didn't you ask? - Sancho grumbled discontentedly.

- Yes, it is about the other! - breaking into a falsetto, Laurus shouted. - I am?

- It turns out, - the colleague had to admit with another sigh. - You are.

In the ensuing silence of silence, Laurel clasped his fingers into the lock, letting off a shiver, and broke into an idiotic smile. Sancho shook his head in disgust, watching the birth of a new oligophrenic before his eyes. And that is exactly how he now saw the eminent kingpin. Debil-moron. Moshkin was afraid to utter his diagnoses out loud, knowing full well that from the idiot of the passive Lavrikov he could instantly turn into violent. And then, as they say in the well-known children's game, "who did not hide, I am not guilty." But for himself, Alexander mentally noted that somehow, under more favorable circumstances, it would be necessary to talk with Laurel on the subject of a medical examination. Only not from geneticists, but from doctors with a different specialization. And as it was not too late.

- I am. - Lavrikov somnambulically rocked from side to side, without changing the Daun facial expressions. - I!..

Moshkin was no longer able to observe this terrible process of degradation. His nerves were not iron.

"That's right, Joseph said," he hissed angrily. - Genetics is a public girl of imperialism!

- Why is it right? Totally wrong! - Laurel approached his comrade-in-arms and laid his hand on his shoulder. - And then, it was not Joseph who spoke, but Raikin.

- Whatever the one who spoke! - Sancho's accumulated irritation spilled outward. "The fact is that now you can never die as you wanted — one of the last ... a real thief in law!"

Laurel smiled openly.

"Stupid it sounds like something." Oh, Sancho? - He himself was aware that he considered his former priorities now in a completely different way. - Childly.

- It is stupid to cross out a lifetime, - he did not retreat.

- Yes, calm down! - Fyodor Pavlovich dismissed his tediousness, as from a bothersome fly. - We won't tell anyone. Nothing. Even a boy.

- But you know something! Said Sancho gravely. - And I know! And this is quite enough not to die as it should be!

- Well, stuck a little light! To die, not to die! .. - Lavrikov, as usual, energetically ran around the room. "Maybe I decided not to die at all!" Why die?

"Die wherever you go," said good Sancho cooled his optimistic views on the future.

- Yes? - Laurel stopped in front of him and thrust his hands into his sides, with his elbows wide apart.

- Yes!

- hre-noo-shki! Even if I die now, then ... - for a second or two he was looking for an opportunity to finish the begun phrase more beautifully, - then with a probability of ninety-nine percent I - Fyodor Lavrikov - will not die!

- How so? - The meaning of his flowery words did not reach Alexander.

- And so! I ... - Laurel was suffocating from overwhelming feelings. - I - continue! I will continue in the next Fedor Lavrikov! - He resolutely fixed his gaze on Moshkin's fleshy face. - The Chinese are not fools.

- What does the Chinese have to do with it? "Sancho was completely bewildered by all this rubbish, spewed out of the thief-in-law, twisted by emotion.

- They have long said: the man who gave birth to a son is immortal.

- What is he carrying, Yeshenki. - Moshkin defiantly rolled his eyes, turning to someone upstairs: whether to God in heaven, or to an invisible opponent on the ceiling. - The Chinese! .. And if the mistake came out?

- Wrong, people are lying, Sancho! - weighty said authority, leaning toward the face of a comrade and grabbing his worried look. - People - yes! They lie! Des-uksi ... srebo ... nucleic acid - never! - Laurel tiredly plopped down on the bed, and the overturned empty tray with a clatter flew to the floor. - I am quite satisfied with her percentage of probability. For the eyes! .. Imagine? Will Lavrikov II! Laurel-next. In the sense of the next generation, they talked about the box about Pepsi! .. Laurel Kosmatenky, ha! - The thief in law is not a joke amused. - There is still time to raise it, to introduce an heir to the business! You have no idea what this ... feeling! - Fyodor Pavlovich raised his chin high, demonstrating Sancho his proud and still quite attractive, despite the years, profile, and rolled his chest with a wheel.

- What?

With every second, Moshkin became more and more convinced of the loyalty of his own diagnosis. He was already thinking that he could acquire his own medical practice. The benefit of customers such as Laurel, wanders the earth in abundance.

- Feeling of infinity! - blurted authority.

- Similarly, crazy. - Sancho addressed this resume to himself more than to the interlocutor.

However, Laurel no longer listened to him. He lay back and stretched out on the bed to his full height, his hands behind his head.

"Bring brandy, be a friend," the lawyer ordered. - I promise: I will have a snack.

Sancho, groaning and shaking his head, rose to his feet and, turning on the sprawling Laurus, grumbled discontentedly:

- I have no additives for stupidity and diarrhea of the brain.

"But I have a son," Lavrikov said quietly, in a low voice, and then shouted loudly: "Get a drink, it's said!"

To interfere with the current desires of the thief in law was pointless. Moshkin dutifully went to carry out the order.

Chapter 7

Sancho slowly put a good portion of semolina in a deep plate with wide edges and put the dish in the microwave. I turned on the timer. In Alexandra, discontent caused by Lavrikov's inadequate, in his opinion, and completely reckless behavior continued to roam, but he was already beginning to get used to the idea that a new dream had now appeared in the life of authority, which had swallowed him up. Laurel has changed, and nothing could be done about it. It remained only to put up and take this fact for granted.

In addition, Sancho at the moment was faced with another important task: not to show his concern to those who were sitting at the table in the cozy dining room of the Essentuki mansion. The head of the security service, having risen today before dawn, noisily sipped hot, strong coffee from a large porcelain glass. At the same time, he periodically gnawed huge teeth into his own sandwich. Essentuki always and everything preferred to eat with bread. Up to the watermelons. That's why he constructed sandwiches in such a way that bread covered ham, butter, cheese on both sides at once. All this was thoroughly heated in the microwave and only then in the optimal state was sent to the mouth. And, of course, coffee. Without him, the chef security guard never got along. He had never been so early before.

Moshkin returned to the table and, sitting down opposite, picked up a glass with his favorite fruit tea.

"At least you wouldn't eat so deafening, eh?" - he frowned.

"And you sniff your nose," Yessentuki retorted, without thinking twice. "And in general ..." He ignored his giant glass for some time and shifted his eyes to narrowed eyes on Moshkin. - Bored we live, Sancho. Like old men.

Alexander, changing his mind about tea, poured himself a plastic bottle of mineral water, drained the contents of a glass cup in one gulp, and again sniffed. Thoroughly do a chronic sinusitis that has long been converted to a chronic state did not have enough time.

"Find a young master," he said casually, but his small eyes looked apprehensive.

Essentuki felt the test for lice.

"You know, such transitions are not welcome," he said peacefully, returning to savoring the tonic. - I won't go under anybody. I would have organized my team.

"That's right," Sancho agreed with his decision without any interest in the conversation. - And let the competitors gnaw throats.

- Why is it necessary to nibble? - Yessentuki did not agree.

- Dialectic. - Moshkin shrugged.

- What is it like?

If periodic communication with Fyodor Pavlovich Lavrikov, erudite and enlightened in many matters, allowed Sancho to occasionally trump with clever buzzwords, then Essentuki's educational level was generally far from it. But he must admit, and did not strive for self-improvement. He arranged himself as he was.

- And so. When all spheres of influence are divided, it will not work out without a fight, - Alexander enlightened him on this issue.

Essentuki concentratedly took an impressive burning sip and scratched his square chin with his fingers. After a short pause, he sent the remnants of the original sandwich into his mouth and completely culturally dabbed his lips with a paper napkin.

- Do you think it's better to roam here and there all day long in a bathrobe between the bedroom, the study and the toilet? He asked, without a bit of irony, based only on his own meager conclusions. - Is this the ultimate dream?

- Who are you katish, friend? - Moshkin threw up, unkindly flashing eyes.

"No, I don't roll, I'm just like that ..." Essentuki frankly perished. He did not expect that his thoughtlessly pronounced words would make such a serious impression on the interlocutor. Nobody could quarrel with Sancho in this house. - I argue.

- So in the State Duma then be elected and argue! - grunted Alexander. - There you will not miss.

The head of the security service set aside the empty glass, completing the process of morning caffeine consumption, and vigorously shook it with huge shovel-shaped hands. Now the vitality of the thug was normal. Not even required any additional calories.

- Why? - he grinned. - A good idea…

Sancho did not have time to morally support the initiative of the future elect chosen by the people who had pricked the skies into the government. Microwave beep, announcing the complete readiness of semolina. Say, it's time to tackle one of the seven deadly sins - gluttony. Moshkin rose from the table, but at the very same second the door to the dining room on the first floor swung open, and on the threshold Laurel himself appeared, already dressed in a refined light suit. Boots are polished to a shine, hair is gently combed back, on the face are wide sunglasses.

- Go! - cheerfully threw authority and, imitating Yuri Gagarin before the first space flight, waved his hand. Her teeth were laid out in a joyful smile.

- But where is the light of dawn ?! - Sancho was taken aback, completely forgetting about the heated porridge.

Laurel laughed heartily, looking at the worried face of his comrade-in-arms, which could also cause genuine emotion.

"The main mass of the people have long ago both light and dawn," Lavrikov uttered with knowledge, morally raising his finger upwards. - To aunt Kostamenky. - The authority has turned a radiant and optimistic look towards the bodyguard. - Essentuki, did you find out exactly where she works?

He rose to meet the boss, bowing his head in a respectful bow, and straightened his stylish jacket.

"Up to the tent room," he said. - Not a great mystery.

- Well. - Lavrikov cheerfully clapped his hands. - Well, let's go, let's go! And they got used to it - the kitchen table, the toilet, the bedroom, here and there ... "He spat contemptuously. - As old fart! .. Act right!

The thief in law famously turned and disappeared into the spacious hall of the mansion. Following him, Sancho jumped out of the dining room. Like a fairytale bun, he rolled on the right side of Lavrikov, barely keeping up with the leaps and bounds of authority. Sinusitis caused Moshkin to breathe with his mouth wide open, which is why any physical exertion, even the smallest, was given to him particularly hard.

- To aunt? To aunt - let's go! - he zabubnil on the move. - That's just on an empty stomach?

- Ay! - Lavr dismissed. - I am fed up with your fears!

For greater persuasiveness, Fyodor Pavlovich struck the back of his neck with an open palm. Quite a bright gesture of authority touched a comrade-in-arms. Moshkin defiantly puffed out his cheeks, which made his round face even bigger.

In many tents trade has not yet begun. Sellers just laid out on display of a potential consumer of the proposed product. Laurel slowly moved along the long endless rows in which nothing could be found. There probably was not only weapons and drugs. And then, if desired, would find this product, distributed quietly from under the floor. But the thief in law today was not at all up to this. He happily smiled at every passer-by and relished the ice cream briquette with inexpressible pleasure.

Beside him, breathing heavily and occasionally wiping off a generous sweat with a wide handkerchief, which stood out with tiny droplets on his forehead and massive neck, he minced Sancho. Essentuki was breathing confidently in his back. The security chef did not relax for a second, gazing at every ordinary man in the street and wondering how real he could pose a threat to the authority entrusted to his attention. For Yessentuki, two more bodyguards of the same impressive dimensions as their immediate superior steadily walked up, but their zeal in the work was not so deliberate. Nevertheless, under the jacket of each of this pair, a formidable arsenal was designated in relief for the enemy.

Suddenly, Lavrikov froze in his tracks near a large counter with a pile of linen. The hand with the ice cream fell down, and the other raised sunglasses on her forehead. In her eyes the authority flashed a clear interest.

"It's not that," Sancho, who stopped with him, kindly prompted.

The rest of the retinue, headed by Yessentuki, also meekly froze behind the backs of a couple that was marching at the forefront. Brave guys tenacious gaze covered all adjacent to this tray space. The rank and file fighters were not informed about the objectives of today's raid, and they had no choice but to keep alert and be ready for an unexpected attack by a potential enemy.

- That, that! - The index finger of Laurus stuck in the direction of a whole pile of underwear. - Cowards for fifteen rubles! Wow! For nothing! - he declared admiringly. - Almost as under communism, to which we never lived.

Agile Khokhlushka, located on the other side of the counter, was not lost. She instantly pushed a whole stack of products that interested him into Lavra and quickly retrospectively, without concealing any personal interest.

- Take, uncle. Cheaper anywhere else bude! - she babbled. - Pure satin, and the peas, and the strip, what you want!

Lavrikov did not listen very attentively to her incursions, mentally casting something of his own in mind. His loyal retinue still respectfully awaited the royal decision. No one hurried Laurus and did not try to influence his opinion. Fedor Pavlovich simply would not tolerate such familiarity.

- About fifty cents are cotton pants? - Authority with a clever look scrubbed his fingers smooth-shaven chin. - With all the cheating? - He turned his head to Sancho and stared intently at the small, piggy eyes of his comrade. - How much are you buying me?

"You're branded," he responded immediately, sensing what the thief in law was headed for.

Lavrikov smiled wryly.

- Who sees the company, except for my ass? - he said reasonably. - And her firm - not care. - Dark glasses returned to their original position, and the eyes of the Lavr disappeared from the eyes of others. - I want such panties. Cheap polka dots. Satin!

- Nostalgia, e-my! - Sancho sadly sighed, pursing his lips. "Take satin ones," he promised, and added with the hope that eccentricities would disappear from the head of authority soon: "On the way back."

- Now! - Fyodor Pavlovich stood stubbornly. - On the contrary we forget.

Moshkin squinted in disbelief at the Khokhlushka behind the counter, awaiting the decision of important gentlemen, and softly gritted his teeth. Behavior Lavrikova became unbearable. He had previously been known as a petty tyrant, but over the past couple of days he had managed to surpass himself. One thing, then another, and now he also needed his underpants in polka dots, which are shameful to look at.

"Like a little child," Alexander grumbled and immediately rushed into a new counterattack. - Now you wanted to see a lady! You can not see the lady with an armful of disposable pants?

Sancho considered his own interests in this matter. He was well aware of the meeting with whom exactly they were being sent, and he was already in anticipation of this moment. Claudia turned the whole soul of the once hardened felon inside out. He wanted to appear before her in a decent form of a true gentleman, and Moshkin could easily have foreseen exactly who of their company would have to drag these satin panties in their arms. How can you impress a lady? However, the argument was convincing for Laurus. He mentally imagined this picture from the side and radiantly smiled.

- It is reasonable. - Fedor Pavlovich nodded. - It is impossible. Where is the lady?

This time, the question was addressed to the troika of bodyguards with Essentuki at the head, sullenly. He turned his head and in a second he delivered his verdict, orienting himself on the terrain:

- It seems, through two tents on the third.

- Sancho, be kind, go prepare the ground. "Lavrikov rubbed his hands together quite a bit, but in his gesture he missed a bit of nervousness."

- Not. - Moshkin even scared stepped back a couple of steps back, as if he saw the plague in front of him. In the hitherto imperturbable and crystal clear eyes of a laurel henchman, grave fear spilled over. - Better by myself. You and your ladies get cool. I'll ruin everything.

Laurel contemptuously appreciated him from under his sunglasses and energetically walked behind Essentuki who had moved forward. Alexander modestly joined the society of two closet bodyguards, trying to remain unnoticed. At that moment, he terribly regretted his multi-pudding build. With this one, you will trickle into the crowd.

Claudia was already in the workplace. She barely lifted off the ground a heavy box with chemical products and put it on a tall box with similar contents. She took a deep breath and turned around. At this very moment, the woman met face to face with Lavrikov who approached. Just for a split second, surprise flashed in her eyes, and then her gaze changed to a majestic, calm and expressed indifference to an inadequate authority visit. Laurel took off his glasses and openly smiled at Klava as an old friend. Sancho was in no hurry to step forward. He needed only one glance at the object of his mental turmoil, like a round face immediately filled with crimson paint, and all attention focused on his own shoes. Essentuki and his two handy thugs showed no emotion.

"Hello," Claudius said first, referring directly to Laurus. - The whole gang appeared?

- Not all, not all. - He continued to radiate genuine cordiality. - From the whole here would be closely. Good morning.

- Has greeted already. - Eyebrow women frowned. "Why did you kidnap Fedya?"

"These are the details," the authority waved. - How is the institute?

"They accepted it," answered Rozgin. - Consider, you extinguished one sin.

Laurel laughed, but the sounds ejaculated by his throat were more like crows cawing. He had already come close to Claudia.

"With your arithmetic, woman, I'm not going to have enough public education to cleanse my sins," he mockingly looked around at the contents of the counter stretched before him and squinted. - Maybe some washing agent would be recommended to wash off at once?

"They didn't come up with such a means yet," Claudia disappointed him and flatly asked: "What did you complain about?"

Lavrikov sustained a two-minute pause, during which he was engaged in carefully studying his interlocutor and now, it turns out, to some extent a relative. She, too, was silent, waiting for an answer to the question asked.

"I want to see a boy," the thief in law honestly admitted. - And I can't think of what kind of sauce ... so as not to be scared. Maybe I should take him to work? Kind of like a stranger?

- Raider to work? She sarcastically asked. - Killer?

Lavrikov sincerely offended. At the moment, he absolutely did not want to spoil relations with this woman. Like it or not, it was the only link between him, Fyodor Pavlovich, and his son. Not the right time for open confrontation. Yes, and not such a monster was Lavr, as it was represented by the household merchant in front of him.

- Well, not so stupid, Claudia, so clearly! - he scolded the woman. "I've seen a lot of shit on TV ... I have quite legal, solid units," he said confidentially. - Computers are gathering dust again ...

- And the institute? - Interlocutor noticeably softened, and it cheered Laurus.

"There will be temporary work," he introduced another resolute offer.

- With a salary?

- How else?

In Claudia, a purely human interest in the conversation that ensued with authority arose. She thoughtful, weighing all the pros and cons. In her presentation, Fedechka was now hanging out without work. The same seat near the computer, in her opinion, was meaningless. And here it seems the case was proposed. Earnings again. What's wrong with it? ..

- Salary Fedechke would not hurt, - Rozgin drawled. - The child is almost naked.

- Here and dress! - happily grinned Laurus.

- Eh! Uh Uh - with wild guttural cries to the tent, Rusik, the immediate owner of the goods sold by Claudia, jumped like a dumbfounded one, and fiercely curled his brown eyes. - Why is the point surrounded ?! Who are they?

Cautious Caucasians were quite understandable. He knew perfectly well how the Slavic lads did not complain about his fellow tribesmen in the market. Locals used every opportunity to drive in and squeeze what is called a foreigner to the nail. Now, according to Rusika, the next disassembly of flights was planned. Two Lavrovsk guys quickly and professionally squeezed Caucasians from two sides, not admitting to Fyodor Pavlovich. The blocked mountaineer realized that his initial fears were hardly groundless.

- Let go! - even more he screamed with a clear threat in his voice. - Now there will be fifty fellow countrymen!

Laurel turned on the newcomer.

- Quiet, mojahed! - he said peacefully. - Quiet!

- I'm a Christian! - Rusik proudly declared, but the hot Gorskii norm still curbed a little.

"Especially," the authority nodded, striding towards the Caucasians. - Come on like a Christian.

"Do not worry, Rusik," hurried to intervene in the emerging Claudia scandal. - These are acquaintances. - And, having already addressed two ambals, she sternly added: - Leave me alone from the person.

- It is said - leave me alone, - in unison she duplicated the order of Laurus, and this time the pumped up guys implicitly parted, giving Caucasians freedom of action.

He quickly rushed to the counter and pounced with claims to his saleswoman.

"You have acquaintances, I have a commodity," cropped Rusik, splashing saliva. - What do they want?

Lavra jarred on the fact that the Caucasian did not communicate with him directly, but with his subordinate. The situation required immediate intervention.

"A woman is needed," answered Claudia Lavrikov with a grin.

- Nothing else? - In the soul of Rusika, male jealousy involuntarily stirred. He turned round. - Woman at work!

Lavrikov shook his head knowingly.

"Then order me to transfer all this household chemicals to the car," he said. - We will assume that your worker has fulfilled the plan for today. We assume? Or not?

At the same time, Fyodor Pavlovich defiantly scratched his chin with his right hand, exposing his personal signet, which was a symbol of real thieves' authority, on public display. To a man who knows a lot about this, one glance at this symbolic decoration would be enough. Eyes Caucasian widened. He can be seen everywhere, he knew how to understand such things. An embarrassed expression appeared on Rusik's face, and he wisely lowered his gaze.

"We will," he said as gently as possible. - I'm sorry if something's wrong.

Laurel smiled openly, thrust his hands into the pockets of his trousers, and looked around at the crowd, looking for Sancho, who had been left behind.

- Sancho! He cried impatiently.

- Yes.

He dutifully walked out from behind Yessentuki's massive back, continuing to experience terrible embarrassment. The thief in law raised his eyebrows in surprise. So he Moshkina never in his life has ever seen how much he knew. But the time for the momentary clarification of the causes of monastic modesty and sluggishness on the part of Alexander, Laurus now was not.

"Sancho, settle with the owner," the authority ordered. - Yes! And do not forget about cowards, - he reminded strictly. "Par twenty-five."

- Cowards are not mine, dear, - Caucasians politely gave voice. - Soslan pants.

"They were exiled, they became mine," Fyodor Pavlovich smiled, and already decisively, with full seriousness on his face, addressed Claudia: "We must go." From Essentuki you will bring ... Legend will you invent for a boy?

The woman slowly walked out from behind the counter, focusing on the same driven thoughts alone.

"I'll lie to something," she said gloomily. - I do not know only - is it necessary?

"It's too late to doubt, aunt," Lavrikov frowned severely. - Brewed porridge - eat! ..

Rozgin sighed heavily in response. In some ways, Fyodor Pavlovich was undoubtedly right.

Yessentuki impatiently drummed his fingers on the dashboard and fidgeted on the leather seat of the jeep in anticipation of too slow, as it seemed to him, passengers. Not for the first time lately, Lavr's bodyguard mentally analyzed his miserable existence that Sancho had tried to complain about this morning. More than anything else, Yessentuki was spread by total inaction. He often caught himself thinking what a nonsense he, a professional bodyguard, sometimes had to do at the whim of the owner. However, Lavr generously paid for his services, and the prestige of working for such an influential and authoritative person as Fyodor Pavlovich was considerable. But Essentuki's rough and hard-hearted soul asked for something more. Something more active, so to speak. Besides, he felt great

Essentuki looked at skinhead guy with a broken boxer's nose, silently sat behind the wheel of the jeep, and was about to turn to him with an urgent issue, as the view security chief snatched in the rearview mirror appeared on the verge of antediluvian Khrushchev Claudius and that red-haired shaggy kid with pigtails , which yesterday so competently and painlessly neutralized Ushan. For some reason, the appearance of the young man did not surprise Yessentuki at all. Even his two brains in his head was enough to understand that this guy is the main character in certain events related to the life of Laurus. Moreover, just after Claudia's visit, it was as if they had been replaced. This, too, could not be overlooked. Essentuki squinted suspiciously.

Meanwhile, the rear door of the car swung open, and Fedechka, first skipping ahead of Claudia and carefully supporting her by the elbow, also climbed into the salon, closed the door. The driver of the jeep kept complete calmness. It is not a person, but a natural biorobot. Yessentuki, on the contrary, turned around and doused the complaining passengers with permafrost in his eyes.

- Whats up? - Claudia's shameless gaze responded rudely.

"I recount whether everything is in place," he said coldly.

"I see," the woman growled.

Essentuki gave appropriate instructions to the driver. The jeep gently pulled away and, taxiing out of the yard, rushed at the top speed to the exit of the city. Outside the window flashed past buildings and numerous crossroads. The head of the Lavrovsky security service looked dejectedly at the lane of the road going under the wheels of the car.

- Hello, mate. - Fedechka, in a simple way, patted the security chef on the shoulder, when the silence in the cabin had become extremely painful.

He turned his head in displeasure.

"How did this one know about me ..." The guy tried to give a voice to careless intonations. - Employer?

"No comment," Essentuki said shortly, imitating a certain distinguished person to whom numerous cameras were aiming. Once he had the honor to contemplate a similar box, and the chip came to his liking.

"You ask me, not him," Claudia's male dialogue didn't take place, and Laurus's bodyguard stared again at the road ahead of him.

- I ask. - Fedechka turned to his aunt's head.

- I went to college. Well, to make sure ... - The woman gently ran her hand through her old-fashioned and inconspicuous hairstyle. - And he is there ... what is the name? - She frowned, trying to recall the instructions Lavrikova.

"The guardian of charitable institutions," Essentuki prompted, using the phrase that Laurel made him memorize. - Patron of the arts.

"That's right," said Claudia's support. - Trustee! I heard about your abilities and, apparently, became interested.

"I don't believe fairy tales," the young man said dryly in response to a not very plausible story.

- What do you believe? - Claudia was confused.

- Causal relationships.

"So trust them, your connections," the aunt did not argue. - Without ties, always - not one step. Or money, or communication. You will work with a month and a half, dress decently, as a student, and not as a punker ...

Essentuki, unable to bear it, turned around in the back seat with a wry grin on his lips, and his gaze unexpectedly met Claudia's prickly hostile eyes. The presence of unauthorized persons at the time of her spiritual revelations with her nephew made her extremely nervous.

- Everything is in place! - She said loudly, and the head of the security service hastily turned away, not wanting once more to bring on her aggressively negative emotions.

Claudia fell silent. Fedechka did not go into unnecessary details either. At this stage, it suited what he was told. And there it will be seen. We will understand. In the end, he himself had an idea of his potential programming skills. So, with the tasks assigned to him must cope.

Jeep, gently rustling tires on smooth asphalt, jumped out of the city and rushed in the right direction. Essentuki opened the side window to the full and put a cigarette in his mouth. I enjoyed smoking. "Damn them, with these thoughts! - he decided. "Work is work, and the rest doesn't concern me." Such an approach to the problem often helped him restore his inner emotional balance.

Laurel in splendid isolation measures the hall on the second floor of his mansion with long strides. Faithful Sancho this time did not deign to join his society, deliberately ignoring the arrival of a young offspring of authority and thereby showing his disapproving position. Every now and then Fedor Pavlovich threw impatient glances at the dials of his watches. Then on the wall near the window, then on the dangling on his left wrist. To say that the authority of the thieves was nervous was to say nothing about his inner state. The cup of patience has already been filled to the ground. It seemed to Lavra that every running away minute lasts at least an hour. He could not even imagine that such confusion would settle in the soul with the appearance in his life of an as yet unfamiliar kosmathenky youth. However, maybe Lavrikov himself screwed up and screwed himself up in such a state?

He did not have time to think out this deep thought. The horn of the automobile horn and the creaking of a metal gate, powered by a hidden mechanism, made it jump to a huge window with armored windows. Jeep majestically entered the territory and stopped in the center of the courtyard. The first of the salon Essentuki got out with a cigarette gripped in his teeth. After him appeared a thin boy with tight pigtails on his head, which at the moment Lavr knew only from a photograph. But undoubtedly, it was he, that same young man. Fedor Fedorovich Lavrikov, whatever it is in his metrics and other documents. The heart of prestige beat wildly in the chest, ready to jump out at any second.

Fedechka again gave her hand to her aunt, helping her get out of the car, and Laurel was already rushing down the stairs like a kid, jumping over three steps. Moshkin would see him in this instant! The thief in law frankly risked breaking off and rolling himself in the fall of the neck. This would be a completely undesirable turn of events.

On the first floor of the mansion are located several gloomy guards with impassive facial expressions. Regular biorobots. Two at the stairs, two at the far wall on a low couch and another one near the entrance with a cypress at the ready. Guys conscientiously carried the customary watch for them, practicing the money received from Fyodor Pavlovich.

- Absorb! - shortly ordered Laurus and personally went to the main entrance.

The Arkharovites did not force them to entreat themselves and repeat the order a second time. They disappeared, as if by magic, but Lavrikov knew perfectly well that the guards had disappeared somewhere nearby and continued to carry out invisible surveillance. Otherwise, Essentuki will tear off their heads, and in this the inglorious career of any careless "bull" will be completed.

The thief in law opened the door and confidently walked out onto the threshold, restoring his breath which had strayed from excitement and sprint up the stairs. Fingers trembling slightly, and the heart stubbornly did not want to go into his usual life rhythm. Towards Lavrikov, Claudia and Fedech were already rising.

Rozgin openly met the gaze of the thieves' authority, and for a minute, probably, the son and father carefully examined each other. Laurel put a lot of hope in this first meeting. It seemed to him that it would be enough seconds to read the whole of his former existence in the Fedechnik eyes. Understand his soul, learn his aspirations, desires, find similar sister priorities.

But that did not happen. So far, before Lavrikov stood an absolutely alien boy unfamiliar to him. And who knows, Laurus thought to himself, perhaps, it would not be enough for the remaining years of his life to get close to the young man and penetrate into the most secret corners of his soul and consciousness. But nevertheless, the thief in law has firmly decided for himself that he will strive for this moment, will definitely try to make up for lost years of communication with the sweat . Now he just liked the boy, caused sympathy, and that was enough for now. The thoughts of Fedor, who visited him for this minute, remained a mystery to Laurus.

Claudia tactfully cleared her throat, and this sound brought the owner of the mansion back to reality. Fyodor Pavlovich even flinched with his whole body. At that moment, the unwanted views of his own bodyguards were fixed on him, and the boss's confusion could be misinterpreted. They will also write about what is good, senile weakness and insanity. Undermining authority. Laurel, as far as possible, pulled himself together.

- I beg. - He stepped aside, passing guests to the house. - Come on in.

Fedechka stepped inside with the first, interested gaze at the luxurious interior of the mansion. Never before had he been in such truly royal chambers. The mere sensation of the dimensionlessness of the house made him respectfully softly chuckle. Everything else and even more so reminded him of a fabulous palace. The boy's mouth opened involuntarily, but he immediately overcame his state of shock and gave his face an impassive passive expression. He was originally going to show unknowingly the employer that he also knows his worth.

Fyodor Pavlovich quietly approached Claudia and quietly whispered to her almost in his ear:

- And you ... you ... maybe wait in the pantry? In the pantry for tea is all there. Tea leaves, boiling water ... - He was not himself, and the woman appreciated his condition.

She did not interfere with the desires of the owner and, accompanied by one of the children of Essentuki, moved in a given direction. Laurel breathed easier. And Fedechka, with a poorly concealed interest, was gazing at a full, chubby man descending a wide staircase and wearing a wide T-shirt in bright red. Fedor Pavlovich involuntarily smiled. He knew perfectly well that the curious by nature Sancho would not be able to sit still for a long time and, under some silly pretext, would definitely defile the boy who had arrived in order to evaluate it live. Lavrikov beckoned his colleague with a finger.

- This is my ... - Authority hesitated for a moment. - Like a butler. Or a valet ... Or a better manager, he finally found. - Alexander Mikhailovich nicknamed Uncle Sancho.

Moshkin could not help noticing the fact that Laurel, trying to hide his own excitement, overdid it with molasses in his voice. But here let him decide how to behave with his son. Alexander approached the young man and extended his hand in greeting.

- Very nice. - Fedech nagged indifferently squeezed the butler's plump palm.

"And this," Lavrikov already turned around at the security chief who had come into the house, "Yessentuki's head of the security department."

"It is terribly pleasant," said the young man with a bit of irony. - We have already met. What is your nickname?

"The nickname is Essentuki," Fyodor Pavlovich repeated again, although the guy didn't address him at all, but directly to the ambalu.

- And then call as normal? - Fedech did not let up, shaking hands with the next faithful minion of authority.

"Yessentuki," Lavrikov called his bodyguard nervously, irritated by his stubborn silence. - What is your name normally? The boy is interested, tell me.

It is fair to note that Fyodor Pavlovich himself did not know the name of the faithful assistant. All those years during which he knew the head of his security service, he remained for him just Essentuki. And nothing else. Do you need passport info?

"No matter how normal it is," he said smartly, and the authority mentally doubted that Yessentuki himself knew his real name.

- He doesn't care. - Laurel with a smile turned his head to his son. - Essentuki is also good. About eight years ago, a man set up the release of mineral water: tap water, soda, a little labels and fat at a thousand percent. That stuck "Essentuki." - Fascinated by the narrative associated with the life story of his assistant, as a result of which he received his nickname in his time, Lavrikov realized too late that he was talking too much. A young lad does not need to know all these criminal details. The thief in law stopped short. "However, this is me, by the way ... We still have Hamlet on economic issues," he concluded, jumping off from a slippery, dangerous topic.

- Hamlet - a nickname? - clarified the young man, losing interest in the individuals already presented to him and turning his back to them.

- Not. "Hamlet" in the passport is written down, - Fyodor Pavlovich almost officially informed the young man, and for some reason added out of place: - He runs around on business.

- "In the despair of mental impasse"? - quoted the young man.

At the moment, Fedech didn't care what to say. He was ready to carry any nonsense, if only he did not immediately have to move on to the main topic of conversation, for which he came here. The same process took place in the consciousness of Laurus. It is frank to admit that a well-known thief in law has not matured a detailed plan of negotiations with his own son. He pondered on this topic all morning, scrolling through various options, wondering about the possible counter questions of the guy, but nothing good came out of this whole undertaking. Just noticing the jeep drove into the yard with Fedechka and his aunt on board, Lavrikov came to the decision to improvise on the go. But he himself didn't guess at that second how difficult this event would be in practice. Before him stood no longer an abstract son, as it was a couple of hours ago, but the real one. From flesh and blood.

- How how? - confusedly asked authority, not catching any meaning in the last sentence of the young man.

"Shakespeare's Hamlet had despair," Rozgin explained. - Because of dad. Mental deadlock was.

Fyodor Pavlovich nervously cleared his throat and squinted at his companions who were silent and frozen without movement. That's always the case. When it is urgently needed, you will not wait for any support from them, but how to wag your nerves or talk over trifles is they always welcome. No problem. Parasites

- Not. - The thief in law shook his head with a smile, carefully choosing words. - Ours - no dead ends. Awl in the ass. He never sits in his office, the current documentation is running ... - Laurel slightly hugged the boy by the shoulders and, dragging him along with himself, moved to a broad staircase leading to the second floor. - Come on, I'll show you. You're in this office and settle down.

The two of them slowly walked to the upper hall, leaving Sancho and Yessentuki provided for each other. Lavrikov did not even turn in their direction, entirely absorbed in the presence of his own son with him. The security chief, staring at their receding backs, squinted involuntarily, dumbfounded by the conjecture that had just arisen in his brain. And how did he not have this idea before? After all, it was enough to juxtapose the disparate facts together, and the answer was self-evident. In addition, Essentuki saw the eyes of both of them when they stood nearby, saw their smiles, and the outlined cheekbones. Ambal vigorously turned to Moshkin, and already ready to break from his mouth the question involuntarily stopped somewhere on the tip of his tongue, stumbling upon the butler's gloomy expression on his face.

"I do not intend to answer any of your questions," he chopped off, warning possible encroachments.

"Well, uh ..." Essentuki said slowly.

- Without "well." - Sancho quickly walked towards the dining room, which the owner of this mansion called just the pantry.

And Fyodor Rozgin, accompanied by his own father, passed a couple of impressive guards on a wide staircase, already tenacious and penetrating gaze, which usually happened to Lavr himself, studied the furnishing of the second floor.

"In these files, the devil will break his leg," Fyodor Pavlovich continued to inform him in the course of his movement to the future office of the young programmer. - E-mail from Cyprus comes, from the Caymans, Antigua, from the Asia-Pacific region. But - no system, nothing is disassembled.

- Protected at least? - the young man busily inquired, mechanically inspecting an impressive collection of paintings owned by the great painters of different centuries. Among them was a lot of what Fedechka read about on Internet sites.

- What is it like? - Lavr didn't get into the way of his thoughts and even for a moment he stopped in the center of the spacious hall of the second floor.

- Have a shared access password? Or not? - said Rozgin.

"There is a password," said Fyodor Pavlovich proudly. After that, he stolenly looked around and, only making sure that there was no one on the floor of anyone else, he quietly whispered into the young man's ear: - "Piastres".

Fedech nodded indifferently.

- Cool password.

- And then! - proudly hemmed authority. - I personally made it up.

They approached, finally, to the cherished place, stopped near the snow-white doors with the host's monograms, and Laurus cheerfully patted the guy on the shoulder.

- Proceed in general. You will be the main programmer.

- Programmer - tactfully, but with some pressure in his voice Fedech corrected him.

"So be it," the thief in law agreed easily and with a smile. - a programmer. - He smoothed out his gray mustache. - A programmer sounds even better ...

Long ago, the blue eyes of Laurus did not radiate such a healthy luster and carefree ease. Authority was now in seventh heaven. For the first time in his life, he felt genuine joy because he had to take care of someone, care for someone. Perhaps this is the feeling of a family, which the thief in law was deprived of throughout his existence on this sinful land due to the rules established in certain sections of society. Now, for the first time in their life, these very rules seemed wild to Lavrikov, somehow primitive. It was time to break such wildness. And for starters inside yourself. Whatever the eternal whiner Sancho says.

The gaze of father and son again crossed, and Fyodor Pavlovich, embarrassed, was the first to hide his eyes. After that, he unlocked the door to the office with a key and pushed it away from him. Fedech in anticipation of acquaintance with the latest technology of modernity stepped over the threshold.

Chapter 8

Claudia slowly walked around the perimeter of the cozy and clean dining room of the Lavrovsky mansion and froze near the wide-open window. Her eyes appeared amazing picture. What could be more beautiful than Mother Nature? Behind a wide courtyard, fenced off from the rest of the space by a concrete fence, there was an emerald shade of a tree planting, immediately behind which a swallow river surrounded by a steep, almost sheer cliff opposite the mansion, turned blue with virgin purity. A woman dreamily rolled her eyes, imagining how good it would now be to plunge into the clear waters of this little river.

Rosgina has long not allowed herself anything like that. All life and all its existence was limited to two things: work in the bazaar and the house, where she still considered her direct responsibility to take care of an orphaned nephew. All attempts at unity with nature, which from time to time arose in a woman in the subconscious, ended in complete fiasco. When to unite with it, if the floors are not washed and the potatoes are not cleaned?

Claudia leaned on the window sill, and her hands stumbled upon some foreign object to which she did not immediately pay particular attention. Opening her eyes, she saw a compact cassette in front of her, neatly covered by someone's napkin, in order to protect sensitive equipment from direct sunlight. A woman took a napkin and automatically drowned a button on the panel with the word "play" she already knew. From the words of her nephew, she knew that this was the way replay was activated. The tape had already been inserted into the tape recorder, and the dining room was instantly filled with enchanting music and singing.

At the same time, the door to the dining room opened silently, and on the threshold Sancho appeared in a red T-shirt. Moshkin did not consider it necessary to dress up for the reception of guests, so expected by the owner, and looked more than homely. Now he regretted his own short-sightedness. Claudia had her back to him, which allowed Sancho, without much embarrassment and trepidation, to observe the appetizing forms of the female body. Alexander's eyes were dull and languid, his throat suddenly dry. What a woman! Fairy tale! He carefully closed the door behind him, but he was in no hurry to discover his own presence in the room. Holding his breath, silently watched the pyshnotely Russian beauty from the side. Even his sniffing at that second was not so loud. Cardiac experiences prevailed over chronic sinusitis.

Claudia, who herself probably did not consider herself not only to beauties, but also to pretty ladies, enjoying the caressing ear and natural beauty outside the windows, plunged into some kind of unearthly dimension, and for a moment it seemed to her that even the wings broke through the blades. She was ready to soar under the clouds at any second. Despite the fact that the woman did not understand a single word in Italian, her round, slightly wrinkled face displayed a whole range of emotional experiences for the characters of this dramatic opera piece. An unexpected tear rolled down Claudia's cheek, after which she fished a handkerchief out of the sleeve of her blouse and blew her nose noisily.

- Have you had a cold? - a voice sounded softly behind her back.

Daring, finally, to the heroic male deed, Sancho not only confidently stepped towards the woman, but even ventured to engage in an interview with her. However, at the moment he was quite seriously concerned about her well-being. Drafts are dangerous business.

Claudia started and turned sharply. From her gaze, Moshkin was unwittingly intimidated. The excitement was read in each of his restless gestures. Again, as at their first meeting, he tried to draw in his beer belly, but the attempt was not crowned with the desired success. Sancho sighed doom.

- What did you say? - Claudia turned down the sound of the cassette, but did not turn it off at all.

- Have caught a cold, I ask? - Alexander feverishly swallowed and involuntarily focused his eyes on the magnificent and appetizing, in his opinion, bust of the interlocutor.

- A bit sulk, - confusedly confessed a woman, hiding a handkerchief in the original secluded place. She looked at this chubby, red man with restraint with reciprocal interest. - In the car, the window was open, so ...

- Yes. - Sancho nodded understandingly. - In jeeps always shows through. I do not like them therefore. Jeeps

"I don't like either," Claudia automatically replied.

There was an awkward deep pause in their incipient dialogue. Moshkin looked around in an attempt to find at least some object that could serve as a topic of conversation. It was at least silly to interrupt so successfully begun, as it seemed to him, acquaintance at this stage. If not to say - blasphemous. The radical decision, which turned out to be simple, like all brilliant things in this world, came unexpectedly, by itself. Moshkin even cheered up.

- I need tea! - blurted out like a cannon Sancho. That's what you need!

He very briskly jumped to the stove for his build and hoisted a kettle with a long spout onto one of the empty canary-colored burners. He kindled a fire like the one that was burning in his chest now. Then he turned again to face the interlocutor:

- I have with dry raspberries, apples are added there, a little pear.

"This is no longer tea," Claudia smiled, watching the man ridiculously and comically shuffle from one foot to the other.

- Why? - blinked Moshkin.

- Compote.

- Compote? - He broke into a smile, showing Claudia is not the worst quality of the teeth of an elderly man. - Exactly! Compote is real! .. Well, we laugh! - The words of the interlocutor really suited him so much that Moshkin, having failed to restrain the laughter bursting out of him, laughed loudly and heartily. - Compote! - He repeated in a fit of Homeric laughter, clutching at his belly, swaying in weight, which at that instant resembled jelly alarmed with a fork.

His fervent laughter inadvertently infected Claudia. At first timidly, and then in full voice she picked up Sancho's fun. They laughed, looking at each other. The tension that hung at the first stage of their unexpected meeting in the mansion's dining room disappeared without a trace, as if it hadn't been at all a couple of minutes ago. Look who is in the room at this moment, for sure would have decided that Alexander and Claudia have long been familiar with each other and between them there were always warm, relaxed relations. Sancho, having forgotten the shyness he had recently been in the presence of this stately lady, famously jumped to the table and habitually engaged in his serving.

"So we'll drink compote now," he said, with tears running in his eyes. - With poppy dryers. Are you drying?

"Oh, yes, I eat everything," Claudia said carelessly, waving a hand.

- Everything? - Pupils Moshkina happily rounded. - A rare woman! And no diets?

"Is that when the money runs out," the woman honestly admitted, which caused a new burst of laughter from Sancho. - Then diet.

The fun has reached its climax. Rozgina again drew her wide square handkerchief into the light of day, wiped her moist eyes, then blew her nose again loudly, not at all embarrassed by the presence of others. Alexander was his board for her. Cheerful, convivial and without any miscarriages there. Cool man, one word. And what can we say about the thoughts and feelings of Moshkin himself, who was one hundred percent sure that he fell into disgust at this high-calorie person. The kettle boiled, and Claudia seated herself behind a quickly laid butler table. Alexander did not forget while gallantly move her chair. Now the Lavrov ally felt like ten years younger. This is at least.

"Well, you're a humorist," Sancho said sincerely, returning to the stove and performing some simple manipulations there.

"It's not me," Klava answered in tune. - This is a humorous life.

He returned to the table with two large cups of fragrantly steaming beverage. Now Sancho himself did not know how best to characterize it. He put one portion in front of the woman, the other opposite, where he intended to settle himself. He landed heavily on a chair.

- Exactly! He nodded, continuing the interrupted conversation. - Break the life! .. Not life - hilarious! Help yourself. - Moshkin, with the kindness of a true owner, swept his hand over sweets on the table.

Every time when his eyes met with Klavdin, Alexander's eyes lit up with ardent passion, but he still, rather out of habit, almost immediately lowered them down, and Rozgin, of course, could not but notice such behavior. She caught herself thinking that she was pleased to get around this slightly clumsy and so funny felon.

- Here. See? - Laurel, as tied, followed Fedechka through the light office, which was packed with all sorts of office equipment for every taste. It seems to be quietly, he watched the reaction of the guy and noticed for himself his interests. - We bought the freshest toys, half of them are not even plugged in. Bedlam - almost strictly concluded the criminal authority.

The young man was fascinated, like a kind of programmed zombie, carefully and with genuine admiration examined the room offered to him as a workplace, and his eyes glittered with excitement. Any boy of his age and with the same interests, naturally, could only dream of such a gift of fate. Here, in this room, everything was not only for the quality and professional work of a good programmer, but also for ordinary children's entertainment in the field of computer games. Lavrikov specifically took care of this aspect as soon as Claudia, accompanied by Yessentuki, went to fetch his son. The costs were considerable, but the thief in law did not regret it. In this particular case, the end justified the means.

The new father noted with pleasure the delight of his newly made offspring, and sincerely rejoiced at the impression so effectively made on the guy. Lavrikov sincerely believed that the first step towards rapprochement had already been taken, and as for the rest, this is already a matter of technology. His father's feelings at the right time will tell him how to be true.

- True cool! - Fedor blurted out in the same breath, having admired with all the latest computers that had appeared to his gaze and finally turned into the standing behind Laurus. - What will we program?

"Anything," he said as casually as possible. - By country. By industry. By casino and pubs. The main thing is not to slyamzili information, - weighty added authority in the end.

Lavrikova was really worried about this side of his financial affairs, and, attracting Fedor to the business, he, as they say, combined business with pleasure. He killed two birds with one stone. Feelings are feelings, but in no case should one forget about the problems existing in our imperfect world.

"We must say:" they did not crack it, "" they didn't open it, "Fedech once again corrected the employer, demonstrating his professional slang.

- A break, open? - Fedor Pavlovich asked worriedly.

- Elementary.

- What meanness! - Laurel shook his head. "You sit behind twenty locks, the security company is growing fat." And someone is rummaging in your wallet by wire, "he went into lengthy reflections. - Neither ethics to you, nor laws at computers ...

- What do you want? - grinned wunderkind. - High technology in the yard. Open world

At the same time, Fedechki, in a businesslike manner, pulled the nearest chair towards him and, without asking Lavrikov for special permission to this effect, assumed a sitting position. Fingers lovingly ran over the snow-white keyboard. The guy was in seventh heaven.

- I do not like it. - The authority, on the contrary, continued to be perplexed to stamp around next to the programmer being hired, now looking down on him.

- Anywhere you will not get to. - Rozgin shrugged, then leaned down a bit and looked at the processor tucked under the table. He was very pleased with what he saw. The latest modification. There is something to come to delight. - We'll have to endure.

For some time, there was an empty pause in the conversation. Lavrikov awkwardly approached the table, leaned against him and absently ran his hand over the nearest keyboard. Fingers clicked on the keys. Mechanically, mindlessly.

"Believe the word," quietly spoke authority, studying the pattern on his own tie with his gaze. - High technology will lead mankind to the lowest abyss without space, you'll see!

"They won't," Fedechka disagreed. - close.

In the eyes of the eminent kingpin flashed professional interest. The collar of the shadow business opened its true face to the son.

- Do you have time until September?

- It is possible earlier, - he assured him.

Fedor openly smiled and once again glanced at the computer equipment. He was already frankly impatient to start some kind of work close to him in spirit. The energy of youth was seething in the body and demanded a way out, expressed in the form of some kind of action. Laurel instantly felt his fighting spirit, and this slightly frightened him. And what if the kid with his innate talents is able to complete the entire planned scope of work in a matter of days? What, then, will Fyodor Pavlovich continue to keep near him? No additional reasons have come to his head.

"You shouldn't hurry," he said weightily, hiding the excitement in his voice.

Fedechka shook his shaggy head, and some despondency reflected in his gaze. Thoughts from the euphoria returned to the daily problems of everyday life.

"It's only uncomfortable with transport," he frankly admitted to the future boss. - Long away. To the house and back - half a day.

- At your disposal - apartments. - The authority has broken off from the table, leaving the keyboard alone. "In the corridor through the door ..." He stumbled in the half-word and then blurted out like a cannon, as if he had rushed headlong into a bottomless pool: "You will live here."

Laurel took an embarrassed glance, and Fedechka, misinterpreting his good fatherly intentions, cautiously and with some degree of apprehension rose to his full height. Pupils narrowed suspiciously. He estimated the persona of the trustee of charitable institutions.

"Uncle ..." he appealed to the authority as gently as possible, trying not to injure an elderly person, not to beat unnecessarily on an already sore spot.

- Yes?

- It would be necessary to clarify immediately. - Fedor tactfully cleared his throat, after which his voice became much more confident. - So that then there was no misunderstanding ...

- Does something bother you? - Laurus responded instantly. - You say do not be shy! Between us should not be omissions.

- I'm confused. - Rozgin nodded.

- What?

Fedechka hesitated only a couple of seconds, and then resolutely asked the gray-haired old man:

- You, forgive, you will not be from a sexual minority?

His seemingly simple and frank question threw the authority into a state of shock. No one has ever dared to even suspect something like that in his thoughts. Lavrikov energetically turned around at the door, fearing that someone would hear the words of his son. His eyes flashed in anger, his pursed lips barely noticeably shaking with indignation.

- I?! - he cried out quite roughly, but, right there, taking control of himself, he died down the rebellion was ardor. - I am a Bolshevik! - Fedor Pavlovich tried to laugh it off, but it turned out that he was not very natural. - And never say that! I'm offended, I'm hot, I'm killed ... "" Laurel stopped short again. - dismiss! Understood me?

- Okay. - A surge of emotions testified to the complete sincerity of the words, and this noticeably calmed Fyodor. The suspicions that arose in the minds disappeared, and the heart, as a result, felt better. "But honestly ... why do I need you?" With an advance, with apartments? .. Good programmers are a dime a dozen.

For Lavrikov, it was the very time of improvisation on the move, for which he had been preparing himself since the morning, but he did not achieve any concrete results. Fatherly feelings also did not suggest anything. They kept mum for some reason. A guy, looking into his eyes, no doubt, was waiting for an answer to the question.

- Why do you need me? - asked Fyodor Pavlovich, while winning a couple of extra seconds to think. - You see, Fedya ... I would like to ... so that the person was there.

- Person?

- Yeah! - The idea has ripened in the head of a lawyer in an instant and has pleased him. - Well, independent is so fresh. That for the salary did not keep. Adults hold on, afraid to speak the truth.

- Why? - I did not understand the young man.

"Why, why ..." muttered Laurus. - They consider me too great authority. And it turns out that there is no one ... sincere around. And it is hard when there is no one around ... And you will. - The thief in law radiantly smiled. - Going?

His explanation more than satisfied the young man.

"Coming," he nodded cheerfully.

After that, the men sealed the deal with a firm handshake. Both were pleased with each other. Until.

"V is being killed," Claudia said melancholy, breaking the silence that had settled in the dining room and nodding shortly in the direction of the included tape recorder.

She and Sancho, having turned on the cassette at full volume, enjoyed classical music, sitting at the table against each other. Steaming cups of freshly made tea created an additional magical aura in their close circle of music lovers. Moshkin was simply inspired by the idyll surrounding him. Favorite music, your favorite drink and, most importantly, the woman you love in close proximity, sprawled on a fragile stool in all its glory. Sancho literally drowned in her green, enticing, like a pool, eyes. His strongest and almost uncontrollable desire was to throw himself at the feet of this lady and, in a rush of surging feelings, would crave her body with passion in his wide and powerful embraces.

However, common sense suggested to Alexander that it was worthwhile to postpone the open manifestations of spiritual affections. His deed could be misinterpreted, but she did not want to push the woman away from herself. In the depths of his soul, Moshkin was now building entirely different, far-reaching plans, on which he had never once thought about in his life. Partly, perhaps, because his worthy woman did not meet on the way. But now everything in Alexandra has changed. He had already painted colorful pictures of family comfort, and even saw in the dreams of children who could well have come to him and Claudia. However, he realized that he was running too far in his thoughts now, and he himself was ashamed of this impulse that was not yet justified in all respects.

The man withdrew his glowing gaze and occupied himself with the fact that he had taken a small sip of tea burning his throat. She and Claudia had already charged on the second glass of the drink. Wow, and here their tastes came together!

"It's a pity, even if not a word is clear," lamented Claudia's opera singing.

"A translator is not required for emotional experiences," Moshkin delivered his own verdict, knowingly hinting a woman to something.

"It is so," she vaguely agreed, not intending to engage in unreasonable disputes with the cute and charming, in her view, opponent.

Claudia was impressed by the kind care with which Sancho treated her by no means noble blood to the person. Moshkina could not be categorized as glamorous men, but he was so funny and childishly embarrassed whenever his gaze intersected in the space above the table with Klavdin that he could not help but arouse in her female emotion. Such modest types in the manifestation of their feelings are now not often found. And even more so in such circles in which Alexander grew up and spent his entire existence.

"Tosca," Sancho said, rolling his eyes toward the ceiling.

Claudia was confused and, putting aside a glass of fragrant tea, made an attempt to rise from the table.

"So let's turn it off if sad," she suggested uneasily. - I turned on without asking.

"No," Moshkin shook his head with a smile, and he did not notice how his plump palm in an attempt to hold the woman covered her hand. - This heroine's name is Tosca.

"Ahhh ..." the woman responded, confused, ashamed of her own blunder.

Sancho cautiously and with grace from where the tenderness which had taken from him shook Klavdin's brush, which caused a pleasant shiver to run through her body. Strange feeling visited Rozhinu. Unaccountable, unfamiliar before, but fully beautiful.

- She will die soon. - Alexander out of habit sniffed. - Completely die.

"Ahhhhhhhh," the woman screamed. - I do not like sad ends. They really are for the eyes. And then there's the opera ...

- In the opera, all ends are sad.

- Well, do not tell me! - Claudia was in no hurry to pull his hand out of the captivating embrace of the man sitting opposite. Absorbed by the music and communication with each other, this couple of middle-aged dove already completely forgot about the cooling portions of tea. - I, when I worked at the Research Institute of Tire Industry, have not yet died the institute, so we have been given tickets to the Bolshoi Theater. The Barber of Seville was called a work. Very funny was the opera. But the buffet there - what a nightmare, - for some reason, lowering the voice and whispers, opened up with the interlocutor lady. - Even for that money.

- Did you work in a scientific research institute?

Moshkin asked a question not for idle curiosity. He wanted to get to know Claudius as closely as possible. He was really curious to comprehend the life criteria by which this woman existed before and, possibly, exists now. It seemed to him that everything, whatever she did, looked in her performance just great. Sancho literally engaged in the idealization of the object of his secret sighs. In addition, now he was ready to continuously change one topic for another, so long as Klavdin's hand remained under the weight of his huge brush for a longer time.

- Yeah. - Claudia also gladly led a relaxed conversation in a cozy atmosphere. - Technologist on the diffusion of rubber resins.

- Oh! - respectfully handed Alexander.

There was so much admiration in his voice that the woman was frankly confused. The hand slipped nimbly out from under the spade-shaped palm, after which Claudia spontaneously rose from the chair. Like any other woman, she could not help but feel the powerful amorous fluids emanating from Alexander. The balding lover was unscrupulously trying to seduce her and incline her to the fall. Sensual feminine nature thrown into a fever, and she, already against her own will, was covered with a thick crimson paint.

- Thanks for the tea. - She frantically tried to get rid of the obsession that rolled on her. She even covered her burning cheeks.

"For compote," the old joke tried to smooth over the rather incoherently embarrassed confusion in Sancho's communication, also assuming an upright position, but Claudia was no longer amused.

She waved her hands to herself and frankly confessed:

- Something threw into the heat ... - The smile on her lips came out confused. - I'll go to the kindergarten, can I?

- Anywhere! - Moshkin pushed back the stool and approached the woman. - you to spend?

There was so much courtesy and a gallant attitude in his voice that if it were not for the tattoos on his fingers and six classes of education marked on the round face, Alexander could easily have passed for a hereditary nobleman from a noble royal family. Now he no longer felt like a timid youth next to Klava. Not otherwise, he noticed a reciprocal sympathy from her side, which he had never dared to hope for before and in her own dreams.

- Do not, do not get lost. - The woman sighed deeply, gaining mental balance, lost a few seconds ago due to unaccustomed treatment for her by the representative of the stronger sex. In order to avoid new encroachments on her female honor, Claudia hastily changed the topic of conversation: - What is the owner of? Nothing?

- Normal host. Gold, - the Lavrovsky comrade-in-arms proclaimed with dignity, but he could not resist and added: - Not without quirks, of course ...

"We are all not without quirks," Claudia retorted with a smile. The local contingent, including Laurus himself, no longer seemed so specific to her, as at the time of the first visit to the mansion. True, they say: with whom you will be led ...

"Absolutely accurate," Moshkin said.

He awkwardly trampled alongside a woman and mentally wondered which side to take another courting attempt. She, unwittingly, threw up such an opportunity to him. With a short look at the served table, Claudia energetically moved in the direction of the potential motive to action.

- Now the dishes only rinse.

- In no case! - Moshkin vividly barred her way and, as it were, casually touched the hand to the place where the idea of a woman's waist should have been. - What are you? Dishes - my diocese!

- Yes? - Her eyes widened in surprise. The positive impression made by the minute grew brighter. - A rare man ...

Sancho was embarrassed, but he liked the praise. Before no one has ever appreciated his exploits, performed daily in the performance of domestic duties, and then suddenly such a review. And from whom? From the one in front of which Alexander sought to show his best side. The image of family coziness and mischievous children dragging Claudia over the hem of her skirt has ripened in her head. Moshkin rolled his eyes to the ceiling. Dreams!

Laurel briskly crossed the wide courtyard of his mansion and plunged into his own greenhouse ownership, as he sometimes jokingly called the garden, located behind the end of the building. He had never felt so happy and complete in all respects a man. She breathed freely, with full breasts, and wanted to squeeze the whole vast world to the joyfully beating heart. The authority stopped and, throwing back his head up, laughed carelessly.

- Everything is good? - suddenly sounded a voice to the right of Lavrikov.

He quickly turned around and only now noticed Claudius in some kind of meter from his person. The woman diligently, sticking the tip of a sharp tongue out of her zeal, broke off branches from some overgrown shrub. Having started this process of ennobling nature purely mechanically, she got carried away with her head.

- Everything is alright. - Fedor Pavlovich approached the lady and stood nearby.

- Gardener would have started! - the woman grumbledly advised, without interrupting her manipulations with the bush. Now she talked to Lavr almost in her own way. Almost on the rights of a close relative ah. - The plant should go up, and you have it spread out like a dough from a pot. Color will not be.

Laurel smiled and put a hand on her broad shoulder in a friendly way.

"Stay, take care," he suggested cordially.

- What more! - Claudia vigorously threw his hand and straightened her hair disheveled by the breeze on her head. "I've come to you, Lavrikov, not for myself, rushed. To help the little boy, while he has light in his eyes." But it's not a long time to repay. And we walk like with belmas ...

Fyodor Pavlovich stared intently, but with a smile playing on his lips, looked at his somewhat relative relative. Among his close associates, with whom he had to come into direct contact from time to time, there had long been no such open and not burdened people with conventions. Not counting, of course, Sancho, but Lavr was already so used to him that Moshkin had long been considered his second "me" a long time ago. The voice of conscience, so to speak. And Klava ... She was a man from another world.

- You ask me to save the light? - asked authority after a short pause.

- You. - Claudia handed him broken branches, and Lavrikov mechanically accepted them. - It so happened that there is no one else.

- Gangster that is asking? - He clarified with a malicious smirk, clearly telling a woman.

For a second, Lavr probably turned the branches in his hands and threw them under the nearest tree. There is someone to remove unnecessary garbage on the territory. Now he was much more interested in the question of what to answer Fedechkina's aunt to the thrown into open challenge. Claudia, with honor, withstood the sarcastic gaze of authority and only squinted slyly in response.

"Not a gangster," she said with constellation. - Father.

Pleasant warmth poured over the thin body of the kingpin. He was very flattered by a short, but, on the other hand, such a capacious word in content. Father! No praises could bring to the ear such a true delight as this short word. Lavrikov failed to conceal the sugary smile that lit his face. It seemed that at this moment even the sun's rays, penetrating through the green crowns of the trees, reflected from his teeth and for a moment blinded the interlocutor.

"Okay, don't worry." - Laurel pulled off his neck dark blue tie and blithely shoved it into the side pocket of his pants. He unzipped the top two buttons on his shirt. - I will teach him how to walk in this life ... Fedor will stay here. For the time being.

In the depths of her heart, Claudia guessed about such a possible turn in her nephew's life when she collected him today before her visit to her parent's house, but her heart still slanted unpleasantly in a loving chest.

- By whom? She asked with a certain degree of fear and caution.

"Son," Lavr answered laconically. - Drive, aunt. Gather his things, come.

A heavy sigh escaped from the chest of Claudia Rozgina. The habitual way of life for her changed dramatically, but with her mind she understood that she should not think about herself now. The future of the nephew was paramount.

"Bag in the car," she admitted reluctantly. Maybe she wanted to change something now, but it was too late. And, being a non-stupid woman by nature, Claudia could not help but understand where the guy would be better. With an aunt who lives exclusively from paycheck to paycheck and counts every penny spent, or with her own father, even if unknown until this point, but capable of changing Fedechki's life for the better. Give him a start in life, so to speak. - I could have done it. Now it's your turn.

"Mine," said Lavr proudly and was already turning around, intending to return to the house, but Klava promptly grabbed his hand just above the elbow.

"And more ..." she added in dismay. - Fedech sweet loves. Candies. But not with chocolate filling and not with white, but as if with jam. "Southern night" are called. "There was never enough for them," Rozgin admitted bitterly. - Previously, a ruble ten cost, and now - do not approach.

She dejectedly laid her head on her chest, as if submissively acknowledging her own financial inconsistency.

- "South night"? - Said Laurus, fixing the name of the sweetness in his memory.

"South ..." She nodded.

- Good. - The face of authority became serious, and he quite unexpectedly for himself intercepted a woman's hand, still resting on his hand, and with a sense of shaking her plump fingers. - Thank you, Claudia ...

She stared at the criminal boss in amazement, and he, instantly ashamed of his own spiritual weakness, famously turned around and walked away, this time without stopping or looking around. Claudia silently studied the retreating back of Laurus, which flashed among the deciduous trees. Treacherous tears came to my eyes.

Chapter 9

At this moment, an older and respectable Lavr in all respects looked like a pimply first-year student looking at naked girls in the keyhole of the door of a women's dressing room next to a university gymnasium. Especially often such phenomena occur in the spring, when hormones stuck in winter frosts begin to wander randomly throughout the body, focusing excessive attention on the brain and genital organs. Sometimes, in the first days of March on the eve of the women's holiday, a whole line of teenagers interested in anatomy gathered around such keyholes, and God forbid, someone will try to squeeze forward without observing the live queue.

But now Fyodor Pavlovich was not at all interested in women, with all their appetizing and colorful forms combined. Through the gap in the door ajar a couple of centimeters, the eminent thief in law, with emotion and other emotions overwhelming his soul, watched his own son.

Fedech, not knowing at all what is the involuntary object of someone's close attention, selflessly conjured near the dimly flickering screen of the monitor, periodically typing something on the keyboard with quick and familiar movements or clicking the mouse located under the right hand. The guy's eyes were burning with excitement, his mouth was wide open, and his legs, long since getting rid of unnecessary shoes, turned up under the skinny bottom of a youthful body and selflessly kept all the rest of the weight on him.

Lavrikov noted that his young programmer had already managed to connect all the personal belongings brought in the morning to the main computer, but he couldn't see what kind of process Fedech was busy with at that moment. The monitor was half-turn to the exit, and the sun's rays reflected from its smooth and flat surface created glare.

Fedor leaned forward, obviously interested in the information that appeared on the screen, and even lowered one foot to the floor. Fingers randomly ran over the keyboard with the agility and professionalism of this computer genius. Laurel smacked his tongue in admiration. He himself never had such a talent, yes, to be honest, he didn't really strive to master these wonders of modern technology. The young man's mother, as Fyodor Pavlovich managed to recall from the tip of Claudia, was a prominent representative of hosiery. To whom, then, did the boy become so clever?

Lavrikov scratched his chin with his fingers, which had already managed to cover himself with a light bristle, and grinned, watching Fedech happily burst out laughing, and leaned back on the leather spinning chair. Wow, he saw something funny there. Maybe a file with jokes? Laurus did not find any other objective motivation for the cheerfulness that surged upon the guy.

The authority, who had already managed to carry out Claudia and deal with the Fadechkin things she had left, changed into her own bedroom and was now dressed in a silk white robe and permanent slippers on her feet. Having aimlessly leaning from corner to corner of the working room and having failed to find a worthy application for himself, the thief in law directed his feet here to his son's apartments. Laurel mentally sought out the reasons why he could invade Fedor's workflow and impose himself on his interlocutors, but nothing good came to his head. It would be much easier if he knew the basics of programming at least at the level of an amateur. One or two questions of interest to him, and the conversation would have started. But in the area in which his son was working now, Laurel did not understand a damn thing, and did not want to fall into a stupid and embarrassing situation. You can shake credibility. Not your own criminal, of course, but much more important and valuable. Parental. Fyodor Pavlovich pulled away from the door ajar, but for a second thought the authority was enough to put his eye on the gap again. Even if it is passive contemplation, it is still better than stupid inaction and scattered thoughts in proud loneliness.

Behind Lavrikov, someone tactfully and quietly coughed. Fyodor Pavlovich swiftly turned and fastened on his face the most vicious expression possible. But it was only Sancho, whose presence could not be shy. He already knew what was going on in the soul of a lawyer and what feelings move him in the first place. Laurel smiled cautiously, trying not to make a single superfluous sound, shut the door to the programmer's office.

"What? .." His eyes turned to his comrade in the bridge of the nose.

"Laurel, tomorrow people ..." began the standard report of Sancho's current activities, but Alexander immediately interrupted his authority, lowering his voice to a whisper:

"I know people tomorrow ..." He tiptoed closer to Moshkin, took him by the elbow, like a young lady on a walk, and took him aside, away from the cherished door. - Do we have "Southern night"?

- What is it? - Moshkin grumbled discontentedly, but I really wanted to know what Lavrikov was talking about.

"Candy," explained the one who instantly killed the interest of the interlocutor in the emerging conversation. - With jam in the middle.

"With jam, I only know the pads," Sancho responded sluggishly, looking away from the window, where three arkharians from Essentuki's office were steadily walking from side to side. - Yellow, sprinkled with sugar. Removed, probably from production.

- Others at all! - Lavrikov said, recalling Klavdina explanations. "Night has chocolate outside.

- There is no such. - Sancho shook his big round head, and then with a feeling added, as if he spat out: - There are none.

But this state of affairs did not suit authority. He was not going to surrender without a fight.

"Throw out somebody," Fyodor Pavlovich ordered. - Let them buy it. In the house - a teenager whose body needs sweet. Catch a topic?

- How many? The face ally asked facelessly.

- How many ... - Laurel was in no hurry to answer, wondering in his mind the actual volume of sweets used by the youthful organism. The calculations have not been successful. "Ten kilograms," he said at last, and immediately corrected himself: "Or twenty."

Sancho barely restrained laughter. With these hereditary and hereditary affairs at the authority exactly balls for videos stopped. He does not know what to do. Only bydate the delight of a child of great age.

- Harmful so much. - Moshkin mastered emotions and only pointedly ran his thumb over his own throat, as if demonstrating Laurus, how harmful and excessive consumption of candy.

- Harmful? - crooked grinned thief in law. - Well, Moha! .. If you were fed with harmful candies, would you have sat down as a youngster for stealing buns? No jam!

Reminders of past years are always unpleasantly distorted Alexander. And as for the "bright" childhood, then there is even more so - a continuous black stripe. The enemy does not wish. However, in the circles where Moshkin rotated throughout his life, all of the past had one other more colorful.

- I would not have sat down! - He reasonably acknowledged the correctness of the laurel words.

- Oh! - The index finger of authority pointedly stuck in the direction of the ceiling. - Why are you pushing me into the arms of the zone?

On his ridiculous and inadequate question, Moshkin sedately tapped his skull with the bent knuckles of his right hand.

- Laurel, you, except for genetics, head should be examined! - he shamelessly rude to the boss. - I do not push anyone! Let him eat! At least thirty kilos! No pity! - And then, unconsciously entering into a rage, Alexander in one breath blurted out the pain: - Aunt would take him to work. As a housekeeper, for example, to save! Why did not take?

- I suggested. - Lavrikov confused shrug. - Does not go.

- Bad, so suggested! - viciously hissed Sancho and, turning a hundred and eighty degrees, rushed to the stairs leading to the first floor.

- Wait, wait, wait! - the thief in law called him, but the colleague did not even turn around. - And you, Sancho? .. Yes? - loudly spoke Laurus, imitating Caesar's legendary phrase before his death, only with a noticeable bit of irony in his voice.

- Yah you! - Moshkin waved his hand and quickly walked down the stairs, already annoyed at himself for not being able to hide the emotions that had fallen into his heart.

But the truth was cruel. Sancho did not imagine further existence without the beautiful eyes of Claudia Rozgina. He firmly set out to persuade Laurus to decide on the need for an aunt's presence next to the young man. Love, huge and merciless, sweeping away everything in its path, firmly seized the consciousness of Alexander. In the end, Moshkin also considered himself a man who had both his heart and soul. It is a pity that others do not understand this. Or do not want to understand.

- Do not disturb? - Fedech resolutely and confidently crossed the threshold of Lavrikov's personal account.

The guy already felt quite comfortable with the new conditions of existence, with the new work, habitat. Even in the heart of Rozgin, those few remnants of fear of an unfamiliar situation that had been a couple of hours ago immediately upon arrival vanished.

Fyodor Pavlovich did not hear the door open, did not hear how the young man approached him a couple of steps, and shuddered in surprise when he heard a mocking voice in the steady silence of his private apartments. Laurel quickly clicked the mouse button, replacing the image on the monitor screen, in front of which, according to the most conservative estimates, had already spent more than four hours. Difficult card solitaire, never brought to its logical conclusion, was quickly replaced by a working file depicting the plan of the urban area and the factory rectangle marked on it. The authority turned in a swivel chair, arms raised on the sleek leather armrests. His slightly confused gaze met his son's slyly narrowed eyes.

- I decided to keep up with you. - Laurel involuntarily caught himself thinking that he was somehow absurdly, childly justified in front of the boy standing next to him. "And a little practice ..." He nodded toward the desktop. - With a mouse.

Fedechka smiled openly. The owner of the mansion caused him genuine sympathy. The way he talked to him, trying to hide his inexplicable awkwardness, manner of holding. Modest and at the same time independent. Encourage him Fedech under any other circumstances, never in my life would have thought that before him a major criminal authority. Cruel and merciless, how he and others like him are drawn to the common man in the yellow press and television and radio channels.

"You are a good fellow," he praised his newly-minted chief, but he could not resist the temptation and sarcastically added: "Only the seven of seven got out of some fig, didn't he?"

- Do not say! - Lavrikov, with annoyance, slapped his knee to his side, showing with his whole appearance that he was taking the sarcastic game of a young man. - Tambourines always get out completely inopportunely ...

Fedech shook his head with obvious understanding. Say, who is not faced with a similar problem. However, he did not intend to discuss such aspects of computer processes for a long time. The young man had more serious questions for Lavr. So say, vital!

- How can you eat something? Got hungry.

Fyodor Pavlovich jumped in his chair, as if he had been stung in an indecent place. The hand picked up the portable handset from the table with lightning speed.

- Why did you keep silent before? - frowned authority, although at that moment he was more angry with himself. It was necessary to miss such an important moment. I almost starved my own son. Too me dad!

"I used to work," the young man replied with dignity. - Now I will think.

Laurel quickly dialed a short number on the keypad and put the phone to his ear. The wait was not too long.

- Uh, what's there with dinner? He asked sternly from an unseen interlocutor. - We get down in five minutes. - The thief in law cut off the connection and looked up at Rozgin. Blame parted his lips in a daring smile. - Five minutes be patient.

- Good. - Fedechka tilted his head to the side and carefully looked at the image on the screen of the laurel monitor. - I also had such a picture in the last working files.

Fyodor Pavlovich turned to the object of study. Before solitaire layout, he really tried to analyze the map of urban developments, which the economic adviser had turned his attention to yesterday. But it was not possible to come to a reasonable solution of this issue.

"A small factory," Laurus informed his son confidentially, tactlessly pointing his finger at the glowing rectangle. - I'm going to buy it.

"I looked at the accompanying data," answered the young man. - There were cross references.

- So how? - interested Laurel. - Found something worthy of attention?

- Nothing. - The young man winced. - The factory is dead. And hardly oklemaetsya.

- The point is not whether he is dead or alive. - The authority offendedly pursed his lips. - The point is ... territorial integrity.

Rozgin shrugged casually.

"From an economic point of view, this is nonsense," he delivered his professional verdict.

- And from the point of view of the order - not at all nonsense!

"What order?"

The perseverance of the self-assured boy slightly angered Lavrikova. Mentally he imagined what he was talking about, but how to explain this position with the help of words? In addition, his own son. It is necessary and not to talk too much in a rush of frank confessions.

"Well, of the way of life, traditions ..." Fyodor Pavlovich set off in some intricate explanations with a certain degree of irritation, but already a second later his gaze faced an inadequate, as it seemed to him, Fedechka expression on his face. - Why are you smiling?

"I'm serious," the young man disowned from the absurd accusation of himself.

- No, you are not serious! - Laurel springily pushed off his hands from the armrests of the chair and rose to his full height. - You're laughing! Internally! And I feel!

"I also feel," the young man retorted, as if nothing had happened. - That way, tradition - well, that's all funny. And so the nonsense comes out.

Lavrikov frowned. The right hand slipped into the side pocket. From a spacious dressing-gown, Laurus fished a pack of cigarettes into the light of God, twisted it intently between thin, long, like a pianist's fingers, but he thought about smoking in the presence of a descendant. Firstly, because smoking, as he knew, is harmful for passive tobacco smoke absorbers no less than for active ones, and secondly, a bad example of a parent. It is not good.

- You are young so far to judge such things! - He decisively besieged his son's attempt to ruin his own life priorities.

However, the tone of the Laurus and his artificial severity did not embarrass Fedech. He continued to stand in front of the criminal authority, with his shoulders wide and his chest rolled out with a wheel. The guy did not consider himself to be subordinates who are obliged to sag under his employer. Youthful audacity - the basis of internal independence.

"You hired me for the position of an independent man," Rozgin reminded Lavrikov of his own maxim. - To judge without regard to your opinion! So?

- So. - Laurel shook his head sadly, and his angry fuse evaporated, as if by magic. - Anywhere you will not get to. Caught on the word.

"I didn't catch it," the young man laughed. - themselves caught. - And he has already more seriously looked into the face of the criminal authority, rapidly changing the topic of conversation: - Are you a gangster, Laurel? .. Sorry, forgot your middle name.

- You can simply Laurel. - Fyodor Pavlovich frankly confused by such a direct and simple-minded question.

"Okay," Fedechka didn't mind. - Just so easy. - With these words, he looked expectantly at the interlocutor in front of him.

Laurel put his hands in his pockets and looked up towards the ceiling. Whatever one may say, but an unpleasant question for him has already been asked, and he will have to be answered.

- Who told you about the gangster? - Lavrikov stepped back and relocated to the window. Turning away now from his son, he leaned forward and rested his hands on the window sill. The back of authority slouched.

"No one," answered Rozgin honestly. - It is enough to look at the nature of the documents, how you live.

In the owner's office again hung a short pause. Communication with his son was not so easy for Lavra as he had originally expected, at a time when he was not yet familiar with Fedechka.

"No," Fyodor Pavlovich finally issued. "I'm not exactly a gangster, Fedechka." I am a lawyer. A respected person who monitors the fair distribution of financial flows in a certain ... uh ... district. If necessary - helps people in distress. Parses the quarrel at a lower level. Reconciles, condemns ...

- Thief in law in Russian, right? - interrupted his youth.

Laurel swung around.

- Even if so, what of it? - Each word was given to the authority with great difficulty. He seemed to squeeze them out of himself. - Everyone has their own destiny. And it is necessary to live it so that it would not be excruciatingly painful ... So that it would not burn the shame, - modestly, without excessive pompousness, he finished his tirade.

- No, nothing. - The guy liked this explanation. "I don't mind, I understand! .. Pull the criminal component out of the life of the country, the country will simply collapse," he put forward his own philosophical maxim, which simply startled Fyodor Pavlovich. - Collapse in five seconds in real time. This is the end of the world happen without crime.

- You think? - Lavrikova eyebrows shot up in surprise.

- Sure. - The guy shook his head in confirmation of his own words. - The electronic exchange will instantly react. Plus or minus a couple of minutes. I can more accurately estimate the collapse algorithm ... Yes, you do not complex, Laurus. You are no worse than any governor or prefect.

- to someone?

"An official of some or elected head of administration," Fedechko explained lucidly.

- Eh no! - The lean finger of Laurus vigorously cut the air at face level. In his voice even the intonations of an undeservedly offended person were skimming. - Found someone to compare! I'm better than the head! And the prefect is better! The prefect is usually lying and hypocritical! Tryndit about the needs of the grannies in the space entrusted to him! .. And I - never. - Authority proudly hit himself in the chest and stepped towards Rozhin. - I try not to deceive anyone.

- From the point of view of your profession - in vain, - the boy smiled.

- Why?

"In the wild, deception is as effective as force and speed," was the position of the young man.

Laurel stared at his offspring. And where he just picked up such clever words? Even at the institute has not yet studied. Or maybe these are genes laid by mother nature? Such an answer to the question posed Fyodor Pavlovich arranged most and pleasantly caressed the soul.

"I prefer the latter," he remarked gravely. - Strength and speed. For we are not in the wild.

- Is it? - Fedech slyly squinted.

The eminent thief in the law did not find what to say to the last short sentence of his son. For a minute, probably, or so, they silently looked into each other's eyes, and as a result, Laurus was the first to look away. Hiding the awkwardness, he checked his wristwatch and happily proclaimed:

- Five minutes have expired. - He amicably patted Fedya on the shoulder and headed for the exit. - Let's go for dinner.

Rozgin moved after him, but at the threshold Fyodor Pavlovich stepped aside a little and let the guy go ahead. They walked down the stairs.

- Why do not you change the hair, nerd? - threw in the back of a young man Lavrikov.

"Because it suits me," he replied with dignity, without turning his head.

- And I - no, - confessed the new parent.

Rozgin shrugged indifferently. They reached the bottom steps of the wide staircase, and only after that the young man turned around. I waited for the oldest satellite to come near.

"A matter of taste," he said, and then continued: "And it cannot be changed." It can only shave. Do you want to see me shaved?

Laurel grimaced like a toothache.

- You - for nothing! - he honestly admitted. - I had a shaven look - in!

The authority with a characteristic gesture struck the edge of an open palm over his throat. Fedech laughed heartily. He was perfectly clear what exactly Fyodor Pavlovich meant by these words, and he no longer intended to develop the topic of an unpleasant conversation for the host. Father and son walked cheerfully side by side in the direction of the dining room of the mansion, from the opened doors of which seductive aromas of cooked dishes were bursting into the common hall. Fedechka licked his lips. He really felt terribly hungry. Approximately the same sensations were in Laurus.

With great difficulty, Sancho managed to restore the balance of his overweight body, tilted over the expanse of water lit up at night in the pool. It seemed another second or another, and he could not stand on a smooth parapet. A loud splash of his huge carcass that fell into the water would surely be heard by all the inhabitants of the country mansion. But the unpleasant incident Moshkin managed to escape. He threw aside the fallen leaves collected by the fish net and took a breath. Reasonably believing that no one hears him, Alexander snuffled hard, like a wounded beast, and was already fluttering under his breath in a completely human way. Having poured out his own soul, Sancho again threw the tool of his labor into the water and began to fish a new portion of yellow and purple leaves.

Fedech stopped just two steps behind Moshkin and for several minutes watched with interest the efforts of the Lavrikov manager. Sancho could not notice the presence of an outsider for the simple reason that he himself was in the light of the illumination of the pool, and the guy was located in the darkness.

- Hi, squire! - finally gave voice to the young man. - What problems?

Sancho interrupted his acrobatic etudes for a moment and turned his head, gazing into the night darkness. It was absolutely impossible to discern the one who started the conversation with him, and he didn't recognize the voices of the new inhabitant of the mansion. Rozgin made his task easier, emerging from the darkness into the lighted space. Moshkin recognized him and immediately erased the brutal expression from his face. Pier to him with similar inquiries someone else, Lavr's ally would have found something to answer. And this little word would be very strong. Would send on mother - and all business. And the son of the owner is another matter. And he did not cause negative emotions in Sancho himself.

- I have? - just in case Moshkin specified and, having waited for the confirming nod, answered: - At me - any! But with the pool of problems you can not get it!

With vexation, he threw the net to the ground and landed wearily on the low bench on the right. His face fully reflected the universal grief of all mankind. Lonely sweat trickled slowly down the voluminous cheeks. Sancho wiped them off with a sleeve of his shirt, not really caring about what she would look like in the future.

- No, I do not know how it is on Beverly Hills! - He said in an empty space in front of him. - Maybe there palm trees do not fall off and the water is always poured with pure emerald. But here - leaves, cones, needles, sticks, dead beetles, birds serut! Soon crocodiles will start in this puddle, which gave a fuck to someone when the bath is normal at hand! Right evil is not enough! Pool!..

- Is there a filtration system? - interrupted his lamentations Fedechka, speaking forward.

- Look, Paskudin! - Sancho's sausage finger poked in the direction of the far side of the pool. - Thousands of bucks patched! An hour will work, cut down, repairmen will come to repair, another two hundred goodbye, and an hour later the old parsley!

Rozgin no longer listened to him. He silently threw off his T-shirt, then the Bermudas and, remaining in some tight-fitting underpants, famously rushed headlong into the pool. He entered the water gently, without any extra splashes, like a professional ski jumper. His youthful body disappeared under abundant foliage, gently swaying on the water surface. Sancho, having lost a potential interlocutor, was silent, but he was in no hurry to rise from the bench. He dejectedly looked down at the net thrown at his feet, slightly faking his toe.

- Sancho! Someone suddenly barked loudly over his ear. - Baby where?

Moshkin reluctantly turned and met his eyes with Fedor Pavlovich's concerned pupils. Laurel was already dressed in home pajamas and, apparently, was getting ready to go to bed when the thought came to his parents head to visit his son's apartment and wish him good night. But it was not possible to catch Fedech on the spot. That rushed into the garden in a frustrated sense.

- At the bottom! - Alexander shook his head in the direction of the pool.

- You sent? - frowned Lavrikov.

- I, Laurel! - Sancho rose to his feet and fiercely curled his eyes. Bushy eyebrows converged to the bridge of the nose, nostrils swollen, like a fire-breathing dragon. - I! All I! And I also attached a brick to his neck! And my name is Gerasim!

He wanted to add something else to the above, but at that moment Fedechka's shaggy head appeared with wet, pigtails stuck to the skull. The look of him was quite funny.

- A knife would be! - said the guy, quickly breathing.

Moshkin's right hand instantly disappeared into a spacious pocket of trousers and fished out a Finn. With a whistle pop out folding blade. Alexander's movements were precise and well-adjusted, without undue fuss. Lavr glanced at the comrade in disgust, but he did not pay the slightest attention to this fact.

- On, baby! - Sancho stepped forward and handed out to Fedech his own cold steel.

- Why do you need a knife? - Fedor Pavlovich asked worriedly. - He is sharp!

In response, the guy just grinned crookedly and, taking the knife from the hands of Moshkin, vigorously pushed off from the side of the pool.

"The gate is in the kovyrnu," he answered laconically, and the very next second the shaggy head disappeared under water again.

Laurel stepped forward and stopped near the very edge of the pool. On his face, replacing each other, reflected a diverse range of experiences. The faithful Sancho trampled next door, but he looked much calmer. Impartiality itself, in a word. It seemed to Fyodor Pavlovich that an entire eternity had passed before the viscous swill of leaves, branches, and the like was set in motion. The real whirlpool began to turn, and the pool's fullness level began to plummet. And an instant later, Fedechka, standing on the tiled bottom of an artificial reservoir, appeared in the field of view of the criminal authority. First, his head was marked, then his shoulders, torso, and so on.

Lavrikov relieved the air that had accumulated in his lungs. Sancho, who was watching him, shook his bald crown only with concern. As for Rozgin, all of his attention at the moment was focused on some part extracted from the drain. The Fedechka, entrusted to him by the Finn, diligently picked out rotten leaves from an oval object. Finally, the face of the young man, who has digged down to the real reason for the incapacity of the filtration system, has lit up with a happy childish smile. He raised a mocking gaze to the two men who stood at the edge of the pool and gave them a friendly wink at them with both of his left eyes.

- How many times were the repairmen? - asked Fedechka.

"About nine times," Sancho replied, lifting himself up on tiptoe and trying to determine what kind of boy was there. - Then I got tired of calling.

- And every time - two hundred? - Rozgin enviously smacked. "All my preparatory courses ... Nine times, gentlemen, you had it in an unnatural form!"

- Well, not bitches, eh? - Alexander could not resist such an objective assessment of the repair brigade.

"Don't swear at a child," Lavrikov immediately straightened him, painfully plunging his sharp elbow into the fleshy teles of his comrade. However, such physical attacks for Moshkin could be compared only with a mosquito bite.

"They specially set the booty upside down, head down," explained Fedech, continuing his manipulations with the cleaning of the waste filter.

Laurel proudly raised his chin and with a smile turned to Sancho.

- How clever guy! He said softly.

But Moshkin was now clearly not up to it. Former raider at the present moment was overcome by completely different emotions, far from being admired by anyone's abilities. He spat on his feet and squeezed his already fragile teeth with a creak.

- I'm going to pool this company without yours, Laurus, will blow up the order! - viciously hissed Alexander.

- The handy guy. - Lavrikov, like numerous characters of Anton Pavlovich Chekhov, continued to indulge in self-indulgence of his own thoughts. - The heady ... Fedor! He called Rozgin. - Water treatments immediately after meals are contraindicated!

However, the young man, having not paid due attention to his father's instructions, had already squatted beside the drain he had disassembled and began to screw the filter on to its rightful place in a new way. But by the side that was supposed to stand.

Sancho frowned at his double chin.

- And let's make a pit of it compost? - he made an alternative proposal, referring to the boss.

- From whom? - Laurus eyes widened in dismay.

- From the pool. Bath is worth it. And so - the grandchildren grow up, and you have fresh humus nemer.

Moshkin has already managed to suppress his wrathful attitude towards insidious repairmen. Now he was occupied with purely economic concerns characteristic of the ordinary Russian person.

- Whose grandchildren? - Fyodor Pavlovich didn't immediately understand his train of thought.

- Yours. - Alexander cautiously nodded in the direction of Fedechka, who was curled at the drain. - Look, Apollo what. In a year, you can easily become a grandfather. Here and compost. Plant strawberries for granddaughters - I do not want.

Lavrikov immediately rebuilt a stern expression on his face and stepped close to his faithful ally. Sometimes even tete-a-tete with the devotee Sancho, he recalled that he was a major criminal authority and that no one should talk to him in such a familiar way. This happened infrequently, but if, as they say, the brasserie came under its tail, run away and hide.

- You, Sancho, do not hurry to send me to the strawberry beds! - he sternly laid siege to the manager's loose talk. - You will become a fertilizer first!

- Yes, I'm kidding! - Moshkin smiled apologetically, feeling that the jokes today are clearly out of place. Not in the mood of a big boss.

"But I don't," Fyodor Pavlovich replied harshly.

Inspired by the conversation, neither Laurel nor Sancho noticed the fact that they were already watched by extraneous eyes for several minutes, and the man, lurking in the shadow of the spreading trees, was perplexedly catching every word uttered by the company gathered around the pool. At first, Hamlet wanted to go out and harmlessly discover his presence outside the immediate proximity of authority, but then he changed his mind. Silently backing back, he completely disappeared into the darkness, and then, turning around, swiftly strode toward the mansion.

Such moments in his life he loved more than anything else. What could be more beautiful than sitting in the evening on the porch with a cigarette in my mouth and silently enjoying the moonlight dimly illuminating the country space? It was this evening, before going to bed, that Essentuki liked to do. He dressed in homemade silk pajamas and with great pleasure went out into the fresh, heady air. As a rule, he spent here something for about an hour. He achieved unity with nature and thereby restored inner balance in himself. The picture that opened every evening to Essentuki's gaze pacified him. Clear starry sky, slender treetops stretching under the clouds ... And if you add to this a gentle breeze, the sounds of nature replacing each other, then life seemed completely different. In the most favorable for perception.

Essentuki flicked a lighter, and his tso momentarily lit up in the light of a dancing light. He lit a cigarette, with pleasure he inhaled the acrid tobacco smoke with his lungs and let it out through his nostrils. He closed his eyes for a moment. For the sake of such a feeling, he was ready to come to terms with his miserable existence as the head of the security service at Laurus. At that moment, he got rid of a nagging longing for another way of life, full of risk and adventure. Simple work was a boon not for people like this bruiser.

Somewhere on the right, branches cracked, and Yessentuki instantly alerted. With a tenacious wolf gaze pierced the space adjacent on this side. Another second or two, and the head of security could personally jump on a potential enemy emerging from the darkness.

- Do not kill, brother. - Hamlet with a smile went to the lighted area in front of the mansion. - It's just me. Sorry if scared.

A Caucasian in his own way is located next to the first bodyguard of Lavrikov, and he had to move slightly on a low wooden porch.

- Resting? - Hamlet asked good-naturedly.

Essentuki nodded silently and again inhaled himself with a fragrant cigarette. The presence of someone else in his personal idyll was not included in the plans of the security chief, and he sincerely hoped that Hamlet's society would not be too long and intrusive.

But the native of the sunny Caucasus has granted for a reason. After a brief pause, he turned his head toward the interlocutor found in the night.

- Essentuki, you answer me, right? - he carefully threw the bait, although in general he didn't count on great luck. So, for the sample, he asked: - What have we got for the lad?

Essentuki threw his head up and slowly released a thin stream of smoke. He frowned at Hamlet, and then turned his gaze to his bare feet. Going out into the evening in the evening, the security chief didn't wear any shoes on principle. He loved to feel the feet of the cool surface of the soil.

"Son," he answered shortly.

- Whose?

The Caucasian squinted slyly, but Yessentuki could not notice this in the dark. Yes, to be honest, he never turned his face to the interlocutor. He cleverly looked at the gnarled nails on his feet and mentally wondered when it would be possible for him to seize the right moment and do a long-standing pedicure. Not surprisingly, most of the shoes seemed Essentuki narrow. Feet grown up in front in a natural way.

"We are all sons of somebody," the bodyguard said slowly, with an arrangement. - It happens as a daughter. So said the owner, - he hastened to explain, so that Hamlet did not suspect him of a penchant for philosophical sayings, which for Essentuki could never be found. - Is it clear?

- I see. - The Caucasian lowered his voice to a whisper and looked around, checking if anyone was listening to their confidential conversation. - His son?

Essentuki leaned forward and put out a half-smoked cigarette on the lower edge of the porch. Butt did not throw away, but gently put it next to him. Everything was calculated on schedule. A smoke, then fresh air, then a smoke again. The head of the security service did not take two cigarettes into the street. Satisfied with savoring one.

"I didn't tell you anything," he said shortly, still not giving the interlocutor a glance. He stretched his legs forward, and he buried his elbows on the plank surface of the porch.

Hamlet broke into a sweet smile. His suspicions, originated there, near the pool, after accidentally overheard a piece of conversation between Laurel and Sancho, were justified by one hundred percent. That's what it means to show up at the right time in the right place. Consider half the battle done. Then everything depends on the brain. From the degree of intelligence. And by the way, Hamlet did not consider himself a stupid man. Even the opposite.

- I did not ask anything. - Caucasian springy rose to his feet and straightened the folds on their fashionable expensive pants. - Moreover, we are one team, yes?

Essentuki said nothing, but this did not offend Hamlet at all. He did not even notice such negligence. Without saying goodbye, Lavrovsky economic adviser walked away from the porch and headed for his car parked nearby. Thoughts were digging in his head, but he still could not concentrate on one, the most important one.

Hamlet climbed into the car, looked around again and started the engine. The foreign car grunted invitingly, welcoming the rightful owner. Hamlet squeezed the clutch.

The metal door of the gate creaked back to the side, releasing the belated visitor. Hamlet thoughtfully whistled an indecipherable tune to his ears. The full moon disappeared behind the clouds for a moment.

Chapter 10

The appearance of a shaggy boy in a sun-drenched hall on the second floor, where three or four people were sitting on a curved sofa and chairs attached to him in front of Fyodor Pavlovich's private apartments, caused genuine surprise to the criminal elements who came to visit. All these people knew each other perfectly by name and by name. They either had to take part in the same case more than once, or someone sat with someone. In short, a tight, closed world, where everyone is tied with a thin thread. The appearance of an outsider in their circle is in itself an amazing fact, and even a little alarming. Fedech, on the contrary, cheerfully looked around at all the gloomy forty-year-old men present here and with joy he saw the already large figure of Essentuki familiar to him near the wide-open window.

- To Lavra can? - He turned directly to the head of security.

Essentuki in response only vaguely shrugged. Say, I do not care. But the guests gathered in the hall did not think so. One of those sitting on the couch, a short-haired blond man with a small beard with a wedge, cleared his throat dryly and turned his hostility towards the young man.

"The line," he said harshly.

- Yes I see. - Rozgin funny wrinkled sharp nose. - But I, how to say ... I am a thug.

The bearded neighbor on the sofa, dressed in green, the color of his eyes, his jacket, yawned lazily and casually threw over his lip:

- Here all are thieves, - and, imitating his fellow man, weightyly concluded: - The line.

"I see," Fedech grumbled discontentedly. - If anything, warn me, I'm behind you ...

With these words, the lad spun around and headed for the wide staircase leading to the first floor. But as soon as he managed to take a couple of steps, the snow-white door into Lavrikov's office swung open sharply, and jumped out into the hall like a rabid, pink-cheeked man in a black, buttoned under his throat. The left cheekbone of this venerable gentleman was decorated with an oblique scar in the shape of the month. He froze on the threshold and focused his eyes on Essentuki. Broke into a happy smile idiot.

"There is good, Essentuki," the red-mighty man nodded happily, splashing his saliva. - Get this pizza-cook!

The chief of security, as if he had been waiting for this stellar hour for a long time, bounced back from the window-sill and nodded curtly.

"At least something," he grunted to himself, and, forgetting everything, he headed for the stairs.

Stomping loudly with huge shoes on the floor and wincing painfully at the discomfort caused by uncut nails on their feet, Essentuki rushed past Fedechki and, jumping over two steps, hurried down. But the agile young man, which, no doubt, was Fyodor Rozgin, it was not difficult to overtake the ambala at the foot of the stairs. The guy grabbed Essentuki by the arm just above the elbow.

- Take me with you, hear? - followed by an unexpected offer.

Essentuki was even taken aback for a moment by such an unexpected turn of events. For many years, during which he worked in this difficult field of the shadow business, especially in the submission of Fyodor Lavrikov, the big guy used to live according to strict and implicit instructions. That is, according to a pre-agreed schedule. Essentuki did not fundamentally acknowledge abnormal situations, and, frankly speaking, was afraid of them in the depths of his soul.

"There was no team," he protested and tried to pull his powerful hand out of the youth's tenacious fingers.

Of course, he did not apply special force, but Fedech, on the contrary, intuitively felt that some interesting event was pecking, strengthened his grip even more.

- How was it ?! He exclaimed with frank indignation. - I enter the course of affairs! And there was a team to promote.

- This is not the case. - Yessentuki zoiziratsya in search of support, but nearby, unfortunately, no one was there. - Here is a fight.

- It turns out disassembly - not the case? - Rozhgin squinted, easily catching bodyguard vibrations.

The head of the security service, free of captivity, puzzled his shaven nape in a puzzled way. Reflections did not take too much time. The answer to the question was quite obvious.

"A point," finally, Yessentuki had to admit with obvious reluctance in his voice.

- What was required to prove! - happily concluded Rozgin.

Fedechka smiled openly, let go of the bodyguard's hand, and was the first to go out of the mansion. Together they went out into the street. In a black jeep, parked at a distance of no more than two meters from the porch, the driver familiar to Rozgin is already located. A pair of strong guys from the Essentuki brigade impatiently stomped around, awaiting the appropriate order of the boss. The boys looked like each other like Siamese twins, and they could only be distinguished by the color of the shirts. One had yellow, the other had lilac. But Fedechka did not go into such subtleties. Now he was interested in something completely different.

Essentuki jumped off the porch and confidently waved his hairy hands. This was the very long-awaited signal. Militants took it quickly and correctly. The jeep rumbled, and the twins instantly squeezed into the cool cabin, squeezing tightly on the sides of the already managed to sneak in and fit in the back seat Fedechku. The security chief sat down next to the driver. The metal gates, powered by a hidden mechanism, were kindly let out from the territory of the brigade that set off for dismantling. A deathly silence was immediately established inside the car, and in this state there was something oppressive. None of those present wanted to bring up to date a young lover of fights. By virtue of the fact that again there were no relevant instructions.

But Rozgin did not like this way of posing the question, and he decided to take the initiative in his own hands.

- What is this thing? - The guy hardly fished his puny body from the tight embrace of the brothers sitting on the sides and leaned towards Essentuki. - Why pizza?

The bodyguard of Laurus is clearly aware for himself that he simply cannot get away from the meticulous lad. We'll have to share information with him, and then, as a result, get used to the obtuse presence of ballast in the face of a beginner. So it fell like snow on the head. Now babysit with him. Essentuki quietly and unnoticed by others gritted his teeth.

"Well, one type opened not so much a restaurant, but ... Neighboring houses to order are served, the street boys are hauling pizza in apartments," he began to make on duty explanations on duty, portraying genuine boredom on his face because he, an experienced fighter and a professional, you have to interpret such simple and elementary things to your salaga. Say, and he could have guessed, not small. - Cinema, in one word. Clienteur on the move overgrown. At home, the new people are young, they don't like cooking. Only here with a roof, bastard, blefanul. - The head of security scornfully spat into the open side window and slowly reached into his pocket for cigarettes. "And the Redskin checked ... The Redskin looks here ..." Essentuki interrupted in mid-sentence and turned his attention to his subordinates. "Today is just a pogrom," he told the twins. - Without a massacre. Once in the teeth I will give him myself, and for now - everything. Purely preventive event.

Bratki obediently shook their heads, like Chinese dummies, thereby confirming that all production tasks are completely clear to them. By this time, the jeep had already rapidly rolled up to a glass establishment with a colorful sign, made mainly in yellow and red colors: "Pizza by phone". The driver hit the brakes sharply, pressing the black SUV against the curb. One of the twins, dressed in a lilac shirt, located in the cabin to the right of Rozgin, intensively shrugged his shoulders, kneading his stagnant muscles, and was the first to leave the car. Following him, Essentuki stepped into the fresh air. Fedech got out at the same time with the second arkhar member in a yellow shirt. The boy with might and main tried to look like his companions.

- And how much should he? - the descendant of Laurus busily inquired.

- On a piece, it seems, in a month. - Essentuki put a cigarette in his mouth and slowly lit it with a jewel-encrusted lighter. - To start.

- Just? - Fedech grimaced scornfully and, having removed the resolute twin who had stepped forward with his palm, made his own adjustment to the brigade's plans. - I'll be the first to start.

- What? - Essentuki didn't catch his thought right away.

"Bazaar," the boy briefly informed him, but, noticing with what distrust the security chief stared at him, he considered it necessary to explain in more detail to him and the others at the same time the plan of the upcoming operation: "I'll start the conversation." Do you understand? .. It will not work out for me - you will be busy ... with your dentistry.

- What? - I did not understand Essentuki.

- Option "teeth".

Essentuki swallowed nervously. To argue with a guy, in his opinion, was a meaningless and unproductive waste of time. All the same, do not retreat. Do not push it with a force in the car? The boss will not understand this rush. Like each other like two drops of water, the brothers silently waited for the orders of their immediate superior. Essentuki did not hesitate for long. Seconds ten. Silently he nodded in agreement, and, following this silent order, the lilac twin stepped forward. He kicked the glass on the door and stepped aside, passing Rozgin ahead. Fedech resolutely entered the room. Search for private apartments of the owner of this institution for a long time did not have to. Not so extensive was the area. The office of the presumptuous businessman was directly opposite the main entrance.

The owner of the pizzeria was still quite a young man of about thirty, with a small tail. Slim, lean, with long, like a whip, well-groomed hands. Huge brown eyes on a pale narrow face were not at all combined with a small nose-button and a thin line of lips, almost completely hidden from prying eyes with a wide hanging mustache. On the sharp chin and hollow cheeks of the owner of the pizzeria, a three-day stubble appeared. Noticing who had come to his place to visit him, the guy turned pale even more, made a desperate attempt to rise from behind the black office table, but could not. I sank down limply to my place.

Essentuki did not enter the office. As for the two of his henchmen, both ambala were picturefully frozen in the doorway, propping up the shoals with their broad backs. With all their looks, they simply emphasized the seriousness of the situation. Fedech confidently approached the table of the owner and sank into a chair opposite. A couple of minutes or more in the room remained oppressive silence. Rozgin was in no hurry to start a conversation. Carefully studied the potential interlocutor from under narrowed eyelids, mentally pretending something. Pause for the owner of the pizzeria with every second became increasingly unbearable. The psychological pressure was too great. The guy broke down. He found in himself the remnants of internal forces and sprang to his feet. Brown eyes flashed in his pale face, but Fedechka noticed that it was only a disguise of purely human fear,

- I can not wriggle out! - shouted the pizza-making without any prefaces, from personal experience, knowing that having soulful and explanatory conversations with fraternity is a dead and obviously ungrateful thing. The desired result will still not be. To consciousness skinheads will not reach. - Yesterday the sanitary epidemiological station was for the tenth time! Pozhnadzor, cops! - As a result, his voice broke into a falsetto.

"Sit down," the young man calmly responded to this emotional outburst. - And do not yell. A soldering iron in the intestine you have not yet inserted, to turn out outside.

- Pasted! - he did not let up. - Already pasted! I live with him!

Fedechka smiled openly and good-naturedly. He was by no means stupid and understood perfectly all the emotional experiences of a cornered businessman. The only consolation was that the type before him was not alone with his problems. All businessmen have to go through this. Law of life. Dialectics.

"But they didn't turn on the soldering iron," Rozgin said reasonably.

The owner glanced in dismay at the two mordovorotov who were frozen in the doorway and literally fell on the flimsy creaky chair behind him. Fingers trembling with excitement, they picked up a pack of Chesterfield and fished out one cigarette. The mustache man with big eyes attached this poison in the right corner of his mouth and scuffed in his pockets in search of matches.

- For what, for what, and for this it will not be! The country of electricity is not enough, but there is always a kilowatt on my ass! - He was still talking in a raised voice. - Soldering, strangulation - this is called "state support of small business"!

- Yes, do not yell, in actual fact! - irritatedly besieged Fedech, having heard enough of the wailing of a mid-sized businessman.

He instantly fell silent and again glanced at the silent twins behind the young man sitting in front of him. Rozgin turned in the same direction. The ardent faces of the arkharvtsev Essentuki looked more terrible than the fiercest grimaces. These cold-blooded butchers.

- Close the door! - sternly ordered them Laurel offspring.

The guys simultaneously looked at each other, but they did not dare to disobey the order of the young man, who, as they saw, did not even cross their immediate boss. Both stepped back and the door gently closed. The businessman breathed a sigh of relief, left alone with the young man. This one did not seem particularly formidable. Fedech turned to face him and leaned against the black tabletop.

- Why are there so few regular customers? - A boyish finger poked in the direction of a sheet of paper lying on the table.

- Where is little? - sincerely surprised interlocutor. - For a hundred!

- Could more? - said Rozgin.

- And then! - The businessman proudly threw up his pointed willed chin. - The sleeping area, one neighbor recommends one another. And I keep the recipe. There is no time to engage only with clients, - he darkened at once. The unfortunate matches finally found in the left pocket of a gray jacket, and the owner of the pizzeria gladly lit it.

- Gang, sanepid ...

- Wait a minute! - Fedech cut him off in mid-sentence. - We will solve with this station once and for all!

The owner of the institution stood in amazement in a ridiculous pose, forgetting to put out the match. She immediately reminded herself, licked her fingertips with an orange twinkle. The businessman cursed rudely and dropped the match on the table. He pulled an ashtray to himself. Having made a whole series of energetic puffs, he was completely enveloped in bluish clouds of smoke, due to which he was now looking at his young interlocutor. The brown eyes reflected doubt and distrust of the young racketeer.

- And who are you? - with interest in the voice asked pizza, dispersing tobacco smoke by hand.

- I? - Rozgin smirked smugly. - Suppose an assistant godfather. Can not see what?

"It's obvious ..." the interlocutor squeezed out not very confidently.

- Here come on. - Fedechka vigorously slapped his palm on the tabletop.

- No! - automatically retorted the businessman.

- Yes, not grandmother! - he was stunned by a strange visitor with the next answer. - Prepare me calculations. It would be good until the day after. How much equipment costs, personnel, repairs.

Saying these words, Rozgin with a businesslike look continued to study the documents before him. Orienting on the move in a situation, he already knew which policy to choose in relation to the pizzeria and its rightful owner. However, having considered everything in his mind, the young man would like to see the project on paper. So to speak, for verification.

- Repair what? - With every passing second, the mustached gentleman's wonder only grew.

- Do you guys run local? - asked Fedechka.

- Run, - he nodded.

"Through them, find another three or four rooms suitable." To start. I will have a look, count. - Rozgin left the documents alone, imposingly leaned back in his chair and folded his arms over his chest. - If there are many potential customers, maybe it makes sense to create a network.

- Who makes sense?

- to us.

- To "us" ?! - The businessman was still in some prostration.

Fedech sighed heavily. It seemed strange to him that such hard-thinking people were able to create anything worthwhile. It is impossible, in the end, to chew this gentleman every word. It was time he had to turn on his own brains. Rozgin shook his shaggy head.

"To you," he said after a minute. - And my company. I will draw up a business plan - we will see our share. The network is always more profitable than one point. - It is surprising that the young boy still had to tell an already accomplished businessman such immutable truths. - And there - a closed joint-stock company. Catch?

- I catch it. - The thin lips of the owner of the pizzeria, hidden under the mustache, was touched by a timid smile.

- What do you catch? - decided just in case the fire to clarify Fedechka.

But piztsedel did not answer his direct question. His thoughts had already moved in a completely different direction. What is there to say? Not every day you will meet such an assistant godfather, who comes to you not with threats and demanding immediate cash payments, but with a proposal for mutually beneficial cooperation. The businessman fumigated his nostrils and rolled his eyes to the ceiling.

"Your work is wonderful, my God!" - only he said.

The road in the opposite direction was not so rapid. Rather, it resembled a mourning procession. The Essentuki guys, who, thanks to Fedechkina wine, were not allowed to work today with stagnant muscles, did not feel at their best. Gloomy, dissatisfied people testified that today they clearly did not ask. In any case, they did not conduct it as they had planned a couple of hours ago. The head of the security service Fyodor Pavlovich himself looked annoyed. The consensus reached during Rozin's negotiations with the businessman didn't suit Essentuki. Much more productive, in his opinion, it would be to slap pizza in the face. And with the attendants would be back, no doubt, and the boss would deserve the praise. Here is an option. And the boy, with his ideas of expanding some kind of network, let everything go under the tail.

Having disguised a couple of cigarettes, the security guard turned the case back, leaning back against the seat, and stared intently at the boy's face, as before squeezed on both sides with broad-shouldered ambers.

"You will explain yourself with Laurus," he sternly warned Rozgin, hoping in this way to spoil the mood.

"Of course, my problems," he replied nonchalantly, but immediately added with a malicious grin on his lips: "No, not only mine." Only the last idiots beat the teeth of a chicken, which will soon begin to bear the golden eggs.

Essentuki wanted to respond to this statement with some inherent rudeness or, even better, to punch the offender in the jaw, but prudently restrained this unwanted impulse. The massive cheekbones began to play on the face of the head of the security service, and tight jaws stood out in relief. The subordinates Yessentuki knew very well that such physiognomic metamorphosis testifies to the extremely bad mood of their boss.

- Brakes at the shooting gallery! - the main bodyguard of Laurus harshly addressed the driver of the jeep and, for greater persuasiveness, indicated the necessary place on the road with the help of a finger looking into the distance. - There!

- What else? - innocently curious Fedechka.

- I want to shoot. - Essentuki grinned his teeth in a bloodthirsty grin. "Like the last idiot." At least on targets.

"Adrenaline ..." Rozgin shook his head knowingly.

But the security chief did not hear his sarcastic intonations. The SUV stopped, and the brave guys quickly jumped out of the car. This time, even the driver was not in the cabin. By a friendly company, the whole four and Fedechka, who had again linked up with them, headed towards a modest semi-basement room, located on the corner of Makarov and Lermontov streets. We descended down a small concrete staircase and found ourselves in a dimly lit room.

The people in the shooting range at the gun shop, where Lavrov's militants often liked to visit, were not at that time. Fedechka stood a little apart and impartially watched while Essentuki and his henchmen slowly fished their pistols from under their jackets, checked their combat readiness, and already after that, knowingly, began to have a good time.

They fired their lads, selflessly, sticking their tongues out of pleasure and flashing their eyes with excitement. The accumulated tension finally found for itself the most suitable way out. The booming cannonade was silent, and the guys started to reload the weapon. All their movements were clear, well-adjusted. Professionals.

Yessentuki happily turned to the young man who had died away. He had no previous insult to Rozgin.

- And you? - The security guard offered cordially.

"I don't know how," Fedech honestly admitted.

- Now we will teach. - Essentuki confidently stepped to the counter and in his own way turned to the weapon seller, a well-fed peasant of fifty, with a broken nose: - Grisha, give the young man something for the first puff.

- smooth? - He specified, out of the corner of his eye, squinting at the boy, as if he was asking the price of him and his physical data. - Or in cutting?

"Cutting, of course," said Essentuki, vividly.

- Moment. - The well-fed salesman dived under the counter and, hiding with his head, groped somewhere below. - Let's look for the beautiful ...

The head of the security service spun around. Fedechka already approached him closely and with much greater curiosity he studied not the weapon, but the face of Essentuki glowing with joy. However, how little a person needs in order to fully feel happy. A couple of loud pops from the gun, and that's it. The barometer of inner mood showed quite different results. The three assistants of the first bodyguard of Laurus looked exactly the same. Following the established routine, they did not start a new firing at the targets, but dutifully waited for the chef to join them and give an appropriate follow-up gesture. The trunks are now modestly downcast, staring at the floor.

"You smell the air, smell it," advised Fedechka Yessentuki, breathing deeply.

- Sniffing. - The guy really deliberately nodded a couple of times, but he couldn't grasp anything essential that could cause him such a genuine delight, like in four healthy men.

- And How? - the security guard did not lag behind him.

- It smells thick.

- Yes, smells ... - Essentuki dreamily rolled his eyes. - Lubrication, metal ... Kaif!

The seller's head reappeared above the counter, and after it the obese body emerged. A man with dignity put his chosen gun on the counter.

"Welcome," he said. - Almost no recoil.

"Take it," Essentuki grinned, winking at the boy. - I'll show you how this toy is played.

"No, I won't," he unexpectedly responded.

- What will not be?

- Take, shoot. I will not.

On the face of a hefty Umbal displayed sincere bewilderment. He often blinked his eyes and confusedly glanced at the seller. He only shrugged.

- In gives! - Essentuki exclaimed dumbfounded. - Yes, any kid! .. I would have fooled at your age!

- I do not need this, Essentuki. - The young man smiled disarmingly. - I do not need it.

The eyes of all those present in the dash at that moment were fixed on Rozgin. Yessentuki shook his short-cropped head. At this moment, he was full of genuine sympathy.

"You, boy, have a psyche," he made the final medical diagnosis.

- I thought - on the contrary, - casually threw Fedechka.

Essentuki grinned, but at the same time he involuntarily looked away from the young man's honest and open eyes. Some awkwardness that had never been known appeared in the soul.

"You hurt," he said frowning, shaking his head. - Three times offended. And this ... - the head of security service nodded at the gun, to which the boy did not even bother to touch - this is detente. Self esteem

- It can be otherwise, - quite good-naturedly, smoothing out previous friction, turned to Rozgin's bodyguard.

- How?

In the cold eyes Essentuki flashed interest.

- Pass me! - wildly screaming shaved bare two-meter block with a square jaw.

- Where, dumbass ?! Barked a moment later, a stocky roll, whose mighty muscles stood out in relief through a snow-white shirt with short sleeves. The tie's knot is weakened, sweat is streaming down my cheeks, in a shoulder holster a dreadful, but at the present moment useless weapon carelessly dangles.

- Bolt, come on the left! - Yessentuki became furious and rushing at full speed along the improvised football field, whose stylish trousers, especially in the area of the knees, already resembled the garb of a homeless man who had fallen in the garbage.

Brothers with light Fedina hands really had an hour to chase the ball around the area between the house of Laurus and the steel entrance gates. The game, which, apparently, the children have been deprived for many years, fascinated them with their heads. This was what Fedechka had in mind when he told the security chief about a different, most pleasant way to discharge. The boy was not wrong in the predictions. For a long time already Essentuki did not feel so immensely happy. Especially in those moments when he succeeded in successfully directing the ball into the opening made of bricks, which served as a football goal. The fraternity of the gdel and the hive is like a flock of frisky first-graders in a big break or in physical education classes.

The shaven-headed ambal, baptized by Essentuki Bolt, promptly walked around the left flank of the waist-naked waistline with colorful tattoos all over his body and famously faked the ball with his toe. The blow fell a bit at a glance, and instead of an improvised gate, Bolt struck an old "Seagull" of the Laurus standing on the side. The ball bounced off the iron body, and he immediately jumped on the spot, caught another fighter with hairy hands.

- It is impossible hands! - a man with colorful tattoos frantically screamed.

- Can! - disagreed with his opponent. - Out of the field!

Players keen on a long-forgotten process did not notice how Sancho and Lavr appeared on the porch of the mansion. Both were frozen in place with their mouths open and for five minutes they watched in dismay over what was happening on the site. Moshkin's eyes got out of orbit, and he even more than usual, began to blink with his fleshy nose. Laurel squinted at his companion who had become stunned in perplexity, who just a few minutes ago selflessly indulged in his inherent moral teachings.

- What is this?! - loudly asked Lavrikov, without waiting for the moral support from Alexander.

The screams and the hubbub of the brothers on the court instantly subsided. Despite the lack of full ammunition, skinheads stretched out at attention, and the spotted ball remained in the hands of the fighter who violated the rules. Fedech emerged from the crowd and, breathing heavily, approached the criminal authority. He, too, was a great sweat from running around, and his tight pigtails stuck to the skull in places.

"This is called football, Laurus," he explained to the host intelligibly. - With a touch of rugby and massacre. The guys got stuck ... - He smiled full-faced and continued to look fearlessly at the owner.

The view of authority has again shifted towards Sancho. I really wanted him to say his weighty word about everything he had just seen. Fyodor Pavlovich himself was in complete confusion. He had never seen anything like it before.

"Actually, there is no football without a goalkeeper," said Moshkin reasonably, and his small, piggy eyes excitedly caught fire. - I can stand up...

He already rushed forward, but Laurus intercepted his hand.

- No, no! - He cooled the fighting fervor of his loyal assistant. - Stay where you are!

Sancho meekly stopped, but his actions cheered Rozgin even more. He proudly looked over his shoulder at his improvised football team and confided to the authority with a radiant smile on his lips, lowering his voice almost to a whisper:

- Did not play out in childhood ...

Laurel squinted suspiciously.

- Where did the ball come from? He asked sternly.

"I bought it," the boy admitted, and immediately added for some reason: "For my own."

However, Lavrikov did not like such an innocent explanation. He even frowned more.

- Your money is intended for your needs! - hard, quite fatherly, he said. - And the ball is intended ... - Fyodor Pavlovich faltered, unable to continue his own deep thoughts about the true goal of a football in the fate of humanity. - Well, to hell with him! - Carelessly waving his hand, he immediately hurried to jump on a new topic for complaints: - Answer better, what did you study with pizza-making machine?

- Nothing yet. - Fedechka brushed sweat from his forehead with the back of his hand. - Obshchakovskaya box office dead weight? It lies. And so we launch it into a completely legal joint-stock company, and after a month and a half, the ticket office begins to legally multiply and multiply. Come, I'll explain in order.

The guy went up to the porch and first went inside the house. From a careless kid who just chased a ball across the field, he instantly turned into a businesslike, serious person who knows the value of every word he utters. Sancho involuntarily smacked his tongue and glanced at Laurus.

- Let's go to. - He briefly nodded fellow at the door. - He will explain in order.

Moshkin obediently flooded in the indicated direction, painfully hurt by the fact that the boss did not allow him to realize the unfulfilled childhood dream and show the children of Essentuki what he could still be capable of as a goalkeeper. Do not forget about frolicking bodyguards and Fedor Pavlovich. For a moment, he lingered on the porch of the mansion, scowling at the muzzled and flushed faces of the Arkharians. Drooping his eyes in the mass stood in anticipation of severe punishment and Essentuki. Laurel snorted shortly.

- Play, just did not finish playing! - he graciously allowed. - Just what to do if it turns out that you are not sucked boobs?

With these words, he rushed after Fedechka and Sancho, who had disappeared from view. The brothers stood for a couple of minutes without moving under the scorching sunshine, not daring to return to the pastime they liked, until Essentuki shouted loudly over the whole territory:

- Do not touch the ball with your hands, you started!

He obediently opened his fingers, and the ball fell on the emerald grass. The game resumed instantly. Bratkov was not even embarrassed by the absence of the instigator of the event in the person of Rozgin.

Chapter 11

The monotonously humming printer relieved spit out of the womb the last sheet of paper and fell silent. Fedech picked up the printout, combined it with the previous ones, and leaning back in the spinning chair, carefully looked at the results of his own titanic efforts. The readings were quite satisfactory for the young man, and he, putting the pile of papers on the left corner of the tabletop, with the help of the mouse successively closed all his work programs. Then the computer itself was turned off. The monitor screen went out. Rozgin famously pushed his foot from the table and rolled away for some distance. The boy's long, dry hands hung limply along the body, and he, with his head thrown back, tiredly attached his eyelids. A computer is a good thing and, of course, necessary in our age, but now his eyes get incredibly tired. Fedech knew about it better than whoever Tony would be.

Having explained with Laurel on the subject of his far-reaching plans for pizzerias, Rozgin returned to his immediate duties. After leaving the working room, the young man with a pile of papers confidently headed towards Fyodor Pavlovich's personal apartments.

This time the hall of the second floor was absolutely deserted. A live queue of thieves, hungry for an audience with a powerful authority, dried up. Fedechk involuntarily smiled and bravely took up the gilded door handle. He turned it and stepped on the threshold.

In the office of Lavrikov there were six people. In the center, near the wide, wide-open window at the table, Laurel himself was placed in a snow-white suit and a gray tie with the image of small dolphins. To his right, on a leather sofa, sat side by side with Sancho and Yessentuki. Both serious, focused, with pursed lips. On the opposite side of the table from Fyodor Pavlovich, Rozgin noticed two unfamiliar men to him. Caucasian in a black double-breasted suit and patent leather shoes, with dark, licked back hair and an obese gentleman with gray hair, dressed in a blue shirt with short sleeves of the same shade wide tie. Behind the gray-haired one more type stamped with a languid expression and fussy, not finding their proper place hands.

"The hearings in the arbitration, which Dowel inspired, were able to be postponed," Hamlet reported fervently, and he was the very Caucasian, opposite Fyodor Pavlovich. - For a month, yes? .. Expensive taken, but moved.

- Why did not they cancel? - Lavrikov asked displeased, linking his fingers into the lock and setting them in front of him on the tabletop.

"We will need the judgment ourselves," Hamlet smiled openly. - Only with a different layout. Director of the plant - a hard-nosed goat, donkey! He does not understand his advantage at all, or Dubel has pressed him very hard.

"Everything is relative," said Yessentuki philosophically, giving a voice from his seat. The head of the security service, who had already spent a good half hour in the office of the chief, was madly wanting to smoke, but he selflessly restrained this addiction in himself, postponing it at the time when Laurus deigned to let him go home. - Though now I can roll, drive. And see who is stronger.

- What are you? - Caucasian frightened turned to the closet bodyguard, and his eyes rounded to the size of tea pots. "It means immediate war!" Do not have time to return!

- A little earlier, a little later - what's the difference? - instead of Essentuki, dryly reacted to the last words of Hamlet Lavrikov. - I still have to.

- Wait with your war! - a gray-haired gentleman in a blue shirt wedged into the conversation. He lazily threw his legs and very displeasedly glanced at the militant Yessentuki. - I open a line of credit for the operation? And if you open, which one? Estimate where?

There was a brief pause in the conversation, during which Laurus frowned over the situation and, most importantly, at its successful resolution. And to dot the i's should be today. Loss of time in the financial issue was unacceptable.

"Open the big line," Hamlet broke the silence established in his office, feeling that Fyodor Pavlovich was not yet ready for a final decision. - Oily.

- We can crack, - the gray-haired expressed doubt. For several years already, he fruitfully cooperated with Lavr and his subordinates. Of course, predominantly he solved all the necessary issues with the financial adviser of authority, which Hamlet was, but sometimes he, as the head of a large bank, had to personally meet with the thief in law and depend on his opinion. Anyway, during large-scale operations, no one else, except Laurus, had the right to give the green light. - As I understand it, some bribes will pull five million people ...

Rozgin, whose appearance on the threshold of the room so far no one had noticed, tactfully cleared his throat into a fist. The eyes of all those present at the production meeting were instantly turned in his direction. Laurel smiled openly, and at the same time life ceased to be painted in black and white. The banker stopped short, and in his eyes was clearly bewildered.

"Excuse me," Fedechka casually threw and impressively walked to the Laurel desk. - Go on, gentlemen.

The young man flopped into a free chair on the right hand of the criminal authority, took it almost lying down and in a way he put his legs on the tabletop. The views of those present synchronously shifted to the master of the cabinet, everyone was waiting for his reaction. Lavrikov cut an indifferent grimace and, imitating Rozgin, also threw his feet on the table, showing the gray-haired banker and his economic adviser a embossed pattern of shoe soles.

"We continue," he said idly through his lip, and half-turning to Fedechka, explained: "We exchanged views here." About ... - Lavrikov stopped short and pretended that he had just now noticed the surprise of others. He slapped himself on the high forehead, looked around the audience with a radiant look. - This is my new economic adviser, if someone does not know ... Fedechka. The nickname ... uh ... - Fyodor Pavlovich for a moment hesitated and blurted out the first thing that came to his head: - Shaggy!

Fedechka slowly raised two folded fingers to his temple and foolishly saluted high advice. Gray-haired and Hamlet briefly exchanged glances. Sancho suppressed a spiteful chuckle in himself. Essentuki indifferently stared in the opposite direction, as if what was happening did not concern him at all. The Caucasian nervously fidgeted on the chair, and then vigorously leaned the body forward.

- He is an adviser, yes? And who am I? - The voice was clearly confused.

- You? - Lavrikov thoughtfully scratched his chin. - I would say ... you are a senior adviser, Hamlet. Fedya is a junior adviser. With a bias in analytics.

- Where with a bias? - the Caucasian did not get the idea.

- Where necessary, there and with a bias! - the authority has already irritatedly responded, but then, having changed the intonation to the benevolent, he turned to his son: - You seem to have moved into the factory business?

He nodded shortly in response:

- Entered. Very well driven.

Lavrikov gazed with affection at his direct descendant. By the nature and style of communication, Fedechka perfectly reminded him of himself in his youth. With a certain amendment, of course, but in general, the similarity was striking. Or maybe the thief in the law just wanted to see this very similarity and he saw him? Anyway, Fyodor Pavlovich every day more and more attached to the young man and no longer imagined further existence without him. And how did he manage without Fedechki for many years before that ?!

"We will have to fight a little bit," he told his son confidentially. - We define tactics and strategy. And expenses.

"Well, I can only guess about your tactics," the young man said ruefully. - But there is no competent strategy here.

- I.e? - Laurel guarded. Even he did not expect such a turn in the conversation.

Rozgin changed his legs on the table in some places. He shifted his left limb to his right, and crossed both hands on his chest, stared with unblinking eyes into the brown eyes of Hammer sitting opposite.

"Give the plant back," he said quietly, but quite clearly. - And pay extra to be taken away. Cheaper will rise.

The young man only hypothetically assumed that the initiative of this transaction comes from Caucasians, but he probably could not know this. However, natural intuition did not disappoint the boy. The blow came, as they say, not in the eyebrow, but in the eye. Hamlet's swarthy face went purple with stains, he crept all over and glared fiercely.

- Laurel! He shouted sharply. - Remove the boy, huh ?! Otherwise, I'll be out.

"You'll get out when ordered," Fyodor Pavlovich calmly parried, but faithful Sancho, who knew the boss as a peeling one, managed to catch metallic intonations in his voice that did not foretell anything good for the person to whom the authority addressed. - In the meantime, have patience to listen to your opponent.

- Is it an opponent? - contemptuously grimaced Caucasian.

Fedka did not hurt the last words. On the contrary, he very dismissively parted his lips in a smile and finally assumed a decent position in the leather chair. Even leaned forward slightly for persuasiveness.

- What is the bazaar guys? - he asked cheerfully, winking at the gray-haired banker. - Because of the scrap dump, on which the debt - the Himalayas! Nineteenth century it! The plant should be demolished, the land should be cleared, then a billion investments should be invested ... Why? - He abruptly threw on the table a stack of papers brought with him. - On the contrary, across the road - a wasteland!

"Wasteland — Dowel," Lavrikov shook his head, but his gaze involuntarily focused on the printed sheets of paper. What is there still dug his genius son?

- So exchange it for a rusty monster, - offered Rozgin. - Take a wasteland, no one is offended - there is a change of chendzh, the city will thank you. And we will set up a compact production in the wasteland ... "He shrugged picturefully. - Well, for example, vortex generators.

- What? - asked financial tycoon in a blue shirt.

- What other generators? - from the move picked up Hamlet.

The hostility towards the impudent kid in the soul of the Caucasian grew with every moment and acquired quite real outlines.

"A peasant invented one Tver," Rozgin continued to develop his thought just as calmly. - A conventional electric pump plus a few iron pipes, in which the water is twisted so that heat arises in bulk! Heat the house though, at least all the Ministry of Energy. Efficiency - one hundred seventy percent, almost a perpetual motion machine! .. Yes, I'll scam the Internet - dozens of projects will be selected for you with a penny investment that the big bosses do not need in FIG!

Fedech smiled smugly at the gloomy men who had gathered in the office. He was bursting with pride from his own words, and the guy sincerely wanted his ideas to be supported by those around him. But as a result, his fiery tirade led to something completely different. You can say the opposite. The corpulent banker, with difficulty, freed his body from the captivating embrace of a leather armchair and rose to his feet to his very full height.

- Young man! He sarcastically said, not without a hint of coldness in his voice. - Nobody needs penny projects, because they are penny projects, there is nothing to steal from them. This is the axiom of our reality, young man. It's a shame not to know! - He smiled and turned his head in the direction of the criminal authority. - Laurel, do not be offended, I have to go. At eleven of the Central Bank Commission. - Gray-haired man glanced at his watch and turned to the assistant who was fussing behind him: "Genula, let's go."

With complete deathly silence, the banker walked to Fyodor Pavlovich's exit from the apartment, but turned from the door itself, hoisting a plump brush on the gilded handle.

"You, as agreed, put me on notice," he said gloomily, and at the end glanced at Rozgin. - All the best!

Gray-haired left the room, and after him the devotee to the chief, like a guard dog, a fussy referent in tight trousers, left as well. The door slammed shut, and in Lavrap's office still no one was in a hurry to break the established silence. Even Hamlet, with his natural talkativeness, kept his mouth shut, waiting for further developments. He only gritted his teeth softly and incinerated the opponent imposed on him by his junior advisors with a hated look.

Fedech was taken aback and, with some apprehension, glanced at the big boss. Laurel sighed heavily.

- I'm right! - Rozgin moaned almost plaintively, thus childishly making excuses in the eyes of others, and in his own.

Fyodor Pavlovich did not respond to this desperate remark. The passivity of the criminal authority finally hammered Hamlet. He hoped to contemplate the storm, which fell on the head of a snotty youth, but this did not happen. His father's feelings turned out to be in the powerful Lavra stronger than his unquestioned authority. Only now the Caucasian realized this fully. He jumped to his feet and grabbed his black briefcase from the arm of the chair.

- And I'll go, since I don't need it! - with a call he said.

But as subsequent events showed, not for all Lavrikov was so soft and fluffy.

- Sit down! - he growled ominously, like a trainer in a circus arena, dealing with vicious predators. Only the whip was missing in his right hand.

Hamlet froze in place as paralyzed.

"Guys," said Sancho, who had been preserving the entire silence of the whole time, was content with a voice from the couch, and so far was content with only passive contemplation of what is happening. - Let's live in peace. At least among themselves. After all, the truth. - Moshkin expected to smooth out the tension in the room. - Why is it needed, this plant? Do we have enough plants? And the bathhouse was drowned ...

"Sancho," Hamlet hissed angrily. - You also became an economic adviser? Average?

The peace-loving intonations of Alexander Moshkin allowed Fedech to take himself in hand and return the lost internal aplomb. He no longer looked so confused and miserable as he had been a few minutes ago. One interesting little thought originated in his head. But it should be checked.

"I know why it is needed, this plant," he said firmly, carefully glancing at Hamlet's dark face. - There is only one reasonable explanation.

- Well, and? .. - interestedly requested the continuation of Laurus.

- You want to be dragged into an absolutely pointless disassembly, they want to exhaust, suck, bleed. And the controversial plant is, you know ... - just a second left for Rozgin to select a suitable comparison, - a string from an extension. You see her, but you stumble - out of pride, out of principle! And Babahan blower. And instead of Laurus - scraps from Laurus. It is not even algebra. Arithmetic. - The young man bent over the table and moved in the direction of the authority of the paper, containing all the necessary information on this subject. - Here is the printout. Results on the whole complex of your affairs. Fold, take away, divide. Even a baby will understand: one small explosion is enough for everything to shatter. Everything! - With each spoken word, he got more and more started. He entered into a rage, as they say. It seemed a moment more, and Fedechka would fall for a hysterical cry. - Because everything is stupid, not efficient,

However, even earlier Hamlet broke into a scream. Deserved, as he knew, the accusations against him threatened to destroy the Lavrovsky financial adviser. And this almost sought at the moment Rozgin. No matter how ardent and passionate his speech was, he did not forget to watch the Caucasians standing in the center of the office. Hamlet first turned pale as a sheet, then turned purple. As a result, even turned green with anger. Well, just not a man, but a chameleon of some kind. Rainbow. The long, well-groomed fingers of a native of the sun's edges danced nervously, and the owner hurried to hide them in his trouser pockets. Rozgin had noticed this, and his suspicions were only strengthened. The case is left for small. Get proof.

- Where did this sucker come from? - The lips of Hamlet, who was gagging at full throat, were shaking like a jelly disturbed by a fork.

Fedechka paused and grinned wryly. At least one positive result was achieved by him.

"From the womb of the mother," Lavrikov said, barely audibly, exclusively for himself, but the next moment, raising his voice to natural intonations, added: "Go out, Fedor."

- Yes please! - Rozgin got up from his chair and swiftly walked to the exit. He left the papers he brought on the laurel table. "I am in the city," the youth threw, without turning around.

- What for? - Fyodor Pavlovich instantly forgot all existing production and financial problems. It woke up an elementary parental concern to the ribs. And it does not matter that the son is already out of infancy.

- Get some fresh air! - Rozgin reported arrogantly and, stepping over the threshold, slammed the door loudly.

Essentuki immediately rose from the couch, tracing the expressive look of authority.

"Arrange," Lavrikov ordered sternly. - Let him not take his eyes off him.

The skinhead Ambal nodded and briskly rushed after Fedech, who had left the room. Only Lavr himself, Sancho, and Hamlet blurred in a malicious smile remained in the office.

- Why would such a concern, Laurus? - unobtrusively faked a legendary thief in law Caucasian.

Fyodor Pavlovich measured his advisor with a long attentive gaze. Hamlet's last question didn't like the crime boss at all. But to stand in a pose is clearly not worth it.

"A good programmer should be protected," Lavrikov remarked morally and quietly exchanged glances at the same time with Moshkin. - He knows a lot of secrets. And you ... - The thief in law rather hastily turned off the topic of conversation that was undesirable for him and switched to the remaining open question about the ill-fated plant. - More precisely, we ... We will try to add, take away, divide and, if possible, multiply. Arithmetic is not forgotten, Hamlet Otellovich?

Laurel took from the table lists of printouts, on which he focused the attention of the boss Fedechka, and carefully plunged into the study of what was written. Intuition told Fyodor Pavlovich that the son was not just crucified here for tyrannosaurs and the like heresy. Somewhere near the truth was hiding.

Today was a particularly sunny day. Warm rays pleasantly caressed the tops of passers-by, who chaotically moved in space for some business. Some stayed in the center of the street and, having set up mirror glasses on the bridge of their nose, enjoyed sunbathing with pleasure. The beeches not located to such procedures, on the contrary, tried to hide as quickly as possible in a shadow, mainly underground, where numerous metro branches were located.

Fedechka stopped at the very entrance to the subway and enjoyed indulging in Italian chocolate-coated ice cream. With a careful eye, he cast around each person passing by, marveling at how different in character and mode of behavior can be the inhabitants of the same city. Rozgin's mood gradually improved, and he began to forget about the unpleasant incident that occurred in the office of Laurus an hour ago. The only thing that did not leave the guy out of his head, so this is the identity of Hamlet and his inadequate reaction to Fedechkiny proposals. That's where it was worth a good dig.

From working thoughts Rozgin distracted appeared on the horizon Nate. The girl decorously stalked along the avenue, wagging her buttocks vulgarly. She, like at their last meeting, was dressed in a short skirt, which hid little, and a bright orange topic raised above the navel. Fedechka with a smile noticed that many of the stronger sex involuntarily turned their heads toward his girlfriend's heart, and some even whistled. What is there to say? Nata could make a proper impression if she wanted. And she always wanted.

- Hello, Fedechka. - A seductive little thing came close to the guy and playfully flashed her bottomless eyes.

- ABOUT! - Rozgin cast a sidelong glance at a large clock, mounted into the wall of a building opposite. "Not even late, hello ... Do you want ice cream?" There is a thin strip of jam under the glaze. Very tasty, "he said confidentially.

- That's disgusting. - Nat's lip curled.

- And I love. - The young man blithely shrugged.

- What? - She squinted slyly.

Rozgin immediately caught the essence of the proposed game. Not so bad, he knew this girl.

- Jam and you.

Nat smiled, clearly flattered.

"That's right, I suddenly remembered," nevertheless, she could not refrain from venomous intonation.

- And when there is no money, why bother? - Reasonably noticed this young man. - Right now I received an advance payment from one gang, escaped from the embrace of the mafia and immediately called you so that you could spend a little advance before you took it back.

Fedechka knew what he was talking about. His words made an impression on Nata. All girls at her age are prone to romance and adventure. For them, this is an additional stimulus to existence. We saw lots of beautiful films, read love books - now they dream about intimate relationships with a sentimental killer or something like that.

- Is it true that you work for a gang? - Nate asked incredulously, but Rozgin noticed how her eyes glittered brightly. She even had a voice involuntarily almost to a whisper.

"True," he answered honestly, and immediately found it necessary to add: "Until classes at the university begin."

- How interesting! - A young and romantic-minded girl threw up her hands in admiration.

- What is interesting there? - Fedech twisted. - Mesozoic Tosca. - And, wearing a mask of utter indifference on his face, he gallantly picked up Nata by the elbow. - Where to move?

- At the movie enough advance? - She asked.

A couple of young people slowly moved along the sidewalk towards the Revolution Square.

- Well, if you do not particularly shy, - Rozgin smiled.

- And I wanted - especially. In Planet Hollywood.

The guy categorically shook his head and for a moment even let go of the elbow of his companion. They stopped at a busy intersection with heavy traffic.

"No, I don't want to go there," Fedechka said absolutely seriously. - There popcorn chew. Gum in the ears, firing on the screen. A cup of coffee costs like my aunt's weekly earnings.

"Well, I would have sat with my aunt at home," Nat said scornfully, frankly wanting to prick her cavalier more painfully.

She even pointedly turned in the opposite direction and made a decisive step in that direction, as if intending to leave the society of the stingy young man. Her whole appearance at the moment testified to the clearly deeply offended state of the soul. Say, the guy in full growth is working on a large mafia group, but does not want to reduce his beloved in the movie. Cups of coffee regretted, you see.

- Nat, Nat! - Rozgin quickly jumped to the girl and grabbed her by the snow-white wrist. Affectionately looked into the huge radiant eyes of his beloved. "Let's go to the old cinema, let's go to an empty one and with a balcony."

- What for? - Natas narrowed her eyes in disbelief.

"Let's make love," said the young man, without a hint of a smile, as something taken for granted. - We had the same planned. On an empty balcony is very exotic.

He gave her a reassuring wink with her right eye. However, the girl did not take such ingenuous and tempting prospects with the expected cordiality. On the contrary, the noble and passionate impulses of the gentleman came at all to her liking. Gaze Nata froze and became somehow prickly.

"That loft, that balcony ..." she said gruffly. - The hotel could then invite, Romeo, if love is a hunt. Or in a motel in case of emergency.

"The motel-hotels are all gangster too, Nat," Rozgin informed his potential partner on planned intimate relationships. - It suppresses my sexuality. The criminal atmosphere kills an erection right in the bud.

Nata snorted loudly, and involuntarily attracted the attention of two elderly women, who stood to the left of her at the crossroads. Noble ladies simultaneously turned in the direction of a defiantly dressed maiden and shook their heads in disapproval. The red peephole of traffic lights went out, being replaced by a bright yellow, and even a moment later, the pedestrians smiled a friendly green light. Women confidently walked to the opposite side of the street in the general stream of fellow citizens, and the newly minted employee of the criminal structure in the person of Fyodor Rozgin and his obstinate girlfriend remained tramping on the sidewalk, figuring out personal relationships.

"With such sensitivity, Fedechka, you're walking to retirement as an un-kissed boy," Nat snapped, but the guy missed her next attack past.

- Nat, maybe then to the porch, eh? - he introduced a new romantic proposal.

- With an advance, with money, and again - in the doorway?

"I will return the advance payment to the gang, do not worry," Fedechka assured her. - I'll quit as unprofitable.

The girl sighed heavily. Argue with Rozgin was useless. He will never change. Traction to adventure or to something associated with high ideas about life he was completely absent. In any case, in Natinu understanding. This must either be tolerated or ...

"Let's just go," the girl suggested hopelessly.

- Let's go to. - Fedechka happily stretched his lips in a wide smile. - Just walking is also useful. And sparingly.

He turned around and threw the ice-cream wrap into a roadside bin. At that moment, his gaze fixed the familiar outlines of a black jeep parked just meters from the intersection. Fedechka hastily looked away. With a lean expression on his face, he again grabbed Nata under his elbow and slightly bent his head forward.

- By the way, for me - the tail! - he said in a mysterious whisper, letting out as much espionage intonation as possible. The girl twitched nervously, but Rozgin squeezed her hand even more with her fingers. - Quiet, do not look back! Look in the window.

They turned to face the glass store at the crossroads.

- See the reflection of the jeep?

"I see," Nat said, just as quietly.

- So, we are not just going to go, and rip.

- I have never in my life left my tail. - The girl's eyes lit up again. Real romantic adventures finally burst into her life. - How interesting!

- And you say - "Planet Hollywood" with popcorn ... - Rozgin really felt like a real James Bond. - Life, Natul, richer than our ideas about her ... Take the right! Quickly!

Instead of crossing the intended intersection, the young people turned into a nearby street and quickened their pace.

- We are on the planet "Russia"!

Turning over his shoulder shortly, Rozgin managed to notice how a black jeep swiftly darted off and rushed to the intersection. Having disappeared from the pursuers' sight, the guy vigorously tugged on his companion's hand, dragging her into the low arch of the panel structure. Towards taxied a grocery van and cautiously made itself felt by the shrill whistle of the car horn. Nata cringe scared.

- There!

Fedechka pulled her to the left to the iron containers for garbage and forced to bend down. Young people did not pay attention to the fact that, by the will of circumstances, they were not in the most pleasant shelter for the organs of smell. But from this point they could perfectly see the jeep of pursuit that had slowed down near the arch. The doors of the SUV swung open, and a couple of strong guys in spacious silk shirts jumped out onto the sidewalk. Brothers were worried about their shaved heads, trying to determine in which direction the object was hiding with its lady of the heart. Fedechka put a finger to his lips, and Nate dutifully nodded.

- Where to go? - the driver already familiar to Rozgin, who was leaning out of the open window of the jeep, loudly addressed the ambals.

One of the assistants of Essentuki spat relishly at his feet, and with annoyance he slashed the air with his open palm.

"Call Mineralka," he said gloomily to his accomplice. "We seem to have lost them ..."

Brothers famously loaded into the car, and Nata, inspired by the event that fell to her share, ignored the presence of a trash can in her immediate vicinity, opened Fedechka's face with both hands, and passionately dug her lips into his mouth. Kiss turned lingering. Rozgin pulled away first and frowned into the shining happiness of her friend's eyes.

- No, all this ... How to say? - he blurted, dropping his gaze. - All this - just to ... - The words were not easy for the guy, but he ventured: - Sorry, Nat. Everything is great, you are good. You may have matured long ago, but I, probably, not too much.

"I don't understand anything," the girl blinked in surprise.

- I want to remain as I was. Yourself. I need.

- What is necessary, Fedechka?

"Persist," he said gravely. - Until.

- Gosha! What for?

Rozgin shrugged. He himself could not understand what was happening to him.

- And the devil knows. It is necessary ... The feeling is.

Nata's eyes flashed unkindly, and she rose abruptly to her feet. Now the girl looked at her negligent gentleman from top to bottom.

"Mummies have no feelings," she said dryly. - Let's save. Best of all - in the freezer.

Fedechka understood perfectly well that the love date was hopelessly flawed. However, he could do nothing about it. He didn't even hold onto Nata, but only frowned at her retreating figure in the arch. The mood finally fell to zero.

- Yes! I'm listening!

Laurel grabbed his mobile phone as a drowning man grabs a straw. It was practically impossible to find out in Fyodor Pavlovich a respectable businessman and an impressive, self-aware prestige today. Never before has the famous thief in law been so distracted and worried. Throughout the evening, he was worn in his country mansion as a wound, unable to find a suitable occupation. Nothing could distract Laurus from restless thoughts. He glanced at his wristwatch every five minutes, panicky watching the second hand moving inexorably in a circle. In addition, he also checked against the wall dial, in the insane hope that his Rolex produces incorrect results.

At about ten in the evening, the melodious trill of the mobile phone sounded like a crushing blow to the bare nerves.

- What is a casino? - Lavrikov frowned, hearing the voice of an invisible interlocutor. - I don't have to go to the casino ... Call the police, why should I jerk me? I do not care that the State Duma deputy, - with every second more and more authority began. - Do not wait, who's reputation will suffer - from the casino or from the deputy? Call cops, said! Let the salary increase work on the deputy!

With a fury, he pressed the button to turn off the connection with his index finger and casually threw the mobile phone into the right pocket of a spacious dressing gown. The embittered look of the kingpin stumbled upon Essentuki's mansion with his three assistants standing near the front doors. The security chief quickly hid his little eyes, but such an act failed to save him from the righteous wrath of the big boss.

- All need to drive! - Fedor Pavlovich broke into a cry, confidently walking in the direction of the arkharivtsi, frozen like wax figures. - So that on the train newspapers and clothespins traded! Essentuki! - The authority stopped right in front of his gorilla-like ally. - Why the child did not give a mobile? To the aunt sent?

"Ours are on duty," he said in confusion. - He has not appeared there yet.

- Army contain! - Lavrikov did not let up. - And in actual fact army - parasites! Petrovka, thirty-eight, by golly! Yellow house!

Having put forward such offensive comparisons for brother, Laurus headed for the wide staircase. However, at that moment when the lawyer's leg had already touched the first oak step, a videophone sounded appealingly in the hall of the first floor. Fyodor Pavlovich turned his head.

"Calm down, Laurel," said Essentuki with relief, checking with a matte screen. - Kostenky himself arrived. Getting out of the taxi ...

- Thank God. - Lavrikov noisily released air from the lungs. - Kill the blockhead! - And then, gazing at his guard, he added weightily: - Not a sound to him!

Brothers intelligently shook their huge heads. The authority, having lost all interest in them, overcame a ladder flight and disappeared on the second floor of the mansion. The son should not have seen him in such an agitated state. In addition, despite the successful outcome, Laurus has not yet fully calmed down. A middle-aged age already made itself felt.

Chapter 12

Already almost in the region of midnight the silence of the Lavrovsky mansion ruthlessly broke the musical explosion. Fyodor Pavlovich, alarmed, jumped out of his own office and almost face to face ran into Alexander Moshkin, who had run up the stairs to the second floor. Sancho was already in his underpants, over which his imposing belly was pictured hanging. In the eyes of the governor, there was frank anxiety. He tried to understand what anxiety was in the mansion, but he could not.

- What is this? He shouted, shouting over the music.

- I do not know! - in the same key Laurel proclaimed. It seemed to him that he didn't even clearly hear his own voice. - It seems music!

"This is yours!" Moshkin oriented himself in the situation, nodding at the closed door of the Fedechino office.

- So what? - The authority also managed to determine the source of concern and hurried to change the topic of conversation: - Where are the medications? Why don't you give me supplements for the second day? - Lavrikov attacked his colleague. - Not from anything!

- In such conditions it is impossible to work! - continued shouting Sancho. - Without aunt, we can not cope with it!

- Carry pudding! - cut off his talkativeness Laurel. - I want to pudding!

And then, without going into further discussions with Alexander, Fyodor Pavlovich pushed the door to his son's apartment with his shoulder. Moshkin just shook his head and, muttering something under his breath, trudged back to the first floor, tucking his belly into the family panties as he went.

Rozgin sat straight on the floor, cross-legged in Turkish, and swayed gently in the heavy rhythms of the music. The young man's eyes were closed, reality receded into the background. Usually this condition was usually characterized by the term "nirvana". It was in her now that Fedechka was staying. Thus the guy got rid of the troubles of the past day. The council in the house of Laurus and the date with Nata were deposited on the soul by negative sediment.

- Fedechka! - that there is strength Laurus cried out, but the power of his lungs was clearly not enough to drown out the rumble of music in the room.

Rozgin did not respond to the call. Fyodor Pavlovich, irritably, stepped up to the equipment and, after several unsuccessful attempts to turn down the volume, quickly pulled out all the plugs one by one. Chaotic blows to the head instantly ceased, and the office fell into silence. Surely all the inhabitants of the mansion at this moment breathed easier. Fedechka opened his eyes and looked at the boss with displeasure. Laurel, on the contrary, tried to portray a tender smile on his face, but instead on the lips of the authority there appeared a certain painful grimace, as if he had fallen into a dental chair.

- Fedechka ...
- It was possible to ask to make it quieter, - the guy discontentedly interrupted his appeal, without bothering to get up on his feet.

"I asked," admitted Fyodor Pavlovich.
- Is it? Sorry, did not hear.
- No wonder.
Fedech chuckled loudly.
- I just downloaded the very last thing, the Black House group. How do you?
- What? .. - did not catch the meaning of Lavrikov.
- Thing.
The authority looked around in confusion, and only a moment later realized that the interlocutor was talking to him about the music.

"The thing is cool," he reacted sluggishly. - Takes a soul. - Laurel approached Fedechku sitting on the floor. - Maybe you will get up all the same, when the senior talks to you?
- What for? - casually threw the young man.
"We didn't agree to beat each other's nerves," the thief in law reminded the guy patiently.
- Did not agree. And you start. - Rozgin with a smile on his lips sustained a short pause. - And I'm waiting for the dismissal.

Laurel swallowed nervously. It was easy to understand the course of Fedechnik thoughts. The young man deliberately sought conflict. Authority quietly gritted his teeth, but he restrained himself.
- What time did you get home? - He asked sternly, changing the subject.

"First, not home, but to the service," Rozgin remarked sarcastically, tucking his legs under himself. Despite the request of the chief, he was not going to take an upright position of the body. - Secondly, about ten o'clock. Agree, baby time.

- But I was worried! - unexpectedly for himself admitted Lavrikov.
- Drink a sedative.
- No, that won't do!
"Wait a minute," Fedech frowned in displeasure, gazing at the legendary lawyer from bottom to top. - Why are you trying to limit my freedom?
- You are free?
Fyodor Pavlovich caught himself thinking that it was becoming harder and harder for him to contain emotions that were raging inside. Due to the temperuous nature of his character, Laurus involuntarily began to boil. In the voice he was hitting the metal, his eyes narrowed unkindly.
"I," answered Rozgin proudly.
"You are a small, beggar, naked man," said auto- attitude scornfully , and his words sounded like a peremptory diagnosis. - Which totally depends on the circumstances!
"I," repeated the young man, no longer so confidently. - Circumstances, of course, not so hot, but ...
Lavr waved his hand in protest, and the guy stopped short.
- These circumstances are created by me! "The words flew away from the authority's teeth and seemed to cut the space in the small programmer's office. - I am truly free in decisions - to make you a big man or to leave on the porch! Got it ?!
The reaction of the interlocutor was not at all what Lavrikov expected to see. Fedechka threw back his head and laughed loudly.
- You are free? - he squeezed through laughter.
- Stop laughing! - abruptly cut off his thief in law.
But the boy was already rolling on the floor, holding the belly that was shaking with laughter with both hands. Fundechki fun was genuine. Or is he so seriously aiming to bring the employer out of himself and to achieve the desired dismissal from him.
- Oh, I can not! - he screamed. - Free! .. All in chains, all in locks, like the ancient magician Houdini! Just can not get out! Free!..
The cup of Fyodor Pavlovich's patience is overflowing. He himself would have been glad to contain his anger, but he failed. Blood struck the head of authority. Laurel all reddened, swiftly stepped forward and with a sweep hit the guy's foot under the ribs.
- Shut up! - The second hit followed the first strike, then the third.
- Shut up! ..

And only a second later, Lavrikov realized what was happening to him. Frightened, he stepped back and closed his eyes. At that moment it was difficult to say which of them experienced great pain. Father or son.

The laughter of the young man broke off, and the eyes of the opponents met. For a moment it seemed to the guy that tears glistened in the eyes of the crime boss. Lavrikov threw up his hand and rubbed his nose intensively with his fingers. After that, he massaged himself and whiskey. He diligently returned to the harsh reality. Fedechka took a sitting position on the floor and silently studied the boss. Laurel mentally swagged himself with the very last words.

- Sorry, - overcoming shortness of breath, he said quietly. - But - got ... Too much ... you talk cruelly.

The justification for the perfect deed was thin, but at that moment Laurus could not find a better one.

"And you are cruel," Rozgin frowned, frowning.

- I did not want.

"It happens," the young man generously forgave him, and even somehow sadly shrugged his shoulders. - We did not succeed in cooperation. It is my fault. He provoked. And now wash off.

Fedechka attempted to rise from the floor, but Laurus, who approached him, heavily laid a lean hand on the guy's shoulder.

- Nobody drives you.

However, it turned out that the generosity and humility of the guy were in reality only feigned. The young man harbored a stone in his bosom, and as soon as Lavrikov again touched him, Rozgin showed his sharp teeth to his interlocutor. He energetically threw off Fyodor Pavlovich's hand and confidently rose to his feet. The guy's nostrils flared furiously.

"No one gave you the right to spy on any stupid ones," he said harshly. - And you also have no right to crush me with your feet - whether you wanted to or not.

- There is a right! - Laurel could not stand it, feeling that it was still an instant, and he would lose his newly found son irrevocably. In the voice of authority appeared undisguised panic.

- What is a fig? - angrily grinned Rozgin.

He pushed Fyodor Pavlovich with his hand and headed for the exit. Man's palm resolutely lay down on the door handle. Laurel turned impetuously. His despair was utter.

- From such that I am your father! - He blurted out in one breath.

Seconds of ten or even more, the thief in law contemplated the still back of the descendant. Fedech froze on the spot, and not having time to open the door. However, Laurus did not see his face.

Finally, the young man turned slowly, and his right eyebrow arched in relief in amazement. He looked incredulously at Lavrikov from head to toe and squinted suspiciously.

- What? - Rozgin asked, believing that he misheard.

Laurel frankly embarrassed. Honestly, he often thought about the moment when he would have to open up in front of his son, but he never knew how to do it. And then suddenly that's how it happened! Unplanned, spontaneous. In addition, after involuntary physical violence. But the authorities had nowhere to retreat. As you know, the word is not a sparrow ...

- I'm your dad. - A silly smile appeared on his face, but Lavrikov hurried to hide it with a downcast look. - So it happened ... I found out late and ... Do not hesitate. Genetic analysis of all confirmed. Ninety nine and a million hundredths of a percent ...

- Dad? - Fedechka was also confused and shocked.

- Yeah. I have a certificate.

- In the pancake. - The young man briefly ran a hand through his shaggy hair.

- What does "damn"? - in sincere indignation cried Fyodor Pavlovich. - Or mother, as expected, or not at all mother! "Pancake" is a substitute!

- And you - daddy? - Leave the office Rozhinu already got sick. On the contrary, he mechanically dropped the body into a leather chair with curved legs, located next to the entrance door. - Daddy. Argentine TV series.

- Yes, even the Brazilian! - Confusion and embarrassment offspring cheered Lavrikova. He has already spoken more confidently and bitingly. - The fact remains. So, I have rights and even obligations not only to take care of you, but, if necessary, to give it in the neck.

- It's late. - Fedechka looked up at him, obviously interested, and his father could not help noticing it. - A child is formed up to three to five years.

"It's never too late to re-educate," expertly declared authority.

- Pere ... Pere ... - means to change. And what can you offer me to re-educate?

The question for a moment took Fedor Pavlovich off guard. But after a moment, he resolutely put his hand around him.

- At least it. Tip of the iceberg.

- With swimming pool? - clarified the young man.

- With swimming pool.

- Thank you, of course, Dad. - Fedech smiled tightly. - But - do not.

- Why?

- That's not mine. Alien. Even worse! This is a movie, for sure! You ... - The guy stumbled. - You live in a fictional movie. Not real everything, do not you feel? The virtual reality.

- God forbid everyone such a reality! - Laurel majestically threw up a sharp chin and straightened.

- God forbid! - did not agree with him Rozgin. - The film ends or breaks, the amount of electronic memory is also not dimensionless. Or just enough electricity cut down. Will close somewhere and - there is nothing. Posting something on snot.

- I do not understand! - frowned authority. - You're just being clever! If this is not real, then what?

- That will be.

- Soon?

Fedechka shook his head.

- Not. After forty years. When I hit as much as you now. When I build something of my own. From the foundation. On a clean wasteland, and not on rusty fragments with the corpses of "bulls".

- Beautiful chatter, Fedor! - condescendingly smiled Lavrikov, but something inside him stirred.

- I regret…

- Is that all you can say?

- Do you need to burst into tears and fall to your gray hairy chest? - The guy has already recovered from the first shock, caused by the confession of the benefactor, and sprung to his feet, pushing his hands off the leather armrests of the chair.

- No, well, I'm opening up to you, that I am your father! - again blurted out and got nervous Laurel. - You are my son! What about you? No intimate emotions! The virtual reality!

"Then explain how you should respond sincerely," the young man grinned in reply. - Who pays, that orders ... Explain, I will try!

Instead of answering such a mischievous sentence of his son, Fyodor Pavlovich merely spread his hands helplessly and said in a whisper, turning more to himself than to a direct descendant:

- Ha! Here is the next one! .. Cynicism, Internet, files ...

"Speaking of files," Rozgin interrupted his complaints. "Since you are my father, then I must, in a kindred relationship, slip another bitter pill as a farewell.

He resolutely walked over to his desk and began vigorously digging into a stack of freshly printed sheets of paper.

"Go ahead," said Lavrikov indifferently. - By bitterness is no stranger.

"All your secret information on all transactions is automatically overtaken by e-mail," said Fedechka.

"Electronics again ..." the authority mechanically groaned, but the next second, realizing what was going on, the whole crept up and also approached the computer table. - To whom?

- I do not know. Here is the telephone address. - The boy finally found the necessary sheet and just put it in the hands of Lavr, frozen to the right, - The hidden program was revealed on the hard disk.

The eminent kingpin did not have time to clarify anything in his son. The snow-white door to the programmer's office opened without knocking, and on the threshold appeared Moshkin, already dressed in trousers and a chewed T-shirt.

- Pudding is served, sir! He mocked, mocking the English butler.

Perhaps at another time and under other circumstances, Fyodor Pavlovich would have attacked his comrade-in-arms with complaints. And not so much because of the caustic tone, but because of the tactless invasion of the son's apartment. But now was a completely different case.

- Sancho! - Lavrikov stepped forward to meet Alexander and put a piece of paper received a few seconds from Rozin on a tray with pudding. - Bullet find out whose number it is!

Sancho squinted his eyes.

"I already know," he said.

- Whose?

- Home Dowels.

Lavrikov turned as pale as a sheet. He turned back to Fedechka and asked sternly:

- Who could lay such a thing?

He shrugged carelessly:

- Only the one who knew the access password. A lot of people, probably?

"Only one, except for you and me," the crime boss said thoughtfully, and his face lit up with a wry grin that offered no good. Even Rozgin easily caught this change, even though he knew Laurus for several days. "Cut in your last thing, Fedechka." In full, - hemmed a thief in law. - And I'll leave.

- Where? - anxiously threw a young man in his back when Fyodor Pavlovich moved energetically towards the exit.

"You have no right to restrict my freedom." - Laurel just turned his head over his shoulder. - Father to son is not responsible.

"I haven't required an answer yet ..."

"You asked where."

Their gazes crossed for a moment, and in Fedechka's voice suddenly something completely sincere was grunting, without its inherent bravado.

- Do not, maybe absent? Late. Spit.

- I can not - honestly admitted a major crime boss. - When they spit at me ... Even virtually. - Lavrikov guiltily spread his hands.

- As agreed. - Dowel's sleek hand with well-groomed nails emerged from the cabin of a foreign car and casually handed Hamlet a plump postal envelope with the image of an aircraft carrier.

The next meeting of the financial adviser Laurus with the leader of the rival grouping took place at the same place as the previous one. This initiative came from Dowel. He thought that changing the rendezvous point was a bad omen. Hamlet implicitly agreed with this uncomplicated argument, not wanting to contradict the quick-tempered and quick to punish the young authority.

Having opened the envelope, the Caucasian stuck his brisk, thin fingers into it and energetically began to rustle with new notes. The Shakespeare's hero's namesake was able to count the money quickly. And he loved. Sum arranged a corrupt laurel ally. He nodded in satisfaction and, without further ado, fished out of the inside pocket of his jacket, an almost identical envelope, but with a different pattern. He wore an extravagant blonde in a red bikini.

"Copies of the analyzes," Hamlet informed the counterpart, hidden from his direct gaze, and the envelope gently dropped into the open palm of the Dowel hanging over the side window of the car. "Show this genetic stolnik to the hungry lab technician, but she will confirm it in all details."

Caucasian literally glowed with happiness and tearing his pride. Still would! Dig a bomb that could kill the Laurus in a matter of seconds! The ultimate dream of any informer. Correspondence disappeared in the depths of foreign cars, and Dubel finally deigned to put on display the interlocutor his oval face with a nagging antenna.

"The steward is much cheaper than full-scale hostilities," he said, openly looking at the brown eyes of the Caucasian. - And destructive. But with Laurel paper is not needed. Just enough to know.

The dowel grinned crookedly and in the next instant turned the key in the ignition lock. His silver car resolutely drove off.

The money received from Dowel as a reward for the slaughter of slaughter on Laurus, allowed Hamlet not only to come to a great mood, but also to have a hearty dinner in one of the most fashionable restaurants in the capital. An unpleasant aftertaste, formed on the soul of an economic consultant after the morning council, evaporated irretrievably.

Now Hamlet did not feel resentment or anger towards the arrogant youngster, who turned out to be the son of a distinguished thief in law. He did not feel anything like it and to Lavrikov himself, who put him very harshly in place with outsiders. Now Caucasians all this seemed far from essential. Being a man more or less versed in the laws of the thieves, Hamlet knew perfectly well what the genetic analysis threatened for Laurus. The dowel will not miss such a colossal chance to press a competitor to the nail. Fyodor Pavlovich, on his own initiative, dug his own grave. So it was a sin to complain about anyone.

Hamlet, whistling an unpretentious little motive under his nose, confidently drove the car into a spacious garage, located two steps away from his house, and, adjusting the tight knot of his tie under the snow-white collar of his shirt, headed for the entrance. It cannot be said that the native of the sunny country felt safe. On the contrary, since Hamlet began to play a double game, he feared every suspicious rustle. I tried all the time to be alert and fully aware of how severe and brutal the Laurus massacre would be, he would learn about the secret games of his adviser.

The Caucasian put a cigarette in his mouth, looking around, walked into the porch and took off the fourth floor with a bullet. Only here he was able to completely calm down and take a breath. The musical lighter clicked, and Hamlet burnt the tip of a cigarette stuck to the lower lip, smiled happily. An armored door with a complex system of built-in locks has always instilled in him confidence in one hundred percent inaccessibility. Having dealt with cunning constipation, the Caucasian entered the apartment. Throwing off his fashionable shoes and unbuttoning his jacket, he stalked into a spacious, richly furnished living room.

Hamlet was already tipsy, having pleased his body with a glass of favorite wine, but by the time he returned to the legal home of this dose, it seemed to him not enough. But in the built-in bar of the Lavrovsky financial adviser there was always a bottle of Georgian wine, which was once approved by Joseph Stalin himself. Here it was worth it now.

The bar flung open and blinded Hamlet's cigarette rolling in his teeth with bright lights. The hand resolutely reached for the matte bottle of red wine, but the fingers barely caught it by the narrow neck, just as another Caucasian source of illumination flashed behind the Caucasian's back — a crystal chandelier under the ceiling. Hamlet flinched, the bottle slipped out and, unable to resist on the shelf, splashed onto the floor. The owner of the apartment abruptly turned back.

The brown eyes of the burning dark man fixed what they were most afraid of at the moment. On an elegant low couch color safari side by side Laurel and Sancho are located. Two steps away from them, beside the wall switch, Essentuki stood grinning. Hamlet swallowed frantically, who was running into his throat, wanted to say something like a friendly greeting, but could not. The language, treacherously stiffened in the mouth, did not want to move. Intuition and a sense of self-preservation suggested to Hamlet that the strange visit of the crime boss with two assistants was by no means accidental.

Laurel slowly rose from the couch and took off his snow-white jacket.

- Hamlet, have you heard about Yorick by any chance? - Fedor Pavlovich sang gently.

- No, why? - Hamlet's voice trembled, and all his attempts to control himself were shattered into dust. - Who is Yorick? I do not know him!

Laurel grinned:

- It is bad not to know the classics. This skull was like that. His name was Yorick.

- Skull? - The Caucasian swallowed again and wiped small drops of sweat on his forehead with his palm. - And you visit, guys, yes?

"It's not time for guests," Yessentuki said, pushing off the wall with massive shoulders and approaching the interlocutor like a huge locomotive. - We - chat. For the economy.

Hamlet automatically backed away, but his back rather quickly met the open door of the bar. At this second, the economy consultant felt a cornered beast. There was nowhere to retreat. Lavrikov with a gloomy expression on his face hung his fashionable jacket on the back of a high chair and pointedly snapped his fingers. Caught look Caucasians moved in the direction of Sancho, but Moshkin only painfully threw up his hands. Say, he is to blame.

Essentuki has already come close to the intended victim.

"You have a stain on your shirt," said Fedech quietly, looking down at Lavrikov. - Blood.

Fyodor Pavlovich raised his head and met his eyes with his son standing on the topmost step of the oak staircase. The mansion was already plunged into complete darkness, and even the night that stood out without a moonless night did not allow any lighting from outside to enter the room. The wall clock, breaking the deathly silence, beat off two hours in the morning. Laurel looked tired and exhausted. Rozgin was able to determine this even by his walk. Hard walking middle-aged man. This time, the guy himself had to worry. For all the time of lack of authority and two of his assistants, Fedechka did not for a moment leave his observation post near the window in the hall of the second floor. He was able to breathe a sigh of relief only when he saw the old "Seagull" approaching the mansion. The first came out of the cabin Essentuki and springy gait headed for the garage. Sancho appeared behind him.

The thief in law did not immediately notice the young man who blocked his way. Moreover, in complete darkness, he first heard his voice and only after that he guessed the boyish outlines. He smiled at his son. Fedechka went down a couple of steps and pointed to Lavrikov with a finger at the brown spot he was talking about. Authority squinted eyes. As Rozgin noticed this evidence of a crime committed in the dark about a staircase about half an hour ago, it remained a complete mystery to Laurus. Or did the son assume that the blood should have stayed somewhere? Intuitively?

"Ah, this ..." The thief in law smiled tightly. He was already on his feet after the eventful day. - Mosquito stuck. I slammed him ... In the dry cleaners wash. Trivia ...

There was a tense pause between father and son for three minutes. Fedechka dropped his head on his chest and shook it from side to side.

"No ..." he said sadly. - In the morning I will return to my aunt. So it will be better.

Without adding another word to what was said, he turned and quickly ran up the stairs. Laurel did not catch up with him or hail him. The feelings that gripped the young man were quite clear to him. The criminal authority slowly rose to the very top of the stairs and sank down on it, clasped his head in his hands, running his fingers deep into his gray hair.

Chapter 13

Having thrown his scarce belongings into a sports canvas bag with dirty white stripes across, Fedech resolutely fastened the zipper, threw the bag over his shoulder, and once again took a long, sad look at his office in the Lavrovsky mansion. At heart the guy was a chore. What is there to say? He clearly did not want to part with all of the equipment proposed for his full use of the equipment. Another such chance in life is unlikely to be presented to him. Yes, and the found father played in his mind not the last role. Oddly enough, but Lavr managed to firmly establish himself in the soul and heart of the young man. However, because of him, Fedechka was leaving the mansion now. He really believed that without him Fedor Pavlovich would have far fewer problems. They have different lives, different worlds, different priorities. And nothing can be done. So fate decreed.

Rozgin sighed heavily and headed for the door. Trying to make as little noise as possible, he slipped out of the office into a common hall. Somewhere below, on the first floor of the building, the morning silence was broken by a shrill phone call. Fedechka checked his wristwatch. Quarter to six. According to his calculations, both Laurus and his loyal Sanchoosche were obliged to rest peacefully. The guy was hoping to leave the mansion unnoticed. An additional meeting with the father would have caused even more confusion in his soul. And for the execution of the decision, the young man needed a maximum of decisiveness and firm will.

However, the fate of the villain again itch to dispose of a different way and throw the boy a new test. As soon as Rozgin came downstairs and only half crossed the spacious hall hung with numerous paintings, one of the side doors swung open and half-naked Moshkin jumped out into the open space. Alexandra's little eyes were running restlessly from side to side, sparse hair on a pumpkin-like head was sticking out in different directions, a carelessly tucked T-shirt peeking out from under the panties.

- Fire? - Rozgin asked him anxiously when his gaze met in space with the agitated gaze of Sancho.

- Worse. - In the voice of the manager slipped frank condemnation. Moshkin himself did not want this, but it happened. - At ten gathering appointed. Extraordinary. Your name is ... ”He shook his head vaguely toward the broad staircase.

- Yes, I'm leaving! - Fedech burst into hysterical cry, and uninvited tears appeared in his eyes. - I'm leaving! Live as you lived!

"Sorry," said a calm, monotonous voice from above. - How we lived will not work ...

Sancho and Fedechka turned at the same time and looked up. Fyodor Pavlovich stood majestically on the uppermost step. His face was drawn and sleepy. Blue bags appeared under his eyes, his cheeks and forehead were paler than usual. The authority took off his silk robe and tightened his belt more tightly.

- Now I can not pretend that you do not exist. - Laurus open eyes were fixed directly on his son.

Rozgin quickly turned away, hiding his eyes wet with tears, stepped impetuously to the threshold and cried out with anguish in his voice, turning to the duty clerk in a tuxedo and bow tie:

- Unlock the door! Rather!

He unquestioningly obeyed, unlocked the lock and stepped aside, passing the young man. No one stopped Fedechka, no one began to contradict him. Lavrikov only gloomily watched his son's back disappear behind a massive door. He silently stepped one step down, then another one, swung and, in order to maintain his balance, clutched at the railing with his fingers. Agitated by what is happening, Sancho approached the boss.

- Breakfast serve? He asked, breaking the lingering pause.

- And how? - Laurel forced himself to smile. - Of course! Today is oatmeal or semolina?

- What would you like?

"Pork on charcoal," the authority honestly admitted.

- It is impossible. - Sancho guiltily shrugged.

- I know.

Laurel winked at his comrade-in-arms and patted him on the rounded shoulder in a friendly way. However, experienced in such matters Sancho could not help noticing the sadness in the blue eyes of the eminent thief. That is just to speak out about this inappropriate.

At ten o'clock in the morning in the semi-basement, dimly lit room of the restaurant "Alexander Nevsky" gathered about fifteen people. All these people of different ages, apparently different in their appearance from each other, belonged to the same social class. Thieves in law. Recognized authorities who received their crown for those or other services to the thieves' community. At their meetings, they had the right to jointly take important and sometimes fateful decisions.

On the long table covered with a white tablecloth, there was nothing but ashtrays. When discussing business matters, lawyers adhered to strict rules: no alcohol and no food. All this was intended for the second, unofficial part of the gathering, and only when the authorities reached the necessary consensus during the discussions.

At the head of the table was the presiding, intelligent elderly man in wide glasses, with a cigar clamped in his mouth. He was dressed in a strict dark blue suit, a white shirt and a solid bronze tie. On the finger of the right hand there is exactly the same massive golden signet as that of the Laurus, located on the right hand of the presiding person.

Next to Fyodor Pavlovich, dressed in a chic white suit, sat loyal Sancho, on the occasion of the gathering, also deigned to squeeze his overweight body into a jacket and ironed trousers with arrows. Moshkin frowned at everyone present, and especially at the Dowel sitting on the opposite side of the table. There was no victorious expression on the face of the competitor. The gathering that lasted for about half an hour did not go at all in the way that the young authority expected. Events turned in such a way that the Lavr, so successfully hooked by the Dowel to the hook, was ready to break at any moment. And only because everyone present treated Fyodor Pavlovich with great respect. Dubel was ready to bite his elbows with annoyance. If you could, of course.

Laurel did not take the word, waiting for the moment when he was asked about it, and during the lengthy debate he was busy only with looking at his thief's sign with interest, with the air that he saw it for the first time in his life.

"We all know well the merits of esteemed Laurus in front of society," the presiding judge spoke loudly and with great pressure in a pleasant baritone, shrouding in bluish clouds of cigar smoke. - We know how scrupulous, even to the detriment of himself, Laurus relates to the mutual aid fund, to the observance of all norms, rules and laws. It can not be perceived otherwise than as a person of the highest, standard sample ...

Those present in the restaurant nodded approvingly, agreeing with the arguments of the speaker.

"Therefore, I propose," continued the authority with a thick cigar in his teeth, after sustaining a short but weighty pause. "To cool the heat of the dowel, to put it in appearance ... it is ..." he hesitated for a moment, looking for a suitable expression, "the rudeness of his behavior."

Again, a rumble of approval rolled over the table, which made Dowel unpleasantly ache somewhere below the belly. He frowned involuntarily, and his trembling hand reached for the printed pack of cigarettes. Competitor Lavrikov fished out one cigarette and put it in his mouth. He flicked the lighter, inhaled.

- I have not done anything yet! - He did not speak very confidently in his defense.

- And do not do anything. "The chairman's bushy eyebrows, with only half hidden glasses, came sternly to the bridge of the nose. "We all need order and stability like air!" But ... - he released another club of gray smoke from his mouth, - Laurus, just as the standard of a lawyer, must answer one question. Do not even answer us, my friends, but to myself ...

Having coughed dryly into a fist, the presiding judge slowly turned his gaze to Lavrikov, who was sitting on the right, and without any pathos or mock grandeur turned to the respected lawyer, as to his good old friend:

- Fedor Palych, you have a family. Child. A son...

Laurel looked up at the interlocutor, from that cold gaze he felt very uncomfortable.

- I got the information here. You, Fedya, justify somehow. Well, at the worst, do not live together promise. Anything can happen, I understand. Other times you will not follow ... - The presiding judge smiled guiltily. - A simple promise in your mouth will be quite enough. Right?

His last question was addressed to all those present in the hall, and the authorities nodded again, like Chinese idols. Say, who is not without sin. Not only did they spawn descendants of the world for their reckless life in this regard. The main thing is different. Do not admit the fact legally. Sancho squinted at his boss, but he still did not react to everything that happened at the gathering. Lavrikov, for some incomprehensible comrade-in-arms, kept complete silence.

- Well, Laurel! - In the chairman's voice, impatient and slightly irritated intonations appeared. - The matter is purely formal. The views are liberal, tolerable. There is a child, and God be with him. Let him live. Promise only that you will not legally recognize anyone. And - everything! - A half-reputable authority cigar vigorously poked into the ashtray's crystal bottom and broke. A thin wisp of smoke from the smoldering cigarette butt rose to the ceiling and dissolved in a dim space. - Closed question. Otherwise, because the crown will have to be removed ... Foo! - the thief in law twisted. "I said it, even to the wildest one! .. And Dubel ..." - A scorching gaze pierced the young lawyer through and through. - If you rypnes once again - you unscrew the head with the whole team, you understand?

Dubel was ready to fall through the ground. It was necessary to rude so rude. At that moment, he hated Lavrikov more than ever. However, the dude had no choice but to agree as to nod in a sign that he understood everything perfectly and was aware of his own short-sightedness.

- Come on, Fedya! - the chairman once again addressed Fedor Pavlovich. - We are delaying ourselves.

A smile touched Laurus's lips. For the first time ever, he looked up at the crowd and peered closely at their benevolently-minded faces.

"No," he said simply and blithely. - I will not promise anything.

Sancho gritted his teeth. He was not afraid of anything in life more than such non-standard behavior on the part of the boss. But intuitively Moshkin assumed just such a turn of events at the gathering. Unpleasant expectations and forecasts were fully justified.

- Why? - The chairman raised his eyebrows in surprise.

There was a tense silence over the table, and the views of all the authorities gathered in the restaurant were fixed on Lavrikov. The tobacco smoke hanging in the basement room made the atmosphere even more gloomy and oppressive. The thief in law, who today performed the functions of the leader and organizer of the gathering, even pulled his big horn-rimmed glasses off the bridge of his nose and intensively rubbed his eyelids with his fingers.

Laurel leaned back in his chair, and stretched out his hands in front of him, covering his hands with the table-top taken from the tablecloth. The smile of authority has become even wider and more benevolent than a couple of minutes ago.

- Because. - He noisily released air from the lungs. - Crown - from people. The child is from God. The question is really closed. - Fyodor Pavlovich with both hands pushed off from the table and rose to his full height. - We will not delay ourselves, gentlemen.

Lounging in the backseat of the Seagull, Laurel stared at the side window of the cabin with a blind eye. At the moment, there was not a single thought in the head of the authority. He could not even fully concentrate on the landscape that was sweeping past. The fingers of his left hand still mechanically turned the golden signet with a nominal monogram. Finally, Laurel pulled it off and, slightly leaning forward, lowered the glass to his right. The hand briefly swung, and an expensive piece of jewelry flew to the sidewalk. Not a shade of regret flashed across the face of the recent thief in law. If now he did not have a crown, then why keep the other attributes of the former authority? The glass returned to its original place, and Fyodor Pavlovich leaned back again. His gaze smoothly shifted to the volume nape of Moshkin, who was sitting behind the wheel.

Immediately after the fateful for Lavrikov meeting in "Alexander Nevsky" and the decision taken by the thieves, Essentuki left the owner who had fallen into disfavor. However, just like everyone else. With the exception of the faithful Lavra to the grave Sancho. Yesterday's lawyer did not condemn his old hangers-on for this ugly and treacherous act. Deep down, he even understood them. To be close to the disgrace meant only one thing in a short time: to disfavor himself. In thieves' circles such reckless self-sacrifice was not welcomed. Yes, no one went to him consciously.

"I am giving way to my sister, to Dedovsk," Alexander finally broke the silence, squinting at the face of Laurus in the rear-view mirror. - I built a house for them on the very outskirts. But there is a lot of land, a garden, a bathhouse. Nephews there, grandnephews. A whole bunch of spin-eats, and the sister didn't have to interrogate anyone. So I will ... - Sancho stopped short, noting that his boss was not listening at all. Do not even delve into the meaning of the words uttered by a colleague. - Laurel!

- BUT?

The hail of Moshkin pulled Fedor Pavlovich out of a state of prostration, into which he himself plunged a few minutes ago. What the former criminal authority was thinking all this time for Sancho remained a mystery, but he sincerely hoped to find out the course of these thoughts from Laurus. For this purpose, a conversation was started about a house in the village. In fact, Alexander did not even think about leaving the host, whom he served all these long years faithfully. The prospect of starting your own independent life in the same Dedovsk or somewhere else still looked very tempting and alternative. But Sancho would not be Sancho, venturing on such a life step. He was well aware that Lavrikov would not last long without him. Will be bent either from self-blame or from an ulcer. Who, if not Moshkin, will watch that

The answer was obvious. No one.

- You are not offended? - Alexander squinted slyly, noting for himself the fact that Laurus does not see the expression on his face.

Sancho frankly izgalyatsya over the interlocutor. Say, when will you, damn stubborn, start asking me to stay? The manager of the party intends to verbally recoup on Lavrikov for all his past offenses. When exactly the boss offended him and what, Sancho now did not remember, but reasonably assumed that such incidents took place.

But Laurus was not the same person to beg someone for leniency. He only with difficulty suppressed a heavy sigh, tearing from his chest, and with deliberate indifference he shrugged his lean shoulders.

- Why on earth, Sancho? - he threw as indifferently as possible and even adjoined his eyelids. - All - as expected. The garden is good. And grandchildren - well ...

Involuntarily in his brain yesterday's conversation with his son and the summary rendered by Fedechka resurfaced.

"This is not a movie," added Laurus with a grin.

Moshkin again gazed in surprise in the rearview mirror, trying to understand what this last saying of Lavrikov is related to, but he did not even think about explaining his words. Sancho didn't have time to ask any questions. The "Seagull" managed by him already smoothly rolled up to the territory of a country mansion and habitually stopped near the steel gates. Moshkin resolutely pressed the horn button, but no one responded from the opposite side of the fence. Complete silence.

- We ran away ... - the manager stepped peevishly and with anger gave a characteristic suitable for former colleagues: - Rats!

Laurel just smiled. Sancho's resentment on this issue best of all indicated that he did not intend to attribute himself to the same category of rodents. Hence, it remains with Fedor Pavlovich. It is not known, however, as anyone. Alexander, unaware that his insidious game was so easily and quickly turned open, puffing heavily, got out of the cabin and went to open the steel gates himself.

Laurel also got out of the car, stretching his sore limbs, with a full breast breathed in the country air.

The two-storey country mansion met the owner with oppressive emptiness. Laurel stopped in the center of a huge lower hall and looked around in confusion. Even the pictures hung on the walls seemed too dark to him today. The back of yesterday's authority unwittingly tilted forward, which made Fyodor Pavlovich look like a slouching old man, broken by some sort of serious illness. At that moment he could not even decide what to do next. Either go to the second floor and occupy a wide bed in the bedroom, or arrange a tête-à-tête late breakfast with the faithful Sancho, or ... Laurel has lost the most important thing for himself. Life incentive. Although it could be a temporary phenomenon.

And here, quite unexpectedly, the silence of the mansion was broken by the sound of pouring water somewhere to the right of Lavrikova's hall that had stopped in the center, and then the authority who had fallen into disfavor heard how a bucket rang in the same direction. Surprised eyes Laurel buried in a closed door pantry. For only a few seconds, he reflected on how he should enter, and then resolutely moved in the necessary direction and pushed the door with his foot.

Near the sink, bent in an indecent pose, stood Claudia. She was located with her back to the exit and carefully pressed a rag above the bucket. Without changing her posture, the woman slowly turned her head and noticed Fyodor Pavlovich entering the doorway. Only after that she took a vertical position and smiled good-naturedly. The wet rag was still in her broad callused arm.

- Alive? - Klava squinted slyly. - And then Fedechka said - they can kill.

Laurel blinked in confusion, naively believing that he had developed hallucinations as a result of negative events.

- Nonsense what. - Fyodor Pavlovich vaguely shrugged his shoulders, so far not fully permeating the topic of the conversation proposed by Claudius. "You ... what are you doing here?"

"I'm cleaning up," the woman replied casually in such a tone as if it was a matter of something taken for granted. - The center seems to be clean. And in the corners overgrown everything. Was it difficult to hire a cleaning lady? - she asked strictly Lavrikova.

"The men have vacuumed," he said, very sluggishly.

- It can be seen. Guys ...

Having lost all interest in Lavra, the woman returned to her interrupted occupation. With a few powerful movements, she squeezed the doormat to the end and, dropping down in the nakortochki near the buffet, proceeded to simple manipulations, as a result of which, in her opinion, the territory started by men was bound to become much cleaner.

- And where ... Fedya? - Laurel stepped towards the woman and bent over her disheveled hair.

"On the Internet, probably," replied Claudia, without turning around and not for an instant interrupting her sweeping gestures.

- Where? - Fyodor Pavlovich did not understand.

- There. - The index finger of Claudia's right hand rose up and stuck in the direction of the ceiling. - They have it called hang.

Greater Laurel and was not required. The very feeling that the son is here, in the house, inspired disgraced authority. He again had that lost meaning of life. Everything turned over in the soul of Lavrikov in an instant, and he, a bullet jumped out of the pantry, like a first grader who had sat at the desk, rushed to the stairs to the second floor. Moshkin, Fyodor Pavlovich, who had arisen on the way, only carelessly pushed aside with a lean hand, but he himself, fearing to be brought down by a distraught host, quickly went off to his side for his build. Leaping across two steps, Laurus rushed to meet his blood-related person.

Sancho, holding him with a sympathetic gaze, turned his head into the open door of the pantry and stopped himself as paralyzed. The woman of his dreams, who had already moved towards the window, looked even more beautiful and appetizing in the rays of the midday sun. In any case, it seemed to Alexander himself. He timidly stepped over the threshold and stopped two steps away from the object of his heart feelings. Claudia heard his heavy wheeze inherent in a person with chronic sinusitis, and turned around. Sancho smiled shyly.

"For some reason, I knew that there would be a happy ending in our opera," he ventured to speak, thus building new bridges in relations with a sultry woman.

Claudia frowned severely and gave Moshkin a long, searching look from head to toe. He automatically picked up his stomach and straightened.

"Well, how it will go on, don't guess," she cooled him off his Jujuan fervor.

However, Sancho interpreted these words quite differently. Like a saving straw thrown at him.

"If only there were" further, "he said wistfully, rolling his eyes to the ceiling.

Breathless from a quick run up the stairs, Laurus impetuously opened the door to Fedechka's office and with a happy smile of a not entirely normal person stood on the threshold. Rozgin turned around. In addition to the computer turned on, on the table in front of him stood a whole mountain of chocolates, and next to it there was a heap of crumpled candy wrappers about the same in volume. The guy's jaws were in intensive work and resembled a waste processing plant in miniature. The young man casually glanced into the agitated eyes of the owner of the mansion.

- I'm sorry. - He took his feet off the table and lowered them onto the fleecy carpet. - Klava downstairs found a whole box of "Southern Night". Well, I slept without asking ...

Laurel laughed good-naturedly and carelessly.

"Eat what this is about," he generously allowed, wiping away tears of happiness in his eyes. - Only sweet before dinner is bad.

"Lunch is not soon," Fedech's parent disappointed. - Aunt has not cooked. She cannot cook if the kitchen is not licked.

- Well, it is not necessary!

Fyodor Pavlovich casually waved his hand, while carefully studying every dash of the face of his offspring, for which, some two hours ago, he voluntarily resigned his thieves crown. But once Laurus so deliberately went to her, so proud of its receipt. This was all his life aspirations. And now priorities have suddenly changed. But the thief did not regret it.

"Do you want us to go somewhere?" And order something? - He suggested Rozginu.

- What?

- Yummy. And forbidden. - Laurel squinted slyly and just in case threw a wary glance behind his back. God forbid, Moshkin will hear it now. - The fact that I can not, and you - can not afford.

Fedechka reflected on the alternative for just a second. Then, springily, he threw his youthful body out of a comfortable chair on castors and rose to his feet. His eyes lit up purely boyish passion.

- And let's go! - he accepted the offer of the father.

Rozgin left his workplace in front of the monitor, not even bothering to exit any of the programs, and came very close to the Lavra. They openly smiled at each other, and then, like the most friendly family in the world, left the office side by side. Descending the stairs Lavrikov was no longer so vigorously, as before he had overcome the same space upwards. Fedech slightly overtook him and quickly slipped past the open door of the pantry. Fyodor Pavlovich did the same.

They went outside and stopped near the antediluvian car, the pride of the owner. From the open window of the first floor where the buffet room taken by Claudia on the boarding of sterility was located, came the operatic aria from the Italian classics. Laurel shook his head with a grin.

- Started a barrel organ ...

Then he opened the "Seagull" rear door before his son, and Rozgin climbed into the salon. Fyodor Pavlovich himself got behind the wheel. The key was already ready to roll in the ignition lock, as the unmasked lawyer slammed himself on the high forehead with annoyance.

- In the pancake! He said nervously.
- What does the "pancake"? - Fedek retorted on the move, bearing in mind his recent conversation with his parent. - "Damn" is a substitute!

"I don't know how to drive," Laurus confessed to him in a somewhat embarrassed way.

- And I. - The guy shrugged.
- what a shame! - Fyodor Pavlovich feverishly drummed his fingers on the car dashboard for a few seconds. - It is necessary Sancho ...

"No, Sancho," the youth sitting next to him protested. - The aunt is fascinated by him. Let them be fooled ...

- And how? .. - Lavrikov was frankly knocked out of a rut.

"We will get by taxi," Fedech expressed his idea and left the salon "The Seagulls" first.

Laurel got behind. Such a simple resolution of the situation would never have occurred to him. With the former abundance of vehicles and people capable of delivering authority to a necessary destination at any time, Fyodor Pavlovich managed to forget about the existence of such a service industry as a taxi. He still continued to live in the world of cinema, as Fedech expressed himself. But now it is time to get out of the dreams.

Rozgin resolutely strode to the steel gate and left the territory through the gate. Lavrikov relentlessly and without further altercations followed his son.

Romance fugitives did not even suspect that their sortie did not go unnoticed in the mansion. After completing the process of washing floors, passed under the lyric chords of Italian music, Claudia switched to the dishes. As soon as she took up a working position near the sink, Sancho approached the open window with a thoughtful expression on her face. An experienced gaze of a once-rampant raider almost immediately snatched the back of Laurus, which had disappeared in the alignment of a metal gate. Moshkin frowned and automatically pressed the "stop" button on the cassette at his fingertips. The melody was cut short at the climax itself.

- Where?! - Alexander muttered discontentedly, turning to himself. - Where are they carried?

Claudia interrupted her occupation and also approached the window sill. She looked out from behind Sancho's massive shoulder, but saw no one.

"Let them go for a walk," she said lightly. "They probably have something to talk about."

However, the words of the woman did not convince Moshkina at all. On the contrary, he frowned even more and, mechanically pulling out the tape from the tape recorder, carefully put it in the breast pocket of his shirt. A stylish jacket, in which Sancho sported a meeting at the thieves' Alexander Nevsky, was no longer on. There was no tie tight under the neck. All this at the moment was peacefully resting on the back of the kitchen chair with leather upholstery.

"I won't bother them," Sancho said, almost in a whisper. - But it's not a sin to look after. I'm sorry. Host here, and I ...

Moshkin moved toward the exit, but Claudia grabbed his wrist with her left hand.

- What for? - Her eyes expressed sincere misunderstanding.

"Well ..." Alexander hesitated and absurdly scratched his bald top with thick fingers. - There is a specificity, what you, Claudia, can not understand. As for me, these ... diffusion processes of rubber. We have our own rubber ... Do not be offended. "He smiled sweetly at the woman." - As soon as - so I'm right here. Agreed?

- I'm waiting. - Claudia let go of his hand and embarrassed lowered her eyes.

At that moment, Sancho thought that wings had cut through his back. It is not necessary to have seven genius in the forehead in order to understand, by the views and actions of a woman, how she relates to the other person. In this particular case, of course. Understood it and Moshkin. He felt that he not only loved, but loved. Inspired by such a discovery, he jogged out of the pantry, crossed the hall of the first floor and found himself on the street. Feet easily and naturally carried him to the garage. Sancho turned and sent an ardent kiss to Claudia. The woman did not answer him.

Chapter 14

For a family dinner, they chose a restaurant in the city center, with the beautiful and romantic name "Champs Elysees". Laurel generously paid off with a private trader who kindly threw them to the place and got out of the cabin. Fedechka was already waiting for him on the sidewalk, with admiration regarding a luxurious signboard that could cause an appetite even for the most captious person in this regard.

"Let's go inside or outside? ..," Fyodor Pavlovich addressed his son, nodding in the direction of several tables brought outside under the shed.

"It's better outside," Rozgin decided, and added with a smile: "How will it work in Paris ..."

Laurel nodded and slightly hugged his son by the shoulders. The soul mate who found each other, unfortunately, did not notice at this moment the events taking place around them.

Meanwhile, the private owner, whose services Fedech and his father used, retreated a few meters from the restaurant, stopped his car at the curb and fished out a mobile phone from his pocket, quickly and confidently ran his finger along the soft buttons, dialing the number. I waited for the connection.

"It's me ..." he said, addressing the invisible interlocutor. - No, not at home ... Yes, they gathered in the city under their own power, well, I oriented and drove ... "Champs Elysees." An hour will surely be. A table on the street ... If you turn right from Tverskoy, up from Mayakovka ... You know, yes? Well, frets.

The man's pockmarked face lit up with a happy smile, and he turned off his mobile phone with a sense of accomplishment and put it in his pocket. The motor purred smoothly, and the car slowly drove off.

At this very moment, an inconspicuous "Zhiguli" of green color, with a slightly wrinkled left wing, rolled into the parking lot opposite the restaurant. Behind the wheel of a Soviet car sat Sancho with a grim expression on his face. Moshkin did not go out of the cabin, he was already keeping well in sight of Lavrikov and Rozgin sitting under a canopy. He just lowered the windshield more and, leaning back in the unusually hard seat, pushed the audio tape sticking out of the radio tape recorder. The lights flashed rhythmically, after which the "Zhiguli" of the sixth model was filled with the sounds of the Italian opera aria.

The stooped waiter with a thin mustache line above his upper lip carefully placed a tray with ordered dishes on the table. Two pots with baked meat and tall glasses with fruit juice. Lavrikov happily rubbed his hands in anticipation. Sancho, who was watching Fedor Pavlovich from afar, shook his head and wanted to disrupt the process with his direct intervention, but changed his mind. One exception to the rule will not do much harm. And today, Lavr, in the opinion of the comrade in arms, could afford this exception. But only today.

"... So the laws did not arise out of nowhere, Fedya," continued yesterday's great authority, waiting for the slouching waiter to leave them alone with his son. - Not intentionally. Just in this country can not have loved ones. Having loved ones in this country, you become vulnerable, defenseless.

- Maybe the opposite? - the young man asked slyly, picking up a fork from the table and actively taking up the midday meal.

"I didn't understand," Fyodor Pavlovich stared in surprise. - What is the opposite?

- Well, this country has been like this for so many years, because everything in it is not close?

Laurel scratched his chin with perplexed fingers and with obvious interest felt the gaze of Fedech in front of him. Sometimes the boy expressed very interesting thoughts. Laurel grinned crookedly.

"No, we must first have a drink, since we are having a spree with us," he stated resolutely, and looked around for the waiter.

A young man serving them with a thin mustache disappeared inside the restaurant. No other attendants were nearby.

"I'll bring it now," Fedech volunteered.

He pushed aside a pot of meat and attempted to rise from the table. However, Lavrikov covered his hand with his dry palm.

"Sit down," he advised his son. - Appears - I will order.

But the young man obstinately shook his head. And his brush quickly slipped from his father's captivity.

"No, no," he protested, rising to his feet. - What do you need? Maybe I am pleased.

Laurel felt how blissful in all respects warmly spread over his body. Rozgin cared for him not because he was paid money, as was the case with Essentuki and his like brothers. He did this solely out of love and filial attention. The feeling unknown to Fyodor Pavlovich before seemed to be very peaceful. Still, he was not mistaken this morning at a gathering, when he publicly declared: "The crown is from the people, the son is from God." It could not be otherwise.

"Gram a hundred cognac," he made a proper order with a smile.

- Just a minute, dad. - Fedechka gave Lavra a half-humorous bow and swiftly headed inside the restaurant.

Fyodor Pavlovich spent his long loving gaze and leaned wearily on the back of a plastic chair with rigid armrests. The eyelids of recent authority are contiguous.

The snow-white Ford Scorpio with the side windows lowered jumped out of the nearest corner so rapidly that even the watchful Sancho, conscientiously keeping watch in his unsightly Zhiguli, did not have time to react properly. Except for Dybel, who was sitting behind the wheel, there was no one in the cabin of a wildly rushing car. The squeal of tires on the sun-hot asphalt caught the attention of the nearby rotoeans. Lavr also turned his head rather calmly. At that moment, he was waiting for any stab in the back.

Dowel slowed down in front of the restaurant just for one moment. A hand with a Stechkin automatic pistol sandwiched between the fingers popped out of an open window, as if on a spring. The young authority narrowed his left eye and shot twice. His weapon was not equipped with a silencer, and, following the loud pistol pops, the street in front of the Champs Elysees was filled with shouts of alarmed passersby. Laurel swung back, the chair under him tilted backwards, and the crowned lawyer fell to the ground. Stechkin disappeared into a Ford Scorpio cabin just as swiftly as he had appeared, and Dubel slammed the gas pedal to the floor. Killer's car, picking up speed, rushed away.

In an instant, as pale as a canvas, Sancho turned his key in the ignition with shaking hands.

- I knew it! - Moshkin moaned painfully, touching the light green "Zhiguli" from the spot. - So it will be! And swallowed!

Alexander's despair was complete. He recognized Dubel at the wheel of the Ford and was well aware that the probability that he missed was very insignificant. Involuntarily, tears came out in front of Alexander's eyes when he thought that Laurus lay there, under a shed, breathless, but he immediately brushed them away with the back of his hand, for the moisture covered his road review. Help your boss and, as Sancho himself believed, Moshkin could not do anything with his best friend. But on the other hand, he expected to overtake the killer at any cost and get even with him at any cost. It was this thought that forced Sancho to stop the accelerator pedal of the old "six" all the way. "Ford" Dubel, looming ahead, rapidly removed.

Panic, sown in the ranks of passers-by, was left behind Alexander.

Fedech jumped out of the restaurant into the street with a small thin decanter of cognac. The guy heard pistol shots and cries of passers-by, but in the depths of his soul there was a hope that what was happening was in no way connected with the person of his father. These illusions melted like smoke, he barely noticed lying on his back near the round plastic table Laurel.

Rozgin rushed to him and knelt down on one knee. His father was alive, but his face turned gray, and deep-set sunken eyes rolled under his eyelids. Laurel breathing was heavy and uneven. The decanter fell from the hands of a young man, and the brandy ordered by Fyodor Pavlovich spread under his feet.

"Good ... I give you, son," Lavrikov croaked heavily and with great difficulty forced himself to smile. He even made a desperate attempt to rise on his elbows, but could not, and again fell over onto his back. Fedech grabbed his gray head. - There is a vest ... The frying pan did not help ... It was worn out ...

Rozgin squinted his eyes and noticed a small tear on his shirt under the unbuttoned Laurel jacket in the hypochondrium. So far, a thin rim of blood has spread in different directions and has rapidly increased in size.

- Father! - Tears splashed out of the young man's eyes, and he squeezed the head of the authority degraded and deprived of regalia, and held his hand gently and carefully along the high sloping forehead of Fyodor Pavlovich. He already had a cold sweat. - Dad!

Lavrikov leaned back and closed his eyes. Curious pedestrians already crowded around Fedechki and lamented something in every way. Rozgin did not hear them, as well as the sounds of approaching sirens. After a moment, someone pulled him by the arm and pulled him away from the body that was sprawled on the ground. Fedechka did not tear his gaze from Laurus's chest punched by the enemy's bullet, and with bated hope noted the fact that it still rises chaotically. Fedor Pavlovich breathed. People in white coats, similar to angels who came down from heaven, carefully loaded the wounded man on a stretcher and rolled into an ambulance car. In the same car on the legitimate rights of the next of kin climbed Fedechka. The crowd of onlookers gradually began to dissolve.

Ford Scorpio famously leapt onto the suburban highway and rushed in the direction of the nearest plantations. Dowel was in a great mood. He even let himself happily whistle and slam both hands on the leather steering wheel with feeling. Everything was as he had planned. The competitor is not only demoted from legalists, but also safely sent to heaven. Now, with a new redistribution of spheres of influence in the city, no one will prevent Dubel from snatching a huge piece.

Driving along a low bridge, under which the turquoise smooth surface of a natural reservoir was poured in the sun, the killer swung and threw the used "stechkin" out the window. The authority glanced in the rear-view mirror and only now noticed a lettuce "six" hanging on its tail. The pursuer clearly lagged behind.

Dubel did not know who was driving the Zhiguli, but by the appearance of the car itself, he reasonably suggested that the enemy could not be too serious. He deliberately dropped the speed of the Ford and allowed the enemy's six to overtake him. Cars drew level on the track after less than two minutes. The ferocious face of Moshkin, who had gone on overtaking, turned out to be directly opposite the smiling face of Dowel.

"What can you do, asshole?" - loudly laughing, cried out the murderer. "You are as rusty as your car!" You all go to the dump, lawyers!

Instead of answering, Sancho abruptly threw the steering wheel to the right, and his old "six" slammed into the smooth, polished side of the foreign car. From the blow "Lada" jumped into the oncoming lane. Dubel leveled the Ford and laughed even louder.

- Scratched, goat! - for some strange reason, he happily proclaimed.

However, the very next second, the idiotic laughter of the outlaw broke off as if by a wave of a magic wand. Dubel's startled look focused on Sancho's desperate and determined actions. Alexander furiously pulled his teeth from the grenade clamped in his fingers and threw the explosive ammunition under his feet. "Six" again went to the ram. Moshkin opened the side door and fell out onto the warm asphalt, covered his head with his hands. The dowel hit the gas, but did not manage to escape from the inevitable collision of two cars. An old "Zhiguli" with a wild screech fit into the snow-white case of the Ford, and at the same instant a deafening explosion slammed. The inhuman cry of the Dowel driven into a trap drowned in its peals.

Sancho looked up only a minute or so later. A few meters away from him, the remains of the beloved "six" were blazing. Still, he got rid of her, as Laurel advised, though in a somewhat uncivilized and wild way. But every cloud has a silver lining. From the white "Ford" also remained only burning frame. There was no doubt about the tragic death of a passenger of a foreign car.

Moshkin rose to his feet and looked around. He should urgently leave the crash site and somehow return to the city. And most of all, Alexander was worried about the fate of Lavrikov.

"I'm thinking everything ..." said Lavr quietly, but Fedech did not let him finish the sentence he had begun.

"This is progress," he said, with a grin, but then he asked: "What are you thinking about?"

Father and son were in the hospital. For a whole week Fyodor Pavlovich had the opportunity to move around a flower-strewn garden in a wheelchair. Doctors boldly predicted his speedy recovery. Rozgin all this time was near, only occasionally leaving the hospital, followed by an aunt or Alexander Moshkin, who during this time managed to start a very warm relationship. The young man, without any additional requests from his wounded father, managed to get rid of his shaggy hair with many tight pigtails and at the moment was almost bald. A short hedgehog of hair covered a smooth skull for only half a centimeter.

"About the vortex generator," Fyodor Pavlovich confessed, without turning his head to the youth pushing the wheelchair behind. - Remember, you said? If it is so elementary - a motor, pipes, - where does one hundred seventy percent of efficiency come from in it?

- I do not know for sure. - Rozgin shrugged. - And the man has no money for research. I can only assume ... Water molecules are in contact with the cosmic vacuum.

- With a space vacuum? - interestedly asked Lavr.

- Yeah.

- And from this warm?

"It's hot," said Fedech honestly.

"An amazing thing," Lavrikov pursed his lips. - In an ordinary pipe, space suddenly appears ...

- So! - Fedechka stopped the chair and walked around it. He looked penetratingly into his father's eyes. - To think a lot is bad. It's time to act. Get up

"I forgot the stick," Laurus attempted to sneak away from the process exhausting the body.

For a couple of days, Fedechka insistently demanded movement from his father on his own two feet. Doctors advised to develop limbs and considered it an integral part of the healing process. And the former criminal authority just as diligently filonil and avoided this event. It was much more pleasant for him to realize that his own son rolls him along the flower alleys. However, in matters of health, Fedech turned out to be an even more tyrant than Sancho.

"Nothing," said the young man categorically. - You lean on me. Get up, get up, do not mow under the invalid! His two have to learn.

"A sadist," Laurus scolded the boy jokingly, but he still got to his feet, groaning and groaning like an old man.

Fedechka carefully grabbed it, and Lavrikov leaned on his son's shoulder.

- Come on! - Rozgin encouraged him. - Step ... Another ... Well done! Great we do it! One more step! .. Next ...

Moving only a meter forward along the avenue, Laurel stopped. Heavy breathing with a whistle escaped from his lungs. He swallowed convulsively.

- Everything! I can not more! - Fyodor Pavlovich admitted to his son.

- tired?

"Not ..." The once powerful and influential authority shook its gray head. - It's a shame ... Well, what are you, in fact, as if you were hired by a nanny ... With a crutch!

- I did not hire, - Fedech disowned this assumption. "It's just ... a capable child must take care of an incapacitated parent." According to law.

Brow Lavra displeased converged to the nose. He turned slightly to the left and met his eyes with the young man.

- Again, "by law"? - He muttered angrily and involuntarily rubbed his eyes on the short-cropped head of his son. "What other law?"

- According to human law, Laurus! - proudly and with dignity answered the guy. "Human, do you understand? .. I admit them ..."

After thinking for a second, Fedor Pavlovich nodded in agreement. His hand, wrapped around Rozgin's shoulder, tightened, and his chapped lips stretched into a smile.

- Okay. Then we will live a little more. - Lavrikov even allowed himself to straighten and raise his pointed chin. - According to human laws ...

"We'll live where we can get away," Fedech picked up.

And they moved on. Slowly, step by step, to the far end of the hospital garden alley. The wheelchair was left behind, and neither Laurel nor his son never turned in her direction. Yellow leaves fell under their feet, testifying that the golden autumn, so ardently and passionately beloved by Alexander Sergeyevich Pushkin, had already thoroughly entered into its legal rights. The son and father, finding each other after a long separation, began their new life coil.

Printed in Great Britain
by Amazon

47822063R00132